Taboo Kisses

By

GRACEN MILLER

Mia,
XOXO
Huggles,
Gracen Miller
RTC 2018

The unauthorized reproduction or distribution of this copyrighted work is illegal. Criminal copyright infringement (including infringement without monetary gain) is investigated by the FBI and is punishable by up to 5 years in federal prison and a fine of $250,000.

Taboo Kisses
Copyright 2013 by Gracen Miller
Cover art by Andrea Kozari
Edited by Amanda Wimer

All rights reserved. Except for use in any review, the reproduction or utilization of this work, in whole or in part, in any form by any electronic, mechanical or other means now known or hereafter invented, is forbidden without the written permission of the publisher.

Published by Gracen Miller
Look for me online at:
www.gracen-miller.com

Gracen Miller

Reviews for Taboo Kisses

"Hot and steamy, brought my wild side out!" ~ **Shalisha Cooper**

"Author Gracen Miller has created a sexy, hot yet taboo world that will have you craving permission to enter and begging to stay." ~ **Mindy Janicke, Forbidden Reviews**

"With toe-curling, orgasmic screams of pleasure, the ecstasy achieved in Taboo Kisses is a *supernova* of scorching hot sexiness." ~ **Kathryn Grimes, Tsk Tsk What to Read**

"Another great paranormal story from Gracen Miller! She does paranormal the right way! Taboo Kisses is mind-blowingly sexy from start to finish! It's fun, kinky, and has an interesting and unique plot! Forget 50 Shades! Pick this one up instead!" ~ **Kristina Haecker, Kristina's Books and More**

What the Critics are Saying About Other Gracen Miller Books...

"Blows J.R. Ward out of the water!" ~ **Dawn Hagan, I Love Books**

"What a ride! Gracen Miller delivers an outstanding first book [Pandora's Box] of the Road to Hell series." ~ **Mary Smith, Book Nerds Across America**

"Top pick all the way!! Hell's Phoenix is a *must* read." ~ **Tanna Heitz, Bitten by Love Reviews**

"Hell's Phoenix was just amazing! Again Gracen blew my mind with her wickedly awesome writing skills. The emotions that the characters go through are written in such a way that the reader experiences it in full." ~ **Tich**

Taboo Kisses

Brewster, Loves All Things Books

"*Wow*!! Another fantastic book by Gracen Miller that has *blown* me away!! From start to finish, Hell's Phoenix demands that you devour each and every page. The emotions that you feel for these characters will be a rollercoaster ride and when you are finished you will feel like you have just run a marathon." ~ **Kathryn Grimes, Tsk Tsk What to Read**

"The description of Hell was *creepy* but awesome. I'm sure I wouldn't go there willingly if there wasn't a Micah... This book contains several breathtaking scenes, maybe sometimes you will even cry -I almost did and I never cry!! And good news for adrenaline junkies, there is absolutely no lack of action in this book." ~ **Andrea Kozári, The Secret Sanctuary of Books**

"Genesis Queen will not disappoint! Wow just wow!" ~ **Steph, Starry Night Book Review**

"[L]et me just say this about Genesis Queen...*awesome*, *amazing* and *perfection*!! Of all the books in the series this one is my favorite." ~ **Mary Smith, Book Nerds Across America**

Gracen Miller

~Dedication~

To my husband, Mark, who asked me to write him something kinky. Hope you had as much fun reading it as I did writing it. As always, I love you more!

Nichelle Gregory, thanks for your support and friendship. And our wicked chats.

Thanks to my betas for helping me work magic...Andrea Kozari, Kathryn Vanessa Grimes, Bridgette Dodson, Kristina Haecker, Kelly Silva Fine, Christina Baker Irelan, Shalisha Cooper, and Mindy Janicke.

Chapter One

"**I** want her alive!" Tyron Gryphon slammed his fist down on his desk, rattling the pens and disturbing the paper.

Maximus elevated an eyebrow, fighting back the surge of his vampyr fangs. Beside him, his mate, Gabriel, a tiger-shifter tensed. The multi-billionaire sitting across from them was a brat cloaked in the body of an adult. Getting his desires one too many times, led him to the erroneous conclusion Maximus and Gabriel would do his bidding out of fear or dominance. A huge miscalculation on the drama-king's part.

Gabriel tossed the dossier on Gryphon's desk. "What do you want with her?"

Maximus studied the woman in the black and white photo he'd retained from the file. Dark hair, petite build, and eyes an indeterminate shade in the monochrome picture.

Sameya. No surname. Not even a last known address. Scant facts in the folder, nine pages total, easy to memorize all of the material. Five-three, one hundred five pounds, she'd be itty-bity up against his six-foot-five stature. He preferred diminutive women, favored how tiny they were against him.

Sandwich her between him and Gabriel, and they'd govern her physically and literally. Sliding into her simultaneously...his balls clenched and his gut cramped at the idea. Amazing how a single photograph induced such fantasies. Even more remarkable because he wasn't the woolgathering type. He possessed more of a proactive type of personality.

Gryphon paced behind his desk, the two huge windows at his back like judging glassy eyes. "She's a siren." Maximus bit his tongue to massacre the laugh that hit the back of his throat. What a gibberish declaration.

"Bullshit," Maximus blurted before he engaged the filter from his brain to his mouth. That quirky sieve often gave him fits.

"What Maximus means is sirens are believed to be extinct, have been for centuries." Gabriel adjusted to the edge of his seat, back ramrod straight, while Maximus slouched and tapped the photograph against his leg, considering the agitated male. "You expect us to believe you've located one?" Gabriel continued, snatching Maximus from his thoughts.

"Not just located one, but spent time with her. She dated my son." Gryphon fisted his right hand. Did he contemplate choking the little siren? Maximus wanted his hand around her throat while he held her down and drove into her body. Balls-deep, pounding into her soft flesh until her eyes crossed and they both came in an orgasm so blinding it took them hours to recover.

Gabriel flicked him a glance, a cagey expression in his golden eyes. "If this is true, how could you not sense what she is?"

Being a griffin, Tyron Gryphon was a powerful enough creature to have recognized what she was from the get-go. If he spoke true, then the woman in the photo was of countless age, and her power most likely dwarfed everyone in the mortal realm. Including the griffin.

"I have no idea." Gryphon ran his hand down his face. "The only conclusion is that she's a *timerelic*."

Maximus notched a hank of shoulder length brown hair behind his ear. "All *timerelics* are deceased." True relics that transcended the ages were a myth. Or so his great grandfather decreed and that old man had departed Atlantis when the city was hidden. However, nothing said one of the ancients couldn't escape their notice. But why would a *timerelic* appear now? Leave the safety of Atlantis? "You're mistaken. Sirens no longer exist."

If they remained, why weren't they eliminating the criminals as they had in the past? Instead, that'd become his and Gabriel's job.

Gryphon slammed his fist on the table again. Weary of the theatrics, Maximus rose to his feet, as their would-be employer said, "She turned my son into a babbling fool. That is clear evidence of a siren."

"How are we to know he wasn't a babbling fool before she showed up?"

"Maximus." Gabriel sent him a cautious peek.

"Gabriel, I've had enough of this fucker's bullshit." From the corner of his eye, he caught the silent gasp that froze on Gryphon's face. Honor wasn't typically questioned among the various paranormal breeds. "Sirens are extinct. End of story. He wants this bitch for another reason he's not sharing. And I don't work for liars."

What would Gryphon do if I tossed Sameya on his desk and fucked her while he watched?

Enough with the daydreams already.

"I'll pay you whatever you want."

Maximus laughed. Of course Gryphon would cough up an obscene amount of cash if they agreed to bounty-hunt for him. That had never been open for discussion. He and Gabriel were the best trackers in the paranormal community. It wasn't about the money, though. The idea of this jowly, beady-eyed motherfucker getting his claws on Sameya-possible-siren made Maximus irrational. Had him itching to beat the arrogant bastard into a pulp for simply thinking of her.

"You'll tell us precisely why you want her. The truth this time." Maximus took a page out of Gryphon's book and slammed his fist on the desk, taking perverse delight in rattling the pen cup off the wood-top and onto the floor. "Or we walk. Right now."

And I locate her for my own needs. Best goddamn idea yet!

Gryphon paused, studying Maximus in silence. Most in the supernatural community maintained a safe zone from vampyrs. Even the griffins, that outclassed other creatures, elected to avoid his species.

Gabriel rose beside him, retrieved a card from the breast pocket of his jacket. "This is the figure we'd expect if we agree to locate the alleged siren." Using a gold pen he'd snagged from the same pocket, Gabriel scribbled on the backside of the business card. He flicked the high-grade, cotton square at Gryphon. "Non-negotiable price. Neither is it a guarantee to hand her over to you once we catch her." Because they *would* find her. "Once we verify her race *and* guilt, then she's yours. If we determine otherwise...."

Gryphon looked between the two of them, without sparing a glance at the obscene figure Gabriel had written on it. "You're serious?"

"Very." The hard edge to Gabriel's voice left no doubt to his seriousness. "We don't hand over anyone without proof of guilt."

Maximus smirked. *Take that and shove it up your ass, you prick.*

"I'll find another to meet my needs." Gryphon made a go-away motion with his hand.

Gabriel buttoned his suit jacket. "Good luck."

Tracking a siren—if that's what she really was—would require more than luck.

Maximus and Gabriel exited the office without speaking. Not until they climbed into Gabriel's black Spyder did they engage in conversation. His partner started the ignition, shifted into reverse, and smoothly backed out of the parking spot.

Maximus waited until they hit the interstate before saying, "We're going after her."

Gabriel got heavy footed with the pedal. "I hope you took the time to memorize her file?"

"Fuck you." Of course he had, and Gabriel knew it.

His partner chuckled and threw him a wink. "Anytime, lover."

Chapter Two

The clicks of Sameya's knee-high black, dragon skinned boots hitting the pavement were drowned out by the revelry on Bourbon Street. Gah...mortals. Loud and obnoxious. The useless infantile creatures were a pestilence upon the earth. Since exiting Atlantis, she'd culled many murderers, abusers, pedophiles, and rapists from humanity's numbers. They should give her a medal for the favors she performed.

The best of her species at fact-gathering, she'd left her Empress in the safety of a trusted few and set out to uncover the terrorist in their midst. Thoughts gleaned from a mystic inside Atlantis revealed the source within worked in tangent with a mystic outside the hidden city's realm. She couldn't figure out what the non-Atlantian would gain from assassinating their Empress, not unless he was promised entrance into Atlantis. Over her dead fucking body—

A sharp whistle snatched her head around, and her gaze connected with a brown-haired frat boy. Drunk and noisy, his stride wobbly, and his leer detestable. "Holy gawd almighty!" he slurred, and she could smell his liquor-laced breath from ten feet away. "You're the hottest babe I ever done seen."

Atrocious English. *Imbecile.* "Do you know what I am?"

"Fallen angel for fuckin' sure."

His buddy slapped him on the chest and chortled, making a fool of himself. "Hopefully, the demon in our bed later?"

New age mankind was as alien to her as the elusive orgasm. When she'd gone into hiding in Atlantis over seven millennia ago, she was the stuff mothers frightened their children with. She'd entered a new world where mortals believed her a myth. How could she garner respect like this?

"Fuck off."

Moody, she would take his head off rather than ingest his soul if he were rash enough to come after her. She kicked a bottle with her booted toe. It struck the shin of a tourist and he went down hard, clutching his leg.

Oops.

She probably broke a bone.

Sameya halted her steps and pondered at the unassuming establishment located on Bourbon Street. *Dirty Liquor*. The windows were boarded up as if the proprietor prepared for a hurricane. The scarred door unadorned, the neon light above the entrance the only indication it was open for business. Bold, red power seeped from the building. Tangible evidence a mystic owned the pub. Lots of mojo going on here. Best guess, once inside it'd null the magic of other paranormals, which would make it easier to manage a rowdy group, especially if a magical creature were involved. But this enchantment was not strong enough to affect hers. Hadn't found a species yet that could micromanage her magic, with the exception of a vampyr and none of them resided in Atlantis.

Intel suggested her target would be here tonight. Itching to get back to Atlantis, she wanted to get this over with.

Tossing her hair over her shoulders, she pushed the door open and sauntered in, rolling her hips. The buttery soft, snug Basilisk hide pants showcased her ass. Not that her attributes were required when she hunted because she could lure a man with just her enchantment, but her appearance facilitated the chase.

The beat of the music overpowered her hearing until she adjusted her magical volume meter to a tolerable level. Heated stares skimmed her body while she made her way to the bartender. It was early, so the establishment wasn't as crowded as it would be later tonight. The revelry was already at a hearty swing, and the dance floor sported an impressive contingent of ladies with a few men. A high-polished, walnut-wood bar hosted less than a dozen patrons.

Sameya slid in-between two males and leaned across the bar. "Whiskey. Neat. The best you have."

Not that she intended to drink her order. One sip of liquor and she'd be wasted, all magic neutralized. She had a strict policy against vulnerability.

"I'm Gabriel." The man on her right leaned a little closer, so near she could discern the minty scent of his breath.

Usually her intimidating otherworld vibe was enough to keep the humans back, even if they failed to comprehend why her diminutive stature came across so menacing.

Not sparing a glance in the male's direction, she said, "Not interested."

"Of course you're not, *syreen*."

The Atlantian term for her race. Sameya's attention snatched about. A slight grin hit the corners of the fair-haired, drop-dead gorgeous man. A mystic. Like her...but not similar in many other ways. Cultured, but with a more humanized flair.

Probably born in this mortal world rather than from Atlantis. Some mystics had chosen to remain among the humans when they shielded their land. But she couldn't pinpoint his exact race.

He ran his fingertip along the rim of his glass, lifted the goblet, and drained the liquor in one gulp. "What are you hunting?"

Syn. The only thing she hunted.

Guarded, she tried to play it cool. "I imagine, the same as you."

"I don't hunt."

Elevating her eyebrows, she called him on his lie with only her expression. Dressed like he owned half the world in a charcoal gray suit and baby-blue cravat...the man definitely pursued something. If nothing more than a willing but fast fuck.

His appearance was remarkable, handsome, with dark-blond, spiky hair. She was curious how many had been granted the privilege of running their fingers through it during coupling. His golden yellow eyes assessed her coolly, and they could not be mistaken for human. Clean shaven square jaw. Expensive clothing stretched across broad shoulders, hinted at power that had nothing to do with magic. It was the feral presence he exuded that suggested beneath the refined attire he was deadly. Could strike with the least amount of provocation with lethal accuracy, no hesitation and no remorse.

"Where you from, little lady?" The bald bartender set a glass of whiskey in front of her.

"Far away." Sameya two-fingered the glass and sloshed the liquor in a circular motion, eyeing...Gabriel.

"Never heard your accent before," the barkeep persisted.

If he were lucky, he never would again.

"I'm not interested in conversation." She flicked her finger for him to go away, an apparent universal sign everyone understood because the male took the hint and moved away.

A very long time ago the mystic race had coexisted with humans. Sirens had filtered the scum from society, the criminal debauchery a feast. They'd been worshiped as gods, welcomed into homes, and prayers were sent their way. In return, mystics had received the mortals into their Valhalla—Atlantis. Then an unknown plague had nearly eradicated mankind. When the prayers went unanswered, the mystics had sunk their heaven to escape persecution. They might be stronger and magically inclined, but humans could still kill them.

Swiveling in her seat, she surveyed the room. She sensed the focus of the male beside her, but he remained seated with his back to the dance floor.

Gabriel. What a unique name, nothing she'd hear in Atlantis. She liked it. The way the syllables rolled around in her head was kind of...intriguing.

On the dance floor, bodies were grinding together in the suggestive act of sex, which increased her awareness of the mystic male. Revelers drunk on liquor and pheromones grew more lascivious with one another, less cautious of the company they kept. No way would a *syn* miss this easy action.

"You have me at a disadvantage, Gabriel." She shuddered. Shit. Nothing could've prepared her for the way his name sounded *on* her tongue. Even though he didn't look at her, she felt his attention. "What type of mystic are you?"

He chuckled. The sound vibrated against her clitoris. Odd reaction to him considering no matter how much stimulation she received, she couldn't climax with anyone except her mate.

Am I growing wet? Nah...couldn't be.
"I'm not a mystic." He rotated on the barstool to face her. "I'm a shifter."
That explained his wild charisma, but not her physical reaction to him. Sirens did *not* mate with lesser creatures. In laymen terms, that meant any creature *not* of her race. They were superior, had ruled Atlantis since its inception. Her kind's preeminence wouldn't change because she had a small, practically non-existence twitch in her crotch.
I probably imagined the reaction anyway.
Of course, she had invented the response. Humans were gyrating sex acts on the dance floor. That'd be enough to—
"How did you know I'm a siren?" Unease crackled down her spine. No supernatural creature could feel the presence of her species. They weren't known as reapers without reason, so how had the shifter sniffed her out?
He shrugged. Such a normal affectation, she would've thought it too commonplace for him to execute.
She spied her target entering the establishment and watched as he took a seat across the room. "What do you want?"
"You."
A weird throbbing started between her thighs. Unnerved by the physical response she couldn't deny, she tilted her lips in a forced smile. "Too bad I'm not available."
She went invisible.
Gabriel chuckled. "I can still smell you. So you know, my sweet little reaper, once you're in my database, I can track you."
Sameya laughed. "Best of fortune with that, shifter."

Regardless of the fact he couldn't see her, she sashayed away, feeling his stare in her direction. Coming to a halt beside the unassuming elf, she touched his cheek and coated him in a magical serenade. With a crook of her finger, he followed her out of the tavern without a verbal request.

She led him down the street and into a dark alley. Only when she had him alone did she drop her magic and go corporeal. He presented no expression to her sudden appearance, just gaped blankly, as if she didn't exist. That lack of recognition proved her serenade placed him in a semi-catatonic state.

A tingling down her spine alerted her to Gabriel's presence. The nerve of the man following her from the bar! For his audacity, she'd give him a show.

Sidling closer to the fey she'd trapped in her mojo, she pushed him against the damp brick wall and pressed her body against his. With a finger to his jugular, she commanded, "I want to know everything, elf."

She dug into the creature's mind, the catch of his thoughts and memories an aphrodisiac to her senses. Heat corkscrewed through her, but it was the shifter's presence that disturbed her most. Her leader's life was at stake, and the vibrant male at her back distracted her focus. Her reaction to him was the worst irony, and his interference bad timing.

Gabriel shifted to lean a shoulder against the brick wall beside the elf's mind she pillaged. He was tall. A good foot taller than her, with broad shoulders that made her feel tiny. She lifted her eyes to his golden orbs. Glowing, they seemed feral in the shadows, but she sensed no threat from him. Not that she feared him when she could serenade him in a split second.

With a twist of power, she eliminated the elf and took a step backward. Her victim slumped to the cracked street, his eyes open and glassy. Dead. He'd deserved to suffer, but she hadn't the time to spare.

Gabriel surveyed the fallen. When his concentration shifted to her, his gaze slithered up her body starting with her boots. By the time he met her eyes, she trembled as if he'd caressed her and stimulated her like in those romance books she imbibed from time-to-time.

"I thought you'd climax before you released him."

Having no idea what one of those felt like, she shrugged. "He deserved his outcome."

Dark blond eyebrows elevated. "Did you get what you were looking for from him?"

Not as much as she'd like. "Yes."

He elevated his hand, and the pads of his fingertips slid from her temple to her jaw, his gawk fixated on her mouth. "You weren't what I was expecting when Gryphon...."

When Gryphon what? But he didn't elaborate, and she didn't ask.

His eyes flashed to hers as his touch scraped across her bottom lip. She shuddered at the tingling his fondling elicited at the base of her scalp. Suddenly, she wanted to know what it felt like to have his hands all over her body. What would it feel like to have him fucking her? He couldn't be her mate...not a possibility with his race. But he tempted her for the first time in a long time.

"I have someone I want you to meet."

That request snapped her out of her daze. Shifters weren't the raping and pillaging type, but she had a job to do. Interruptions weren't tolerable. And she'd dallied overmuch.

"No." A moment later, she intentionally lost her visibility and side stepped his attempt to snag her. "Better luck next time, shifter."

She swiped a fingertip along his chin, and static tingled on her flesh. Snatching her hand back, she peered at him. What the fuck had just happened? Nothing good. In the next second, self-preservation kicked in and she fled.

Chapter Three

Gabriel sipped whiskey straight from the miniature bottle he'd snagged from the hotel minibar. He pushed the balcony doors open and stepped out into the humid, New Orleans, Louisiana heat. Past midnight, the revelry on Bourbon Street kicked into overdrive. Tourists swilled liquor like a cheap whore sucked cock. Fast and hard.

He hated this city with its overpowering stench of rotting garbage. The corpses buried in mausoleums irritated his oversensitive sense of smell, and the human congestion increased their risk of exposure and they couldn't chance being discovered.

No self-respecting shifter would reside in this cesspool of iniquity. Following their quarry wherever she went, left them with no other choice but to venture within the territory lines. Being a tracker had landed him in many unsavory locales over the years. Who was he to complain over a little inconvenience when the profits were enormous? Not that Sameya would gross them a single dime after the way they ended things with Tyron Gryphon. When he'd mentioned Gryphon's name, there hadn't been an ounce of recognition on her features.

She did not know the man. Curious that Tyron Gryphon claimed they were more than acquaintances. Were nefarious schemes afoot? No other prospect came to mind. Griffins were known charlatans, willing to do anything to gain what they desired. If Gryphon knew how to collar a siren, then he and Maximus needed to proceed cautiously.

Sirens were known among the mystic community as 'reapers' because by the time mankind or fey realized they peered at a siren, it was too late, they were a goner. They could enthrall almost all species, leading to a willing demise. Sirens had been known to eradicate an entire fey breed. Or so the myth went. He'd never actually met one until tonight. And watching her do her thing to the elf...fuck it'd been hot. Only for a moment had he pondered what the fey had done to deserve his demise. In the end, he simply hadn't cared enough to intercede.

Only a vampyr was immune to a siren's song. That afforded Maximus a safety net, but not himself. As a tiger shifter, she could lull him as easily as another. He could track her now that he had her scent in his nostrils...and goddamn what a scent it was. But what would hunting her down gain him if she could serenade him?

If he wasn't mistaken, she was the third part to his and Maximus's triune. The way his body reacted to her tonight, the tiger pressing against his skin, roaring in his head to get free and claim her. He'd damn near lost control in the pub. His feline responded to her the same way it had when he'd met Maximus...with the irrational need to claim, dominate and mate.

Gabriel slammed his fingers through his hair. What a fucking nightmare. Her red streaked black hair and flawless skin were exquisite. Eyes like violets, a deep purple no one would mistake for human. And her body in those skin-fucking-tight pants—what had they been crafted from anyway?— was made to give men pleasure. Petite, but curvaceous, her hips were rounded enough he could envision holding them tight as he bent her over and fucked her.

This unexpected outcome complicated their lives further. A shifter and vampyr mating was as unheard of as a siren mating outside her species. Gabriel loved Maximus, would die for him, but Maximus had lost everything to be with him. After almost a millennium together, he still carried guilt for his lover's loss. With the siren as a potential mate, he worried she'd mess things up rather than improve their relationship.

They'd spent six months hunting the elusive siren, wanting to catch her before Gryphon accomplished the feat. They caught small leads and followed them until the trail grew cold. A few weeks later new information would emerge, and they'd chase another lead for a couple of weeks. After it'd become obvious she didn't know Gryphon, Gabriel wondered who'd been planting the leads. Had they really been following Sameya's clues or following one of Gryphon's goose chases? That the griffin might be yanking their chain pissed him off and made his tiger edgy.

To bump into her tonight by accident—or had it been a chance coincidence? His gut said Gryphon knew where she was at any given time, so why involve them? None of the turn of events made sense.

"What bothers you, Gabriel?" Maximus plucked the miniature whiskey bottle from his hand. He hadn't even heard the vampyr's approach. Sneaky like that, it was one of the many things he found sexy about his lover.

With his hands on Gabriel's shoulders, Maximus turned him away from the crowd below, and left his palms on him after they faced one another. Only an inch shorter than Maximus, Gabriel peered into his silver-blue eyes.

Gabriel ran his hand over his face. "I bumped into Sameya tonight at *Dirty Liquor*. I...." He expelled a breath. To express his next thoughts would give credence to them. "I believe she's the one that'll complete our tri-union."

Maximus ran the back of his fingers against Gabriel's cheek. "*Naleah*...." A vampyr term of endearment that roughly translated into 'my love'. "You're vulnerable to sirens. It's possible she serenaded you."

"I heard no song." His cat had felt her the instant she approached the bar and his cock had gone instantly hard.

Maximus wore only a towel hooked about his waist and beads of water ran down his smooth, muscled chest. His wet chin-length, wavy, dark-brown hair clung to his neck. He'd come fresh from the shower, but Gabriel could smell his unique scent. "I doubt you would. It's not like she's singing a lullaby."

"My tiger went crazy wanting out. You cannot imagine her scent. The way it incited my beast. Maximus—"

"We're already an unconventional couple, Gabriel." Maximus cupped the back of his head. "What are the chances of our third being another breed totally different from one of ours?"

Gabriel kissed Maximus's wrist. The odds must be one in a billion. Their mating was rare, so to add another variety would be inexplicable. "You're probably right. Except...." He sighed. "You're right." He pushed his fingers through Maximus's damp strands and leaned his forehead against the vampyr's.

"Except your tiger went irrational near her the way it did me?"

Sometimes it felt like his lover could read his mind. "Yeah."

"We'll catch her and put this theory of yours to rest. One way or the other. Until then"—Maximus fisted a handful of his hair and wrenched his head back, his dick jerking against his slacks at the vampyr's aggression—"I'm going to fuck you."

Gabriel smiled. A hard fuck was what he desired, and he loved that his mate could sense his needs. He sidled closer, kissing the other man's forehead. "Shall we go inside, Maximus?"

"No." Maximus ripped his towel off exposing his nudity to Bourbon Street revelers below. "Out here where all of humanity can watch us."

A heartbeat lapsed between them. Gabriel's fondness for voyeurism kicked in, and his tiger purred.

"I want you to growl for me when you come." Maximus nipped his bottom lip and deftly worked the buttons through the holes on Gabriel's dress shirt. The muggy air kissed his flesh and swirled around him. His shifter senses prickled him with gooseflesh, tingling as if to alert him of being tracked. Crazy notion when they were removing clothing on the terrace and many were below. Of course people would watch!

The vampyr bit his lip again, hard enough to draw blood. He swiped away the hemoglobin with a lick. He employed his fangs when he was in a playful mood, which countered Gabriel's animalistic disposition perfectly. "I'll fuck you over the bannister, Maximus." The urge to mark, dominate and mate continued to twist through him. He'd sink his cat canines into the mating mark on the vampyr's neck when he came. It was the only way he'd come close to pacifying his tiger's needs.

Maximus pulled Gabriel's shirt free of his pants and pushed the garment over his shoulders, following the material's descent with his palms down Gabriel's arms. The vampyr liked to touch and Gabriel loved having his hands on him. His lover tossed the shirt over the railing. Commotion from below and someone squealed, "Look!"

They kissed, tongues tangoing as Maximus released Gabriel's slacks and pushed them to his ankles, along with his underwear. Gasps from below, followed by, "So, hot." The clicking and bursts of light evidence photos were being taken. Neither of their faces would turn out, a little bit of magic that always surrounded them.

Gabriel wrapped locks of Maximus's moist hair around his fingers and jerked his head back. He met the vampyr's eyes. Fuck, he loved this man. The only problem they'd had to being mated was the difference in species. Mating was about paring two individuals together that'd benefit nature. Gabriel would die for Maximus. Yet, they needed their third to make them complete, but the effects she could have on their established relationship could cause everything to go sideways in a hurry.

"I'm going to fuck you hard, Maximus."

Eyes shifting from silver-blue to bright green indicated the vampyr had come out to play. His fangs extended. A slight forward tilt of Maximus's head and he buried his teeth into Gabriel's neck. He groaned as Maximus's tongue swooshed against the incisors buried in his flesh. Nothing like having his spouse bite him, feed from him. A vampyr's bite was painful to all but their mate.

Maximus jerked Gabriel's head hard to the right and thrust his fangs deeper. The vampyr's fingers curled around the base of the tiger's dick and he stroked in time with his sucks. Glide and suck, glide and suck, with his thumb slithering over the head. Gabriel's knees trembled and his balls tightened, his crown throbbing. He'd blow any goddamn second, but Maximus only played, and released his length.

Gabriel's inclination was to bend his spouse over and fuck him hard for the teasing foreplay. Instead, he cupped Maximus's ass with a hand and ground his pelvis against him. Hard cocks rubbed against one another. The vampyr hissed against his flesh and downed his blood faster.

Fangs retracted with a pop and his tongue swiped down his neck and across his collarbone. Strong fingers clasped the tiger's cock and gently stroked. Gabriel grew harder. Ached to bury himself balls deep inside his spouse.

Gabriel circled Maximus's pierced nipples with his thumbs as he kissed him, his cat emitting a low grumble. Licking down the vampyr's throat, he nipped his collarbone and scraped his teeth over his nipples.

"It's about you tonight, lover." Maximus pulled him upward, their mouths connecting.

The kiss went on and on as his lover gripped his butt, his fingers skimming through the crack of his ass, tantalizing him. Maximus moved down Gabriel's neck, kissing and licking, until he went to his knees in front of Gabriel's erect cock. Pumping Gabriel's length with one hand, the vampyr cupped his balls with the other and licked the head of his dick. Gabriel jerked and palmed the back of the other man's head.

"Let's give the crowd a show they won't soon forget." Maximus gripped Gabriel's hips and turned him so he stood at an angle to the crowd beneath them, his cock visible to the gawkers.

"When we locate our third mate"—Maximus's lips glided along his erection, back and forth in wispy teases and he thought his balls would explode with the need to plunge into the vampyr—"she'll help me suck you." No forewarning, Maximus swallowed Gabriel's penis into his mouth, his tongue curling around the head, his tongue-piercing tormenting him further. He tangled his fingers in Maximus's hair and tried to urge him to take more, but the vampyr failed to cooperate.

In response, his lover peered up at him as he released his crown and licked down his length, tonguing his balls. The metal piercing ratcheted his arousal higher. Gabriel wanted it fast and rough, but by all appearances, Maximus prepared to take his time.

"Either suck my dick or bend over, Maximus."

His lover laughed and squeezed Gabriel's balls with one hand, while probing his anus with a finger of the other hand.

The sensation was so intense, Gabriel could only concentrate on the bliss, and let his head tilt back, his eyes closing, eliminating everything except the ecstasy.

Without any warning, Maximus sucked him into his mouth and to the back of his throat. Back and forth he moved, his tongue swishing along the underside, the piercing drawing forth more pleasure. He sank him deep within his wet heat, over and over again, down his throat as he teased the underside and the crown with wispy whooshes. Gabriel's balls tightened and a tingling started at the base of his spine. He'd blow soon if he didn't halt Maximus.

Let him swallow me once more.

Maximus took him further, burying his nose in Gabriel's pelvis. His tongue flicked back and forth against the underside of his dick. He swallowed and Gabriel almost came. He jerked Maximus's head back by his hair. His lips suctioned so tight on Gabriel's cock, there was a popping sound when he was free of Maximus's mouth.

"Up," he snarled, his tiger clawing against his skin. It wouldn't do to shift with witnesses present. "Lean over the railing and be ready to take all of me."

Maximus bent and placed his forearms along the bannister. He waived at the crowd below and Gabriel could picture the flirty grin and wink he sent to the spectators. Maximus's easy demeanor enamored everyone.

Leaning over his lover's back, Gabriel reached around and gripped his mate's cock. Erect, the smooth length long and velvety hard. Precum beaded the head and he swiped his thumb across the slit as he pumped his hand.

"Don't come while I'm fucking you, Maximus." Gabriel nuzzled his lover's neck. "I want you dropping your load in my mouth."

The vampyr peeked at him over his shoulder. "Give them a show, *naleah*."

Gabriel kissed Maximus, and then moved down his back with a mixture of kisses and bites. Unable to control his tiger's satisfaction, he purred loud as he palmed Maximus's ass-cheeks and spread them. To groans from his mate, Gabriel tongued the man's rosetta. Maximus pumped his hand along his cock, while rocking back against Gabriel's mouth.

He couldn't wait any longer. Swiping the bottle of lubricant off the balcony's table, he worked the emollient into his lover's ass with his fingers. He coated his cock with the substance and positioned the head of his dick against Maximus's entrance. Below them the crowd cheered and Maximus sent them a thumbs up.

Gabriel thrust balls-deep into him. His tiger roared. Maximus moaned a "fuck", held the railing with one hand and jerked his other against his cock.

Holding Maximus's hip with his right hand, he ran his left along his back and anchored his palm on his neck, flexing his hips to set the pace for slow deep drives. Fuck, it felt good to be inside his mate, to connect with him on this intimate level.

Gabriel leaned over his back, quickening the thrusts of his hips until their flesh slapped. He tangled his fingers in Maximus's almost dry hair and wrenched his head to the side. He licked the vampyr's neck, his lover's soft grunts and moans lost in the revelry below them. Tiger fangs burst from his gums.

He pressed his mouth to the other man's ear. "Feel good, Maximus?"

"Fuck yes." Maximus clenched his ass around Gabriel's cock and his tiger thrust through long enough to execute a low-throated growl. The vampyr released his erection and moved his arm over his head to grip the back of Gabriel's head. Pushing up with his hand on the bannister, he twisted his head to capture Gabriel's mouth with a kiss. They were lost together in the kiss, with Gabriel moving inside Maximus, executing languid glides. Maximus broke free with a heavy moan. "Harder, *naleah. Harder.*"

Gabriel pushed him down over the rail, his hand clamped on his neck. It was a submissive pose and Maximus was as submissive as the tiger inside Gabriel. But together they took turns playing the docile partner.

With his other hand he reached around and grasped the vampyr's cock, timing the pumping of his palm with the thrust of his dick. On the drive in, he stroked to the tip of Maximus's erection, and on the tug out, he dragged his palm to the base.

Maximus panted as hard as Gabriel. The crowd egged them on as Gabriel fought against his tiger taking over. He bottomed out inside Maximus, collapsed across his back and bit the curve between shoulder and neck. Gabriel came with a roar that startled the crowd, and he struggled to restrain the tiger, as he felt the fur pop along his spine. Somehow he managed to contain the beast.

With a flex of his hips, he withdrew from Maximus's body, turned him and went to his knees. Precum leaked from the vampyr's crown. Gabriel licked it away and coiled his tongue around the head. Maximus groaned, wrapped his fingers in Gabriel's short strands and guided the speed of the blowjob. Moans hit the air as Maximus flexed his hips, driving his cock into Gabriel's mouth. The shifter accepted the dick down his throat...and purred. Maximus flew apart, climaxing, a heavy moan ripped from him. Gabriel swallowed, continuing to purr as cum filled his mouth.

"Fuck." A tremor went through Maximus when Gabriel swirled his tongue around the slit of the vampyr's waning erection.

Maximus tugged Gabriel's head back and yanked him to his feet. They embraced to a loud ovation.

Chapter Four

From across the street, Sameya watched Gabriel and the dark haired male make love in front of everyone. Even with her superior hearing, coupled with the noise of the Bourbon Street revelry, she couldn't catch most of their conversation. She'd heard only one thing. They were searching for someone. A female.

Following Gabriel from the pub to his hotel room was either clever or a blunder. She hadn't decided which, but she leaned more toward a serious miscalculation even if she liked what she saw.

Sameya had taken only a handful of lovers during her life, none of them making it beyond a one-night stand. What was the point when enjoying sex wasn't an option except for with her mate? Damn unfair. Sirens were the only breeds incapable of climaxing without their significant other. All of her sexual encounters had been for political reasons.

But what Gabriel shared with this other man...it was revealing. Love and respect guided the act, and damn the shifter had growled when he came. Had bitten into the shoulder of the dark haired male, too, right over the mating mark she assumed he'd left long ago.

Envious of their relationship, she should've walked away. Before she became enamored and serenaded them into slavery. She hadn't kept a pet in a long time. But she wanted Gabriel. If she turned them both into her pets, she could have them perform for her entertainment whenever she liked. The thought appealed to her.

The smack of her palm against the brick building drew little attention. Frustrated with herself for dallying over a shifter, she told herself to leave, this moment. Not another minute should be wasted on Gabriel and his lover. Regardless that he was pet material, her preoccupation with him waylaid her mission. She needed to focus and fast. No matter how many times she thought that, her feet remained rooted to the sidewalk.

Something about that goddamn shifter compelled her to remain. She'd held her breath when she suspected he positioned himself to enter the other male. That'd been when she caught the features of the dark-haired one. Wavy, chin-length hair. Scruff along his jaw, square chin, and carnal lips. Sensuous. Every bit as handsome as Gabriel. His eyes were a mixture between blue and silver that shifted unexpectedly to a vibrant green that glowed.

What do the mortals think of that?

He peered straight at her as he parlayed a thumbs up to the crowd and winked at Sameya. Vampyr. He knew she hid in the shadows. She allowed a small smile to tilt her lips, and he returned her grin.

Can't serenade a vampyr. I'll have to be careful to charm him with magic.

Gabriel had entered the vampyr in a hard thrust that wrenched a "fuck" from him. Those kissable lips had rounded on a moan of ecstasy, and *her* clit had throbbed as if Gabriel were in her.

Holy fucking Empress!

Orgasms weren't her commodity, just theirs, but the delight on their faces...she envied what they had.

Instead of hightailing it like she should, Sameya leaned against the wall and watched them. She suspected Gabriel had a hard time controlling the were-shifter inside him. And more than once she thought she saw the imprint of a beast glimmering over his humanity, but it was so minor she couldn't gauge his breed.

What will he look like in his animal state? She had no idea what type of animal he even was. His vibe was of the 'don't fuck with me' variety, which led her to believe he was either a large-breed cat or a wolf.

Gabriel came with a growl and buried his very obvious shifter fangs into the other man's neck. Not that the vampyr seemed to mind, but rather his sigh and the way his eyes rolled until only the white's of his eyes were visible suggested he enjoyed the bite. A lot. Probably even the man coming inside him.

A few moments later, Gabriel turned his lover and went to his knees. A hot flush swept Sameya's body as he sucked the other man's penis into his mouth.

Heat engulfed her and her channel clenched. Her knees shook, and she swiped her hand through her hair.

What is wrong with me?

Sex never affected her like this. Not when she had participated in the boring act or even when she watched. But these two men had her squirming. She stepped a little deeper into the shadows as the vampyr turned his head to gaze in her direction. That species had the vision of an eagle. And she sensed his awareness of her. He verified that theory when he licked his lips, blew her a kiss, and clamped his hand on the back of Gabriel's head, guiding the blowjob.

Sameya tried to swallow past the thick knot forming in her throat. Nothing alleviated the obstruction. Breathing grew impossible, and her lungs burned from lack of oxygen. Empress E'Neskha counted on her, while she wasted time watching two men get one another off in a very public display. Time for games was over.

She stepped a little further down the side street into the dark shadows. The vampyr shook his head and mouthed, "Stay. Watch."

Her retreat died as a gasp exited her lungs.

His mouth parted, she could just make out the dark-haired male's raspy inhalations. Flexing his hips, he drove his erection into Gabriel's mouth. A loud groan and he clenched the railing with his free hand. Angled so he could maintain eye contact with her, his head tilted backward and deep-throated moans buzzed the air.

The sound hummed across her skin and centered between her thighs.

Is that moisture leaking from my body?

Indifferent to Bourbon Street patrons, Sameya shoved away from the wall and thrust a hand inside her pants, between her thighs.

Wet.

She bit her lip and stared at the couple on the balcony. The vampyr smiled as Gabriel's purr rent the air. The dark haired male came, hard, his entire body vibrating. Through it all his eyes remained locked on Sameya...as if he invited her into their web of intimacy. Her knees quaked at the ramifications of her response. It was likely one of them was her mate.

The vampyr jerked Gabriel's head back and yanked him to his feet. They embraced to a loud applause from the street gawkers.

Sameya collapsed against the building once more, unable to drag in a breath or tear her focus off the men. Rattled by her reaction to their coupling, she wasn't sure how to proceed.

After removing her hand from her pants, she spread the moisture along her lips. What a novelty. She ached where her fingers had been. Wet from watching them…holy shit! She'd given up hope of finding her mate. With the likelihood that she'd found him, she wasn't certain it was a blessing. She'd been alone for so long, she had accepted her fate as an old maid. She was sure to fuck up a relationship. Divorces weren't an option in the mystic world. Once mated it was for life.

Besides, it was unheard of for a siren to partner with a vampyr or a shifter. Just as taboo as a vampyr or shifter mating outside their own breed. What an odd combination nature had put together.

"Holy hell." She sucked her fingers into her mouth, noting the sugary taste of her arousal.

What would the males taste like?

She flinched. *So not thinking about that.* Curiosity in this instance would lead to a whole boatload of trouble. And she had a job to do.

The men broke the kiss and the vampyr traced a finger along Gabriel's jaw. Words were spoken, but she couldn't make them out. They both ignored the hoots and hollers of the audience beneath them.

Sameya couldn't yank herself away from the carnal display. She might be a loner, but she couldn't deny she coveted their closeness. What they shared was special, and only mated pairs ever looked at one another like that.

The vampyr turned his head, his eyes silver-blue once again. Like a homing beacon, he tagged her exact spot with his sight. He crooked his finger at her to come to them. She shook her head.

Gabriel left the vampyr's embrace to white-knuckle the railing. "Where?"

"There. In the shadows. Come to us, siren." Once more, he curved his finger at her. The mortals began to notice, a few swiveling to see who the men wanted to join them.

As Sameya pushed away from the side of the building, she went invisible and strode down the street, careful not to bump into any tourists and draw unwarranted attention. Legs rubbery, her stride wasn't nearly as confident as she'd like for it to be. She made a right, then a left on the next street until she came up on the backside of Jackson Square, making a beeline for the wharf. Water had a way of calming her.

"Vacate the premises." The hobos jerked at her command and gazed about. Sameya went solid. One of them spewed misinformed propaganda about voodoo priestesses, and the other prayed to the Christian deity. "Be gone!" They tripped over one another to evacuate the bench she wanted. Not that there weren't other seats to pick from, but she coveted this particular one. It was at the end of the wharf with the least amount of visitors.

Sameya collapsed on the wood, ignoring the discomfort. The lap of water failed to soothe her frayed nerves. This complication in her life wasn't welcome. Not now. She was happy with the status quo of her life. And she'd made a promise to the Atlantian Empress. Her Empress had handpicked her as security at the dawn of the other woman's reign. Good at her job, more powerful than other known sirens, diversions had never been a problem for her. But then there was no purpose in being social when she might reap a friend tomorrow at a word from the Empress. Not that anyone wanted to be her friend. They were all too scared of her to initiate a rapport. Most of the sirens she knew had become pampered anomalies. Like a wild tiger among unsuspecting mortals, if motivated, they could turn on the mystics at any given moment with little provocation.

She'd been okay with her friendless life until tonight when she watched the relationship on the balcony blossom with something special.

So how could she execute the job she'd been tasked with efficiently if she were playing footsie with a possible mate? She twirled a lock of hair between her fingers. For her future, how could she not investigate?

She exhaled slowly. More information was needed before she could make a decision. She didn't even have an inkling which man could be her partner. Maybe he'd been in the crowd and she'd assumed he was the vampyr or shifter. Yes that had to be the case. She'd put that theory to the test right now.

After she determined her potential spouse, she would get back to the job she came here for and decide later what to do about him.

Chapter Five

Maximus had been surprised when he spied Sameya across the street flirting with the shadows. He'd initiated the sex with Gabriel for his lover's needs. It'd been obvious he required a respite. Once he spotted, Sameya, he'd killed two birds with one stone. Showing her how good they were, while they both got their rocks off.

In the black and white photo he retained from their meeting with Gryphon, he'd been unable to guess her eye color. A lavender-violet combination. What an odd color, but exquisite with her Goth red-streaked black hair. Lips sultry and stained crimson, he envisioned them parting over his and Gabriel's cocks.

Her arousal stunned him. Sirens weren't known to experience lust unless they were mated and then only with their spouse.

"You should've told me she was there, Maximus." Gabriel slammed his fingers through his spiky dark blond hair, giving the locks a more natural flow.

"What would you have done different?" He pulled on black leather pants. "If you'd gone after her, you'd have scared her off sooner. At least this way"—his head burst through the cotton black shirt—"she got an eyeful of how good we are together." He fingered his black top hat and settled it on his head. "I smelled her arousal."

"I did, also, but I dismissed the evidence as someone in the crowd."

"Right now I bet you she's thinking about us. Which one of us is a potential mate? Convincing her we're both hers might be a tad difficult." Sirens mated in pairs, not threes. Should be entertaining convincing her they would be a threesome, rather than a duo. At the moment, all Maximus wanted was to hear her climax for the first time. And get a good look at the wonder in her eyes at what she'd been missing. "My fangs are itching to taste her, Gabriel. I've got to feast on something before I lose control."

He'd rip a pedophile or murderer apart if his behavior wouldn't draw the attention of the authorities. Killing them would have to suffice.

Gabriel stopped him at the door with a hand on his forearm. "You think she's our mate, too, don't you?"

"Yes. I have no doubt. We'll find a way to bring her home, Gabriel." Snapshots of her sandwiched between them as they drove into her in unison went off in his head. She was so diminutive they'd have to be careful not to harm her. Who was he kidding? She was a mystic. A goddamn siren. That put her at the top of the mystic food chain. That meant she was hardier than she appeared, and she could take whatever they dished out. If he had his way, she'd take all they had to give her.

Maximus went out the door in search of prey.

***

Sameya caught the vampyr as he exited the hotel wearing a top hat and a skin-tight, black shirt that V'd in the front. What a fine figure he cut in his black leather pants that clung to his exquisite ass. His shiny black shoes were the only piece of attire that caught the light. Perfect attire to prowl for a victim.

Behind him, she matched her stride to his long-legged gait. Not easy with the congestion on Bourbon Street. He hooked left onto St. Louis Street and glanced over his shoulder. She remained invisible, so he might sense her, but no way could he see her.

"Spoil sport," he whispered with a grin and swaggered down the badly cracked sidewalk, his confidence evident in his stride.

Sameya bit back a grin, gawking at his superb butt encased in leathers. What a waste on a leech.

"I can hear your footsteps, siren."

To acknowledge his comment confirmed her presence. British accent. He hadn't grown up in America.

He stopped walking. She stopped. He chuckled. "We'll play it your way, *naleah*."

She frowned at the endearment but held her tongue.

The farther they moved down the darkened street, the more sparse mortal activity became. "You're with me." The vampyr made a 'come here' hand gesture. A Caucasian, balding male exited a dark alley with a cigarette hanging from his thin lips. Sameya watched as the human made no protest, not even when the vampyr clamped his hand on the back of his neck and guided him down a series of side streets. No objection when they crossed North Rampart and Basin Street and walked to the locked gate at St. Louis Cemetery.

"Be a doll and break the lock for me." He pinned her with his focus.

Sameya leaned against the brick wall and crossed her arms over her chest.

The pathetic mortal, unsuspecting of its imminent demise was the one that spoke. "With what?"

"Don't be difficult, Sameya. I know you're there."

She came away from the whitewashed brick. How'd he know her name? She hadn't shared her identity with Gabriel. And by the Empress's glory could he say her name again? In that foreign lilt, her name sounded amazing on his lips.

The vampyr's silver-blue eyes altered and glowed that vibrant green, evidence of the killer inside him. A clucking of his tongue and he sighed as he palmed the lock, pulverizing the metal. He kicked the gate open.

His body was smooth, graceful even when busting in bolted doorways. Sameya followed him inside the cemetery, shutting the gate behind them so as not to draw attention from a stray drive-by police cruiser. Two steps in his direction, she halted, realizing the vampyr stood staring in her direction wearing an ironic grin.

"I knew my little voyeur was with me."

Sameya slammed to a halt. Heat hit her cheeks and she thanked her stars he couldn't see her blush. A big error closing the gate, especially when she could serenade anything that came to investigate.

"Watch this." The vampyr braced the spine of the man against a mausoleum and sank his fangs into his throat. The mortal struggled but for a moment before going limp. Fangs retracted and he lifted his head, licked the wounds, sealing them. He adjusted his victim in his arms so he could face, Sameya. "It would please me greatly if you would go corporeal while I finish dining."

Once more, he bit his victim. This time with gusto and the male cried out. Glowing emerald eyes stared in her vicinity as he drained his victim. No point in hiding any longer, she released her magic.

His eyes widened as she appeared, traveled from her head to her feet and swept back up again. Gods help her, but his gawk felt like a physical touch and she rubbed her thighs together to alleviate the sudden ache there, deep inside her.

I cannot be the mate to a bloodsucker. But would the shifter have been any better alternative?

Releasing his victim, he lifted his head.

"He's dead?" Sameya nodded at the human.

"No." He licked and healed the wounds.

"You don't plan to kill him?"

"He'll die tonight. With my teeth in his throat."

Sameya crooked her head, studying him. A fine specimen of the male species, it was a shame he was a vampyr. But...she'd enjoyed witnessing him sink his teeth into his victim. "Finish him so I can observe."

"Come closer and you can experience his death with me."

She elevated an eyebrow, silently questioning his intentions.

"No hidden agenda. Do you wonder why I picked him?"

Sameya shrugged. What'd she care for his reasoning? All mortals were unworthy of life; she only focused on the worst of the scum. "Not really."

He frowned, as if surprised by her response. "He's a rapist of little girls."

"Then he should die in pain." She stepped forward. "I can give that to him while you feed."

A hint of a smile graced his lips, and for a long moment she became spellbound by them. Would they feel as good on her body as they were pleasing to look at? A longing sigh escaped her. Most likely, she wouldn't feel anything.

Just like I'm feeling nothing now. What a lie that is!

He repositioned the mortal, tonguing his victim's skin like a medic would a wound with an alcohol swab. "Place your fingers on his neck right below where I put my teeth."

Sameya stared into his eyes a long moment before redirecting her attention to the human's neck. She placed the pad of her index and middle finger centimeters below his teeth. His fangs surged out and pierced the male. His victim jerked, but offered no other resistance.

She slammed him with magic a few seconds later, and their quarry screamed in agony. "Quiet," she cooed to their prey. Tears rolled down his cheeks, and he executed mini-jerks in the arms of the vampyr, but his screams had turned silent.

Curious about the mystic's fangs, she shifted her middle finger to rub along the incisors where they punctured skin. The vampyr groaned.

She elevated her focus; his attention was locked on her. Growing bolder, she slid her digit up his fang to his gum line. His grip tightened on the mortal as a rattling breath left the human's lungs, expiring much too soon in Sameya's judgment.

He released their quarry, clasped her wrist with his fingers and pushed her back against the same mausoleum he'd held his prey against minutes before. In her personal space, with his big body pressed against hers, Sameya didn't back down, but glared up at him. Amusement twitched his lips.

"Unhand me."

"No."

"I will bury you, vampyr."

"You're welcome to try, doll face." He lifted a hand and ran a finger along her shoulder, down her arm. "I've been around the block a few times. I won't be that easy to defeat."

Sameya shivered from his touch. As if she had suddenly ignited with fire, he released her and tucked his hair behind both ears.

"What's with the top hat?"

He sacrificed a boyish grin to her. "It's a statement."

"What does it say?"

"It's a mistake to think I'm trivial."

Sameya glanced at the dead mortal. He could say that again. Following the long line of his legs, she noticed the bulge in his leathers. How could she not notice with the size wedged within those restrictive pants? Ripped abs weren't hidden all that much beneath the fitted cotton either. Broad shoulders made her feel more petite than she was. They didn't grow men like him and Gabriel in Atlantis.

If I allowed it, he could overpower me easily. Feeling as if dragons swirled in her belly, she wondered why that thought tingled her skin with anticipation rather than unease.

The way he watched her with his gunmetal eyes...with such heat it unnerved her.

"What's with your Goth look?"

Huh? She didn't understand the term. "I don't comprehend."

"Don't do the internet much?"

"No." What a colossal waste of time.

"The red streaks in your hair." He indicated by capturing a lock and holding it out. "The black eyeliner, long lashes, and the very red, kissable lips." The pad of his thumb dragged across her bottom lip.

Her skin tingled, felt too tight to contain her soul. Around him she couldn't think straight. She shook herself out of the weird haze he induced. She thought she understood his meaning. "I require no adornment."

"Hmm...." He rubbed his chin with his fingers.

"What's your name?"

He ignored her. "I would've thought this look lured the wrong crowd."

"My appearance is not my choice." What was his problem with her looks anyway? No one else had ever expressed a problem.

"Don't get me wrong, you're hot as sin."

"I eat *syn*."

"Pardon?" He adjusted his top hat to a more secure angle.

"*Syn*. Mortals like your rapist." Sameya indicated his human victim.

"Ah...." Why did that breath of understanding electrify her skin? And what about her statement pleased him so much? "An honest reaper."

"I've never met a dishonest one."

"How many do you know?"

"I'd wager more than you."

He chuckled, and her body reacted with a quiver down her spine to center between her thighs. Again!

Empress' delights, she disliked the jumbled way he made her feel. Confused one moment and aroused the next. "What is your name?"

"Call me mate."

Her breathing died, then escalated. She forced a lame-ass sounding laugh past her lips. "Don't get cocky. I'm not into leeches."

"Don't disqualify me from the running." He sidled closer, aligning his body against hers once more, but maintaining space with his palms on the mausoleum on either side of her head. "Not when Gabriel and I haven't had the gratification of making you come...*yet*."

She gasped, her eyes rounding at his foregone conclusion. "Better men than you have tried."

"None of them were your mates."

"Wait! Mates? As in plural?" She flattened her hands against his chest to push him away, but forgot to add pressure. The hard contours of his body fascinated her more than was practical. "That's...insane." But gods the idea fascinated her. "Sirens don't partner outside our race and we certainly don't have more than one partner."

Sameya didn't realize she spoke the thought aloud until the vampyr thrust both his hands into her hair. After he had her anchored into position, he shifted closer, widening his stride to fit her pelvis between his legs. His hard-on nestled against her abdomen as he tilted her head back by her hair.

"No more insane than a vampyr mating a shifter." His mouth landed on hers. He nibbled on her bottom lip, licked the corners and crease. Distracted by the exhilarating sensations, she was unprepared to counteract his move when he placed the pad of his thumb against her chin and tugged, parting her lips for his tongue to thrust inside.

Sameya squealed her surprise at the wet contact of his abrasive tongue. His fangs grazed her bottom flesh, and her eyelids snapped upward. He watched her, eyes glowing green. He pulled her tighter against his hard frame as his hand moved down her neck, over a breast, and across her belly to land on the front of her thigh. The fingers in her hair shifted, twisting her head to an angle that deepened the kiss.

I should stop him now before it get out of—

The forays into her mouth, thrust inside, withdraw, and repeating the movement, were subtle hints of sex. He fucked her mouth with a skill she'd never known possible. She grew so hot every pore in her body should've melted, or at the very least ignited.

Sameya squirmed against him. Needing more of something she couldn't name. With his tongue in her mouth, thinking straight became impossible.

His hand shifted from her thigh to dive between her legs. She jerked when he rubbed his thumb against her clit. Hard enough she could feel it through her Basilisk skin pants.

Empress save me that feels good. He broke the kiss and lifted his head; his gaze intense as he rubbed her where few had ever touched her. Desire burst in her belly and raced along her flesh.

The vampyr released her suddenly, taking several steps away, his fists opening and closing as he began to pace a small path in front of her.

Sameya slid down the tombstone, panting like she'd raced someone, but that made no sense because running didn't tire her. But...what had his hand between her legs been creating? The elusive orgasm? She hoped not because that meant this intimidating vampyr would be her mate.

A hand to her throat wrenched her out of her thoughts. The vampyr slid his palm upward to tilt her head back to meet his glowing green eyes. "You were this close to coming, Sameya." He indicated how close with the fingers of his other hand. The pads were almost touching. She tried to shake her head in denial, but his grip tightened, threatened without words for her to remain silent. "You're not the only one reluctant about this relationship." His hold on her loosened slightly. "Regardless that you're a reaper, Gabriel and I want you. Come to us, my little voyeur, and we'll show you what you've been missing. Not just the orgasm, but family and people who will die for you."

He kissed her hard before standing. Damn him for not being as affected as she was. Her submissive pose chafed her pride, but she made no move to rise.

He jammed his hand in his back pocket, fetched a card, and held it toward her. She didn't move to take it, so he tossed it at her feet with a smile. "That's where you'll find us. Don't make us wait long."

"I don't want what you're offering."

"Liar." The vampyr canted his head to the side. "You're braver than that, Sameya."

She stiffened. "You know nothing about me."

"You'll come." His eyes said she'd *come* in more ways than one.

Sameya shook her head. Why in all the earths would she join them? She held no control over the vampyr, and she'd bet her palatial room in Atlantis he wasn't the submissive type. As for Gabriel...she hadn't known many shifters, but none of them were docile. Sounded like a nightmare situation.

"Join us soon, Sameya."

She struggled to her feet. "I vow to you, vampyr, that not even on the soul of my Empress will I join you or Gabriel."

"Don't make me force you."

Threats were a bad move. "You may be immune to my serenade, vampyr, but you cannot force a siren to do anything." Sameya bolted, using her magic to speed up her departure.

He surprised her by catching her in a dark side-alley, one block over from the Cathedral. Sameya saw only a glimpse of his face before he slammed her against a wall and sank his fangs into her throat.

Chapter Six

"Goddamn it, Maximus, what were you thinking?" Gabriel paced a small path in front of their bedroom door.

"I was thinking she'd runaway and we'd never see her again." He'd found her defiance entertaining until she vowed on her Empress' soul not to join them. If she went back to wherever she'd been hiding before, they'd never find her. Of that he'd been certain.

The predator inside him rebelled against that outcome. Neither would the man allow her to walk out of their lives without a fucking brawl. Both halves of him would fight for her. Gabriel was the same; he needed more time to acclimate to Sameya's captivity. It was for all their best interest.

When he caught her, he'd been mindless with the need to show her to whom she belonged, so he'd reacted on instinct and sank his teeth into her neck. And sucked unadulterated ambrosia into his body. Her blood *was* nirvana.

Sameya had moaned, sealing her fate with the sound. No more proof necessary to confirm her identity. Only a mate enjoyed a vampyr's bite. Letting her walk away after he'd found her, was more than he could tolerate, so he'd flooded her system with *venome* and promised the next time he'd forgo the toxin so she could appreciate the experience.

"It's not like you argued against bringing her to our home and trapping her here with magic." Right after entering the hotel room in New Orleans, Maximus had placed her on the bed and called for a helicopter to take them home immediately. Less than two hours later, they'd landed on the helipad twenty minutes outside their secluded estate on the outskirts of Chimera, Alabama. A limousine at the ready to see they arrived home safely with no questions about the comatose woman with them.

Their mind manipulation abilities were a spectacular talent to possess, not to mention the obscene amount of cold-hard cash they paid their servants for loyalty.

On the drive to their house, Gabriel had contacted their local gal-pal, Kat, a witch who could fuck you up before she broke a smile. Asking few questions, she'd met them at their home and hexed their abode, locking Sameya within the private boundary. The magic had a one-week time limit. Not very long to convince her to remain with them.

"Congratulations. She's beautiful." Kat ran a fingertip along Sameya's cheek, her gaze locked on his siren. Kat's leather one-shoulder top flattened her ample breasts. That thing couldn't be comfortable. Her long brown hair offset her teal eyes. As far as witches went, Kat was the best of her ilk. Highly sought after, she garnered a huge asking price for her spells. They'd been close friends for over three hundred years. She'd even been his and Gabriel's lover for a short period of time, so he knew how ample her breasts were, and that top did nothing to showcase them.

She spoke a series of words that stung Maximus's skin and a diamond-encrusted collar appeared in her palm. She pressed it into his hand. The magic coming off the piece tickled his flesh.

"She's old, and I'm not strong enough to trap her in the house for long. That snapped around her neck"—she indicated the jewelry in his hand—"will keep her bound to you, Maximus, until you're ready to release her." Kat tossed Gabriel a woeful expression. "The cat in him won't allow him to enslave her." Maximus noticed the muscles tensing in Gabriel's shoulders. The tiger would enjoy dominating her in the bedroom and chasing her, but his feline's sense of fair play wouldn't allow him to take the choice away from her. "Your vampyr, however, will love lording over her." Just the idea made his cock thicken in his leather pants.

Gabriel scowled. "You've done all we asked, and we're thankful. But we don't need further complications. Take your necklace and get the fuck out, Kat."

A slim grin tweaked the corners of her lips. She ignored Gabriel. "The magic activates when you snap the gemstones around her neck. Since Gabriel's too big a pussy—all puns intended of course—you have the honors, Maximus."

A displeased grumble rolled from Gabriel as Maximus flipped the necklace over in his palm. There weren't any discernable clasps.

She must have sensed his confusion, because she said, "Magic holds it together. Place the two ends together, and it'll lock tight. Only you will be able to remove it, Maximus."

He should refuse to enslave her. But when Sameya woke, she'd run first chance she received. He couldn't take the risk of losing her. Not until they had an opportunity to convince her to remain.

"You're not seriously considering this, are you, Maximus?" Gabriel gaped at the sparkling collar. He spoke funny thanks to his tiger being half out. White striped fur mixed with flesh along his arms and his canines were elongated.

He shouldn't be, but...."She'll reject us outright. This will give her time to get to know us." Maximus held no hope she wouldn't wake enraged and ready to bolt. And he wouldn't blame her. Anyone took him down the way he had her he'd want blood, also. The collar would keep her with them.

Gabriel crossed his arms over his chest. "You know this is wrong."

"I'll release her in a month."

"Maximus—"

Maximus bent over Sameya and hooked the necklace on her before Gabriel could talk him out of binding her to him. "I won't lose her without a fight." As the words departed his lips, the jewelry adjusted and tightened about Sameya's throat, turning into a choker. It looked damn good on her. Went a long way in marking her as *his* property.

"Smart decision, Maximus."

"Fucking *leave*, Kat." Gabriel pointed at the door, but glared at Maximus. "You've done enough damage."

Maximus wasn't sure to whom the last comment was intended.

"You'll thank me later, pussy cat." She blew Gabriel a kiss and twirled a dark brown lock of hair around a finger.

"Give us some time alone, Kat." No point in taunting the tiger beneath the surface. While the witch was a long-time friend, she pushed his mate's buttons often.

"Nah...I think I'll hang around." Gabriel snarled and their unflustered gal-pal went on. "You might need me, so I'll be in the game room playing X-box." She trounced out of the room in her black four-inch, calf-high boots and skinny jeans.

***

"You disrespect our *mate*, Maximus." Gabriel fought against the tiger going after Kat. There was no debating with his inner beast. The witch had wronged their woman, and the animal instinct was to make her suffer. In the end, she'd kick his ass with her witchery shit. Clawing her a little would go a long way in taming his cat's fury, though. Ultimately, this was Maximus's fuck up. He'd practically roofied her with his *venome*. Instead of seeing to her welfare, he'd kidnapped her and now enslaved her with the witch's help.

Son-of-a-fucking-bitch! Nothing good could come of this. To bind Sameya to their will was as good as caging a wild animal. His cat would enjoy chasing her and taming her, but confinement would never be an option.

"My actions are justified." The blaze of green eyes testified to the vampyr's broodiness.

"Bullshit." His canines drew blood as he attempted to speak around them. "I thought you capable of many things, but never this."

"She gave me no other choice."

What a cop out! Alternatives were always available. "How would you feel if your freedom was taken from you, the way you've done to her?" Maximus paled and ran his hand down his face. Gabriel refused to soften his words. "I'm disappointed in you, Maximus."

The vampyr's shoulders squared and he notched his chin higher. "When she woke and busted through Kat's spell, how disappointed would you be when she departed our life...*forever?*" He got in Gabriel's face. "I would be devastated to lose her. I know you would be, as well. This way, I give us a slim chance of wooing her into staying."

"It's wrong." It was mulish of Gabriel to continue to reiterate the wrongness of what Maximus had done. His focus would be better served on damage control when Sameya woke. The tiger's sense of honor was irritated. They should be protecting her, not causing her harm.

"Please try to understand—"

Enough of this bullshit. Gabriel shifted. Arguing wouldn't resolve their dispute.

"Goddamn it, Gabriel, your shifting solves nothing." Maximus put his fingers through his unruly hair. Using his feline body, Gabriel nudged Maximus away from their woman. "Don't be like this."

Gabriel barred his teeth and growled. He leapt onto the bed and stretched out beside Sameya, chuffing his annoyance.

Chapter Seven

Sameya's head throbbed. Disoriented, she rubbed her temples with her fingertips and moaned when the touch elicited more pain than comfort. Lowering her arms, her hand touched something furry.

That same hairy object made a chuffing sound. Her eyes flew open, and she winced at the sudden brightness of the room. The sun poured through the window to her right. Using slow movements, she turned her head to identify the warm entity. A white Bengal tiger.

His massive head rested on the pillow beside her. Huge. At least six hundred pounds of muscle and somewhere near twelve feet in length. What a beauty. Yellow eyes peered at her. She'd never seen a white Bengal with anything but blue eyes before. His tail flicked back in forth in short agitated movements.

"Welcome back, siren," a darkly hypnotic voice said.

Sameya jerked into a seated position and regretted it when her head paid her back with a stab to the temples. The fucking vampyr from last night prowled nearer. Wincing at the continued throb, she watched him cautiously. He'd ditched the top hat, exposing wavy, chin length hair.

Beside her the feline made a weird sound, a cross between a growl and a snarl. The creature sat up with so much grace, she momentarily forgot about the vamp. His weight dented the bed, and she adjusted her position to keep from rolling into him.

Like an amnesiac her memories from last night slammed into her. The cat forgotten, she swiveled to face the vampyr. "You bastard. You bit me!"

"That's not all I did."

Narrowing her focus on him, she realized he was still attired in the same clothes from the previous evening. The only thing missing was his hat. The room held a distinct male feeling. Navy walls, dark wood floors, a leather chair and settee near the window, and the four-poster, cherry bed with royal-blue coverlet. Not a touch of femininity in the room.

She threw her legs over the side of the mattress. Thankfully the throbbing in her skull had abated a fraction. A scratch at her throat halted her rise. The vampyr watched her, his silver-blue eyes rapt as she lifted a hand to her neck. An inch thick choker, encrusted with jewels by the feel, snared her focus as the enchantment tingled on her fingertips.

Seeking her well of siren magic, she tapped into the mojo in the necklace. A powerful totem intended to restrain her. When she located the witch who'd trapped her, she'd kill the individual...or better yet, keep the brazen one as a pet.

Sameya leapt off the bed. The Bengal followed as she stalked toward the vampyr. He held his ground as she approached. Reaching him, she placed her hand on his chest, directly over his heart and channeled power into him. Nothing happened.

The motherfucker!

Her magic wouldn't work on the one who bound her. "*You* collared me, not the witch!"

"So it would seem."

"I demand your name."

"Why?"

"I want to know the name of the man I'll kill when I'm free."

He chuckled. "Good luck with that, *pet*."

Cold rage slithered down her spine. She kept pets, but would never be anyone else's. Taking a page out of the human handbook, she smacked him across the cheek. His head snapped to the side, and the throb in her hand was refreshing. As he turned his face toward her, he worked his jaw. A red handprint pinkened his skin.

Fury stole her logic. She wanted to unleash her siren on something, someone, or anything to prove she wasn't suddenly as sterile as the humans.

Breathe through it. I'm only defenseless against him and only as long as this magic is viable. When she broke the spell, she'd rip him apart and enthrall the witch as a pet for eons. Sweet revenge would be hers.

"When my Empress discovers what you've done—"

"Blah, blah, blah." He mocked, rolling his eyes. "She must leave Atlantis first. I cannot imagine even you are that important to her."

His conceit would be her victory. She swung her arm, but he caught her wrist and put her against the wall. The tiger snarled.

"Stay out of it, Gabriel."

Gabriel? She glanced over the vampyr's shoulder as the feline shifted into the man from the bar. Fuck her, he'd said he was a shifter, but she never would've guessed he was the biggest of the breeds.

The shifter's eyes gleamed gold, rimmed in a wide black band. "Release her, Maximus."

Startled, her gaze shot to the vampyr. "Maximus? As in...'MadMax?'"

"I see my reputation precedes me."

"Impressive." And it was. He'd single-handedly taken out almost the entire troll contingent.

"He's not been MadMax for over a thousand years." Gabriel's voice licked over her like a lover's tongue. She gritted her teeth and steeled herself against any physical response.

Didn't matter when he'd held the title of MadMax. He had a name in Atlantis. "Uncollar me, and I'll pretend this did not transpire." She'd still go after the fucking witch.

"No." Maximus's hand slid from her shoulder to her throat. Her pulse leapt, and that odd feeling of heat snaked through her again. "You're mine and Gabriel's mate."

She glanced at Gabriel who hovered behind Maximus's right shoulder. She'd already told the hardheaded vampyr, sirens did not have plural mates. Although the idea of having two men such as these paired with her...she'd be lying if she pretended not to be intrigued by the idea. How many would envy her in Atlantis? Mostly she was feared, and that had served her well, but sometimes the fright grew wearisome. The only friend she could claim was the Empress, and theirs was a complicated relationship.

Sameya shook her head. She wouldn't allow vanity to turn her rash.

Maximus's thumb swished back and forth, drawing her attention to him. "We cannot lose you without trying to court you."

"You think this is the best option?" She yanked on the choker. Had he collared any other siren, she'd probably think him not just ballsy, but exceedingly intriguing. Worthy of a roll in the sack to say she'd done him.

"I was against it."

Maximus hissed at Gabriel's comment. "You would've run, Sameya, and we'd have lost our chance to prove we're right for you."

She'd already advised him once that sirens didn't mate with creatures beneath them. Maybe if she said it a second time but slower this go-around, he'd comprehend the words. "Sirens. Do. Not. Mate. With. Vampyrs. Or. Shifters."

"Incorrect. *You* are mated to a vampyr and a shifter. Which means, sirens *do* have plural mates and do so with those outside their stratum."

Empress, what an imbecile!

Gabriel moved to stand at their side, his golden eyes attentive. Sameya worried she could lose herself in those beautiful yellow orbs. "Don't you want to know what an orgasm feels like?"

Hell, yes, but not with either of them. And no reminder of their lovemaking to one another would alter her mind. But...what would it feel like to have their hands on her the way they'd touched one another? Could they make her come? She highly doubted it. More superior men than them had tried. And failed.

Drawing herself straight, she glared at the shifter. "Can't want what I've never had."

"And yet you desire both of us." Maximus's snarky grin made her bristle.

Did he work at being irritating or was it a natural talent? "Arrogance isn't attractive. I desire both of you as much as I enjoy being collared." She glowered at Maximus.

From the corner of her eye, she caught Gabriel shake his head. "Foolish, hardheaded siren. You have no clue of what you speak."

Sameya snorted. "I know there is more to life than fleeting moments of trivial hedonism."

Gabriel snatched her out of Maximus's grasp. His hand palmed her nape, his fingers massaging her flesh. She stiffened at the skin-to-skin contact. His touch did *not* elicit a response from her.

The tiger's other arm circled her waist and he pulled her flush against his chest. "You'll learn something about me, Sameya. I have zero tolerance for bullshit."

"I have zero tolerance for enslavement."

Maximus chuckled. "She'll be a joy to tame."

"Fuck you, MadMax." She wrenched Gabriel's head down with her hands and kissed him, suffusing her siren song into him.

"Okay," Maximus said from behind her, sounding a tad surprised by her aggression.

Gabriel jerked at the first thrust of her magic, stiffened, his hands clenching on her hips. He fought the spell, but he was no match. The image of him holding her down by her hips as he thrust his cock into her slashed through her mind...his thoughts migrating to her conscious. What a naughty boy he would be in the sack. Shoving the wicked fantasy aside, she concentrated on giving him a piece of herself and enthralling him to become hers. The moment her magic locked on, all tension left his body.

Sameya drew away from his lips, not lingering on how good they'd felt pressed to hers. She whispered against his ear. "Kill the vampyr the moment I shut the bedroom door behind me."

The shifter nipped her earlobe. "As you wish, mistress."

Smiling, she stepped out of his reach and strolled toward the door.

"Where do you think you're going?" The haughty vampyr. Too bad she wouldn't be present to witness his death at the hands of his lover, otherwise she'd gloat her ass off.

"To cool off with a drink. That is allowed, right, *master?*"

"You're not allowed to leave the premises without my express consent."

Sameya flicked him the finger as she shut the door behind her. A roar emerged the moment the lock engaged. She giggled as crashing glass and a curse from the vampyr sounded from the room.

"I win." *As always I win. She* was a master at the games immortals played.

She reclined against the door to listen to the conflict within. The vampyr held no chance of escaping the shifter. Being lovers, Maximus would try to not harm Gabriel any more than necessary. Because of his inability to injure his mate, the vampyr would fail, and the shifter would win. That equated to victory for Sameya.

There for a brief moment, she'd contemplated going along with their game. What harm would it have caused? None really. She would've gotten laid, been disappointed when the sex sucked—as it always did...that wasn't likely to change after over fifty thousand years—and then she would've been on her merry way after she gloated over not being their mate. The 'told you so' would've been sweet. There was one problem with that...she ran her finger along the collar. No one subjugated her without repercussions.

With a tilt of her head and a grim smile, she tapped the jewels. In no time at all, this trinket would be useless. The witch's magic infused into the choker gave Sameya a direct link to that particular creature. That one was near. Very close, indeed.

Keeping the shifter was tempting. He'd been receptive of her siren song. Easy pickings. They made the best pets.

But first things first...the witch responsible for this fuck-up. The streamers of magic painting the air would lead her straight to her quarry. Sameya stepped away from the door, her stride determined.

Chapter Eight

The home of her captors could be classified as a mansion it was so huge. Having no intention of staying beyond the next five minutes, she ignored the obviously male décor and made a beeline straight for the sorceress.

Sameya found the witch in a room full of entertainment...televisions, billiards, darts, eighties arcade-style games, along with a fully stocked bar by her guess. The enchantress felt young, not more than three or four centuries old. An adolescent in paranormal years, but the power coming off her—she'd be extremely powerful in another century, which would make her an invaluable pet when Sameya could wield the other woman's magical clout for her own benefit.

Going invisible just as the witch turned in the other direction, allowed Sameya to go unnoticed. As she approached the enchantress undetected, she attempted to dig into her thoughts...but was blocked. *Stronger than I realized.* She drew abreast of the other woman and felt anxiety radiate from her tall, lithe figure.

"Who are you?" The witch's gaze darted about the room.

Sameya smiled. Throwing her power about the room to confuse a fellow supernatural was one of many siren skills. They'd been useful creatures once, killing the human pestilence that existed among mankind, even killing their own when they'd gone insane or wanted too much control. They'd earned their reaper nickname. Feared by all of the loredom, their friends were few, but they kept the peace at all cost. Many of her kind currently neglected their talents and had grown indolent in life. Pampered in Atlantis they collected friends rather than the scum.

Since entering earth, she'd discovered mankind was plagued with evil; it even festered among their youth. Their justice system lacked conviction, but Sameya wasn't bound by the human law's sense of fair play. While here on her mission, she'd taken out several amoral individuals.

Empress E'Neskha trusted Sameya to locate the would-be assassin, and she would complete her mission. A couple of so-called mates wouldn't distract her or stand in her way.

"Where are you?" The witch's voice trembled.

Smart girl to fear me.

"Here." Her voice projected across the room and the other woman turned toward the sound. "But I'm really here." Sameya laid her palm on the witch's bare shoulder and overpowered her with siren magic. "Mine."

The enchantress' lips parted in a gasp as she spun about, while Sameya fizzled into view allowing her invisibility to drop.

Sameya trailed a finger along the girl's jaw. "Sit."

Her new pet slumped onto the sofa, gawking at Sameya.

"What's your name?"

"Kat."

"How old are you?"

"Four hundred twenty-three."

She could see the frustration and questions burning in the girl's teal eyes. "Speak freely."

Kat gulped. "Why would you serenade me?"

"You helped enslave me." She indicated the choker about her neck. "But that'll cease soon."

"The magic's good for a month. It won't drop before then."

"It is nil when Maximus is dead."

"You killed him?" Kat paled at the idea.

"No." Sameya shook her head. "He will be dead soon, though. I serenaded the tiger and set him on the vampyr."

"They're your mates!"

"Not going to happen." Kat's stricken expression articulated her confusion without the need for words. "Mate is a polite word for master. When a siren mates, the female is serenaded, and loses her freedom. I will *not* allow that to happen to me."

Why'd she confess that, when she normally hoarded siren secrets? She had no idea, but she did know she would never give her spouse complete control over her. No way would she forfeit her liberty simply for the elusive orgasm. Nothing could possibly be that good.

"They aren't like that. Maximus and Gabriel won't want to control you."

Anger spiraled up her spine. Sameya ground her back teeth to resist retaliating against Kat. "Maximus. Already. Does. Control. Me." She jerked hard on the choker. "Thanks to *you*."

"On your knees, bitch."

Sameya bristled at the sound of the British voice behind her, but went to her knees. "How'd you survive?" The tiger should've bested the vampyr. They were superior fighters. *Goddamn!* What was she to do now?

"Release Kat from your serenade." Oh, he sounded angry, very angry. Good! She was pissed that he subjugated her!

How she despised him for his control over her. Unable to disobey, she connected with the mental constraints she'd bound to the witch and cut through them. Kat sagged as if actual ties had been severed.

"Be careful, Maximus. You have no idea how powerful her magic is." The witch rubbed her temples.

"Proceed with caution, Kat." Sameya glared at the woman. "When this is over—"

"Enough!" Maximus stepped in front of her. Capturing her gaze with his glowing green vampyr eyes, he hooked two fingers beneath the necklace and jerked her a little straighter, the jewelry pinched the back of her neck. A cut on his brow healed as she watched. The evidence of clawed material indicated he'd survived an attack. "Come, my little reaper. You have a tiger to release and an orgasm to experience."

Chapter Nine

Maximus watched Sameya pale at the mention of an orgasm. He'd never met anyone that didn't greet a climax with eagerness, but sirens were unique among the paranormal castes and the most powerful of all mystic creatures. Their kind ruled Atlantis. They could've run the universe, but they were obligated to the survival of mystics. They were the jailers, the assassins, and the sin-eaters for the diversity of the supernatural.

Conflicting emotions migrated through him. He wanted to redden her backside with a long and well-needed spanking, but he wanted to see her expression when she came for the first time. To have discovered she would be enslaved to the one who gave her such pleasure surprised him. He wouldn't want to be anyone's slave either. But...she held no qualms about chaining others to her domination.

"We'll release Gabriel from your serenade first. On your feet, Sameya."

"I *hate* you." She knocked at the arm that had two fingers locked around the jewels encircling her throat.

Holding tight, he yanked her against his body by the necklace, angled his hand beneath her chin, and forced her to tilt her head back to meet his eyes. "At the moment, the feeling is mutual."

She was so tiny pressed up against him, the top of her head reached only his shoulders, but his dick responded like a flash fire. Flaccid one moment, and hard a second after she connected with his frame.

"Maximus, go easy on her." Kat gripped his arm. "She's your mate and scared."

He was no fool. He knew she was frightened. Being held against her will went against her nature. Sameya used all available resources to gain her freedom. He'd do the same in a similar situation. The problem they had was convincing her she was better off *with* them.

"Don't tell me how to treat my mate, Kat." A gruff statement uttered to keep Sameya guessing. He wouldn't harm her, but more could be gained if she didn't know it yet. Besides, he figured she'd consider an orgasm detrimental to her well being, especially in light of what she'd just revealed. "Follow me."

Maximus tugged on the collar and led her out of the room. "Lucky for you we had a vault installed in our floor." They'd used it several times to lock their bounty into after capture before transporting them to their employer. He'd never thought to use it against his lover. "Otherwise, I'd probably be dead."

"Lucky for you, don't you mean?"

Employing his vampyr speed, Maximus spun and shoved her against the wall. A hand captured her hip, and he elevated her until they were at eye-level. The fingers hooked in her choker released and encircled her throat. "Spread your legs, Sameya."

"Don't," her voice trembled.

"Do it."

She obeyed, but turned her head aside as she executed the movement. Maximus moved into place between her thighs and released the pressure on her hip, so her pussy snuggled against his cock. His pelvis was all that held her in place. She gasped, eyes rounding before clenching the lids shut.

"Look at me."

She whimpered, but turned her head toward him. Her eyelids flickered upward. Wary amethyst returned his perusal. Such a unique and amazing color, coupled with her dark complexion and red and black striped hair, she was stunning. Her lush figure was made for seduction. Maximus could not wait to sink into her body.

"You ever turn Gabriel against me again and I'll beat you."

"You try it, leech, and I'll annihilate you."

"Forgetting so soon who is in control?" He tweaked her collar. She blanched. "If I told you to go to your knees and suck my cock, you'd do it without a blink."

"No gentleman would force a woman to perform sexual acts."

"Don't make the mistake of comparing me to your elite Atlantis society, my fuckable reaper. I'm no gentleman. In fact...." he ran his thumb along the pulse in her neck; it beat wildly against his pad. "Allow yourself to pretend my mouth is between your legs. Feel my tongue licking you, as if I am really there. Get very close to climaxing, but stop before going over the edge." She'd come with him and Gabriel, but not because of some fantasy-induced release.

Sameya blinked. She shifted and froze with a tiny squeal when his erection nestled perfectly against her folds.

"Are you pretending?"

"No." Staring at his mouth, she licked her lips. "I can't. I have nothing to compare your suggestion to."

"Pity." He'd rectify that immediately. Maximus stepped away from her and watched her slide down the wall. Her shaky legs almost gave out when her feet touched the floor. He'd rattled her, and that pleased him. Withholding a grin, he wrapped his fingers in her jewelry once more and led her back to his bedroom. Inside the room, he slammed and locked the door. "Sit on the bed."

She hesitated, but they both knew she couldn't challenge him. Back ramrod straight, she settled on the edge of the king-sized bed. Maximus watched her for a moment. In the next twenty-four hours, she'd be well and truly fucked on that mattress. In sleep, they'd sandwich her between them and wake her—the tiger's roars coming from the vault jerked him back to reality.

"Release Gabriel from your enchantment."

Her lips compressed into a line of unhappiness, but a second later, she said, "Done."

"Are you lying to me?"

"I cannot lie."

Right. He'd forgotten. Lying was one of the few exceptions to a siren's excessive talents.

Maximus went to the vault's door, unlocked it, and twisted the handle. Once opened, Gabriel prowled out in tiger form. White Bengal and large. Intimidating, but the siren notched her chin a little higher, mutiny blazing from her eyes. Defiant even when she was outplayed. Fuck him, that was hot.

Gabriel went straight to her and knocked her flat on her back. Chuffing, he leapt onto the bed and caught her throat between his teeth...purring. Ruined the aggression with the satisfied noise.

Maximus joined them and met her wide-eyed gaze. Maybe the aggressive move hadn't been destroyed by Gabriel's purring. He'd forgotten Sameya didn't know the many sounds of his lover's moods.

"He's displeased with you." Maximus climbed onto the bed beside her. And a lot turned on by her Hail Mary tactic. They both were.

Fingers clenched in the comforter, she said nothing. A few heartbeats later, she flinched. The wet rasping sounds told Maximus that Gabriel had begun to lick her flesh.

"Is he licking you?"

"Yes." Not more than a whisper.

"I'll remove your boots and pants so he can tongue you elsewhere." The tiger's purring rumbled loud and Sameya's breathing stuttered.

"Can't."

"I'm in control, reaper. I can do anything I want."

"No. My pants and boots won't give for anyone but me."

Interesting. Maximus still tugged against her footwear. When it remained in place, he slid his hands up her legs and cupped her pussy, rubbing. She gasped and tried to squirm away, but with the way Gabriel contained her she went nowhere.

"Release her Gabriel, so she can remove her clothing for you." Golden eyes blinked at Maximus. "Do you want to lick her pussy or not?"

Two breaths puffed from the tiger's nostrils. That was a yes.

"Remove your pants and boots, Sameya," Maximus said as Gabriel laid a final lick to her throat and sat back on his haunches, his yellow eyes focused on their mate. In tiger form, she'd be his sole concentration.

Her hands shook as she sat up and ran her fingertip down the side of one boot. The movement opened up the odd material to the ankle. "Don't make me beg."

Ignoring her plea, he changed the subject. "What are these made of?" He retrieved the shoe from her and studied it. Sharp, but soft.

"Dragon scales." The other foot ornament hit the floor. Maximus elevated an eyebrow, surprised to discover dragons still remained. Only in Atlantis. "Please don't force me. I cannot bear enslavement."

He scrutinized her. Tears shimmered in her eyes, turning their amethyst color into glittering orbs like the stone when it sparkled in light. "You're only enslaved if you climax, right?"

A brief nod. He would've missed the movement if he hadn't been watching her with such intensity.

She'd stalled on the removal of her clothing. Maximus allowed the transgression. "And only your mate can make you come, right?"

"Yes."

"Do you believe either of us are your mate?"

Her bottom lip trembled and she rubbed her temples.

"You cannot lie," he reminded, running his finger along the side of her knee.

"I—I believe it's...possible." Sameya met his gaze, hesitation turning them over bright. "I know enough about both your breeds to know you wouldn't...at least the shifter wouldn't"—she tilted her head toward Gabriel—"be able to tolerate forcing his mate into submission."

Maximus arched an eyebrow. "Then you also know that often when a shifter finds his spouse, he often fucks her for the first time without the female's consent." The act of non-consent was heavy in the paranormal world. It was even more pronounced in the shifter race. He pinched her chin to force her to maintain eye contact. "Tigers like to dominate, but that doesn't mean he'll want to keep you enslaved."

"And you?"

"I'll keep you enslaved until you admit you're ours and better off with us."

"What if that never happens?"

The very idea made his stomach sink and his fangs drop. He licked the incisors. "We'll remove your pants together, Sameya." Her lips parted, and before she could speak he said, "No further arguments or pleas. You're better than that."

Chapter Ten

Maximus held her eyes as they slid her pants off. Sameya wanted to scream in frustration. Yet...there was something intoxicating about these two men. They intrigued her and incited unfamiliar feelings. Scary and fascinating.

"What type of pants are these?"

Why all the interest in her clothing? "Basilisk skin."

"Did you kill the Basilisk?" The article hit the floor with a thud and his palm slid up her leg.

"No." Breath stuttered in her lungs and congealed in a knot. "It's of reptile origins and sheds its skin. Those sheddings come at a high"—her voice squeaked when his palm neared the juncture of her thighs, but the direction altered at the most crucial moment—"price." She couldn't deny she liked his touch. But liking and wanting it were two very different things. "I'm under the sanctuary of Empress E'Neskha." Her last cowardly ditch to save her life and she blamed him for reducing her to such a spineless state.

"That holds no power here, Sameya. And not even in Atlantis against one's mate...or rather mates in your situation." He placed an emphasis on the plurality of the word as his hand smoothed over her hip. "And the shirt?"

"Human origins."

"Good." He quickly unlaced the red corset and drew it over her head.

Maximus took a step back and his eyes went from silver-blue to vampyr green in a breath. Chill bumps invaded her flesh, which had nothing to do with the room's temperature, but rather from the force of his observation as he measured her naked flesh.

Gabriel's sudden purring startled her. She glanced at the huge feline as he rose and leapt off the bed in a graceful move. Maximus palmed the tiger's head and stroked him, pausing to scratch behind his ears. "I'm jealous you'll taste her first, Gabriel."

Sameya covered her face. "Gods, help me!"

The bed jostled and Maximus pulled her hands away from her face, his regard tolerant. "Do not hide from either of us. You want us."

"No." She damn sure did not! To want them ensured her slavery.

"I thought you couldn't lie? I smell your arousal."

Was that why she felt hot down below? "My body yearns. I do not."

"We'll alter that state of mind." Maximus kissed her, his tongue flicking along her lips. The ability to breathe evaporated. She resisted his embrace by clamping her teeth together. A slow lick along the column of her leg from the tiger shocked her and drew forth a gasp. Against her lips Maximus chuckled and plunged his tongue into her mouth.

"Spread your legs for Gabriel." He nipped at her bottom lip, soothing away the sting.

Sameya parted them slightly, resisting the urge to wriggle away from the lick Gabriel placed against her calve. The cat's tongue was abrasive, but not distasteful.

"Wide," Maximus whispered against her jaw.

She whimpered, but followed his instruction. Another set of searing kisses as his hand slid down between her breasts, across her belly, along her hip, to clamp his palm on the inside of her thigh. His fingers slipped beneath her knee and pulled her leg up until her kneecap was braced against his hip. She could only imagine how open she was to Gabriel. No one had ever seen her so exposed. Not emotionally or physically.

Licks to the sensitive flesh where her legs united with her body. Maximus mimicked the same movement against a nipple. Sameya bit her bottom lip to restrain her cry. Too much sensation and not what she wanted.

"I'm afraid she'll climax quickly, Gabriel." Abandoning the teasing licks, Maximus suckled on the nipple. She clamped a hand on his head, and tangled her fingers in his hair with the intention of pulling his mouth off her breast. She'd yank him bald if necessary...but the enjoyment was so strong, she forgot her purpose and instead held his head in position.

Teeth grazed along her flesh, starting at her knee and taking a path straight up the inside of her thigh. A tiny moan escaped before she could suppress it.

"Stop," her voice broke. "Something's wrong." Heat flashed across her body, but gooseflesh cooled her skin. She ached all over, but wanted more. She felt balanced on the threshold of something powerful, and so extreme she wouldn't survive. And if she did endure, she wouldn't come out the other side the same woman.

Maximus lifted his head. "Shh...relax. Nothing is wrong." He disengaged her fingers from his hair and pressed kisses against her knuckles.

The feline's tongue swiped through her folds without any forewarning. Sameya yelped, her hips jerking.

"Fuck, you're extra sensitive to touch." He sucked one of her fingers into his mouth.

The short breaths of the shifter puffed against her skin as his tongue moved over her hot flesh with repetition. Caught up in the sensations, Sameya couldn't rip her sights off Maximus. His green eyes burned into hers as the fur between her thighs dissipated and was replaced with the man. Gabriel's oral bliss changed, he probed her opening, pushing into her with his tongue over and over again. His fingers teased the outer edges of her labia as Maximus's face blurred in her vision.

Maximus kissed her as Gabriel's thumbs spread her lower lips. Softer than the cat's, the curl of his tongue felt different from the tiger's but no less amazing.

"She has a fat clit." Gabriel kissed the nub as Maximus departed her lips to look at him between her thighs. The shifter kissed her clitoris once more.

"What does she taste like, Gabriel?" Maximus's dark voice licked across her body.

"Ambrosia." Gabriel thrust a finger into her and she cried out. Nothing painful about his intrusion, but the pleasure was more than she could've anticipated.

"You're a virgin?" Gabriel executed small thrusting motions with his digit.

"No." Were those noises coming from her? Maximus smiled at her, so she guessed they were. "Five lovers." What was the point when the touch of others had sickened her? She'd only taken a lover when necessary in her line of work. Usually only as a political move to aid the Empress and she'd barely tolerated the intrusion then. Her first lover she had foolishly hoped was her mate. Feeling nothing but revulsion as he rutted her, she'd sworn off sex for a very long time.

Yet...with these men, she enjoyed both of their touches.

"She's terribly tight, Maximus." Gabriel swirled his tongue around her clitoris and Sameya almost catapulted off the bed.

"No wonder she's so sensitive to touch." Maximus rubbed her belly with his palm. "She's not experienced."

She detested being manhandled. Except for now.

More swirls against her clit and she curled her fingers in Gabriel's spiky hair. One of them hooked her legs over the tiger's broad shoulders as his mouth worked against her flesh and his finger pumped into her.

Panting in between the moans and sighs, she became lost in the quivering centered at the nexus of her thighs. Only vaguely was she aware she had begun to grind her hips against his face and pull him against her with her hand.

This couldn't bode well. Not for her at least. Her belly cramped and a high-pitched whimper crashed through her lips.

Fingers tangled in her hair and Maximus drew her head up just enough her gaze locked on Gabriel nestled between her legs. "Oh...*gods!*"

Sameya crashed with a scream. Her body shuddered and it felt as if her molecules melted. Gabriel's tonguing grew more aggressive as a flood of warmth exited her body.

Maximus ran a fingertip around her lips. "You're even more beautiful when you come, my little reaper."

Sameya blinked, but could manage no coherent response. *Dear goddess that was spectacular.*

"You're turn, Maximus." Gabriel rose from between her thighs, his finger still pumping into her very moist pussy. So wet, there were sucking noises where his digit met her body.

"I'm going to fuck you, Sameya." Maximus pinched a nipple, staring at her as if he expected a complaint. Her tongue—right along with her body—had dissolved into such an uncaring state of completeness, she couldn't summon the urge to complain if she'd wanted.

"Taste her first." Gabriel removed his finger and offered it to Maximus. The vampyr sucked the other man's finger into his mouth, his cheeks hollowing.

"Perfection," Maximus said before he kissed the shifter.

Sameya watched them in fascination. Maximus licked her release from Gabriel's lips before devouring his mouth in a kiss. Gabriel was already nude from the shift, so he undressed Maximus, slow and thorough as they fondled one another. She ached at their obvious affection for each other. She'd never anticipated having such intimacy with anyone and to have it this close to her grasp...*I don't want it.* To be that committed to someone else scared her to death.

A serpent tattoo flanked Gabriel's right arm. The tail of a white Bengal tiger began on his ribcage and spread across his back. The front claws ripped into his shoulder blades, the marks were so realistic she almost believed the ink an authentic tiger instead of a tattoo. A Celtic shoulder design spiraled upward to stop midway up his neck.

The shifter kissed down Maximus's throat and then lower when he jerked the vampyr's shirt over his head. Angled away from her, she thought she caught a twinkle of something foreign on Maximus's chest. Sameya sat up and slipped off the bed, sidling closer to Gabriel for a better gander.

"Don't go anywhere." Gabriel palmed the back of her head and she flicked a glance at him. He wasn't as tall as Maximus, but they both dwarfed her. She felt tiny standing next to them.

Gabriel's yellow eyes held her pinned in place, while fascinating her with their odd color...at least odd on a white Bengal. But they fit him.

"He's pierced." She indicated Maximus's nipples.

"Want to lick them?" Gabriel made the offer, but Maximus didn't retract the proposal.

Sameya shook her head.

"So shy," the tiger remarked. "We'll change that."

She wasn't altogether certain she wanted her inhibitions to be altered. Her entire life would change if she accepted them. Where would they live? Atlantis was her home and—

"I have other piercings." Maximus ran his fingers through her hair as Gabriel disengaged the vampyr's belt buckle. A few moments later, the button fly leather pants were open and the shifter was shoving the vampyr's clothing to the floor.

"He's pierced here." Gabriel went to his knees and licked the staggered piercings on the top of Maximus's cock. Like a ladder there were five of them back-to-back. "They feel fantastic inside me. But this one,"—Gabriel swirled his tongue around the head of Maximus's erection, and the vampyr groaned—"the Apadravya piercing is favored by women."

Horrified, Sameya stared at the metal that penetrated the head of his penis vertically. "Sweet gods, didn't that hurt?"

"Yes." Maximus shrugged. "The pleasure it gives Gabriel—and will give you—is worth the minor pain I suffered."

No way could that have been insignificant pain.

"You can tell me if you agree when I'm inside you."

That got her attention. Her gaze swept off his crown and crashed against his. "Will you bite me?" She'd liked it, until he drugged her with his *venome*.

"Yes." He reeled her in by a lock of hair, sandwiching her between them, with his hand on her nape. "But I promise not to *venome* you like before." He bent his head, his mouth so close to her ear his breath teased her skin. "I prefer my lovers aware while fucking them."

A tremor went through Sameya.

"Are you frightened?" The question came from Gabriel as he pressed against her back and palmed a breast.

"I don't like to be touched."

Maximus used his knuckle beneath her chin, tilting her head back to meet his compelling stare. "But you like our touch."

"Yes."

He grinned. "Gabriel made you come. Do you still contend by the act he now dominates you?"

She released a long ragged breath. "He does. He has as much sway over me as you momentarily do." *Only Gabriel's control won't evaporate in time like Maximus's will. I'm so fucked. And not helping my Empress.*

Maximus's hand slid downward, fingered the choker. "And when I make you come—"

"You'll have no need of this offensive necklace."

She couldn't gauge his thoughts as he considered her. Funny how his vampyr shifted to and from the forefront and the evidence was always in his eyes, from silver-blue to green.

Gabriel tangled his fingers in her hair and roughly pulled her head back, angling it to the side against his chest. Just enough he could plant his lips against hers. Their first kiss, and it was very different from Maximus who kissed like he planned to conquer. Gabriel's was slower, more thorough, but just as freaking fantastic.

When he parted from her lips, he peered at her. "I release you from the siren mating call."

Sameya gaped at him. Releasing one from the siren mating call was unheard of. Then Maximus pressed his hand between her legs and she forgot about her astonishment. She lurched against his touch, but was captured in Gabriel's sights.

"Easy...relax," the shifter cooed as Maximus thrust a finger into her, withdrew and plunged two into her.

"Goddamn, you're tighter than I imagined possible."

"Told you." Gabriel fondled her breasts as he continued to hold her head steady. "She'll still take your dick."

"Probably easily." Without forewarning, Maximus sank his fangs into her neck, his tongue flicking against her skin where his incisors pierced her flesh.

Raw desire coursed through her and his fingers quickened, going knuckle deep. Sameya moaned, clutching one of his shoulders in support and digging her fingernails into the back of Gabriel's hand, which plucked at her nipples.

Just as suddenly as he bit her, Maximus released his hold on her neck. He licked the wounds and she knew he'd sealed them. Would there be a mating mark there? Vampyrs usually always gave them. But so did shifters. She was in dreadful trouble.

Maximus kissed Gabriel, and then favored her with his mouth on hers. They proceeded in that manner for a long time, kisses among them while Gabriel played with her breasts and Maximus fucked her with his fingers. But when his thumb flicked across her clit, she shuddered against Gabriel with a high-pitched squeal. Her clitoris was even more sensitive than before.

Maximus smiled down at her as he laid the pad of his thumb directly over her nub. She groaned when it rotated.

"Do you want me inside you?"

"Yes."

"Do you want to mate me?"

"No."

Maximus chuckled. "I will be satisfied only when you say yes." His fingers ran through her hair. "I love your red-and-black striped hair. Your amethyst eyes, petite frame and your lush red lips—they'll look fantastic wrapped around Gabriel's dick." She'd never given a blowjob before. She bet she'd stink at oral play. "I especially love the way you grind against my hand." She was rolling into his finger-thrusts. Shameful, but she no longer controlled her body. "Will you fuck my cock the same way?" Right as he brought her to the edge of another glorious climax—how had she lived without them for more than fifty thousand years?—he removed his fingers from her body. "Let's find out, shall we?"

He abruptly walked away from her, leaving her white-knuckling the reckless need to demand he finish what he'd started.

She groaned and would've crumbled to the floor without Gabriel's support. He turned her to face the bed as Maximus spread out lying flat on the mattress. His erection jutted upward, the piercings glinting in the light. Fascinated by the stainless steel cutting through his cock, she hadn't noticed the size of his dick. Huge summed it up nicely. She wasn't stupid, she knew her body was designed to take him regardless of dimension, but the initial penetration might be a little painful. And she couldn't begin to imagine how the piercings would play into it all.

"Have you ever ridden a man before, Sameya?" Gabriel's lips moved against her ear.

Sameya shook her head.

"Have you ever been taken from behind?"

"No." Wasn't that how shifters typically mated their women?

He nipped her ear lobe. "I'll take you from behind and mark you as mine when we officially mate. I'll bite you here." Gabriel ran a finger along the curve where her shoulder met her neck. "The marks from the bite won't disappear. You'll wear the evidence of our mating like Maximus does." She knew how it worked, but she couldn't locate her voice to comment. "Maximus will bite you, too, leaving another mark. His will be between your legs." His fingers shifted into position and tapped her femoral artery. "It's a touch more intimate, don't you think?"

More than a touch, but all she could manage to utter was, "Yes."

"To finalize the mating, after you're marked, we'll both fuck you. One of us here"—he shifted and pressed a finger into her pussy from behind—"while the other is here." He withdrew the digit and pushed against the opening to her anus.

Sameya inhaled, a ragged sounding breath as he leisurely inserted his digit into her ass. Foreign feeling, but not distasteful.

Gabriel pumped his finger into her tight hole, his pace measured. She bit her lip. "Feel good?"

"Yes." *I wish it didn't!*

"You want to fuck Maximus?"

The question startled her, and she ripped her gaze off Maximus to peer at Gabriel over her shoulder. "It's my choice?"

"It's always your choice." He kissed her nose. "We've already proven we're your mates." Technically

Maximus hadn't, but she'd gotten almost there before he deserted her. "Give us a month to prove we can make you happy."

A month of shattering climaxes couldn't hurt. But it wasn't like she could really leave anyway. "I can't leave." She jerked on the collar to indicate her current predicament.

"Come to me, my reaper, and I'll remove it." At her surprised expression, Maximus tacked on, "As long as you give me your word to stay of your own accord for one month."

Chapter Eleven

Gabriel held Sameya as she watched Maximus, considering his offer. He could smell her fear, but beneath that scent her excitement was an extravagant smell. The spicy twang taunted his tiger, and he struggled against the compulsion to bend her over the bed and take her immediately. Claim her as his mate before she succeeded in escaping.

On the heels of that fantasy was Sameya on her knees with his cock in her mouth. Or Maximus fucking her while she sucked him. So many debauched things he wanted to do to her, but all of it ultimately ended in her joy...and Maximus's.

Tired of defying his innate desires, Gabriel bit the curve of her neck, but not hard enough to break the skin. A strangled sound emerged from her, but she offered no protest. He thrust two fingers inside her and palmed a breast with the other hand. Sameya arched against him as he licked where his teeth held her flesh.

Releasing her skin, he dragged his teeth along the sexy line of her neck and pressed his lips against her ear. "We won't be rough with you the first time." They were animals; they would take her forcefully and soon. "Even when we're wild and out of control, it's always about the pleasure, Sameya. And you have two of us committed to you. Feel how hard I am for you?" He rotated his hips against her ass and from the corner of his eye he caught the gentle glide of her eyelids shutting, while Maximus palmed his cock and stroked. "Won't you fuck Maximus while I watch? Tell me how his piercings feel inside you."

"This is taboo," spoken in the barest of whispers with no real hint of conviction in her tone. She had him there. Their races didn't co-mingle and never mated. As far as he knew, he and Maximus were unique. But his family accepted them.

"Taboo kisses were always my favorite, Sameya." He licked down her throat and shoved her hair aside as he followed the descent of her spine. On his knees behind her, he cupped her ass-cheeks, pulled them apart and dragged his tongue over the tight forbidden entry. She whimpered, trembling.

Abruptly, he elevated to his feet and placed his mouth against her ear, keeping his tone mild. "If you won't join him, I will."

Gabriel stepped around her and faced her once he reached the edge of the bed. He stood proud before her in his birthday suit, palming his cock and stroking. Well, maybe not his birthday suit, since he'd been born a pup and hadn't shifted into human form until he was five. Her gaze traveled his physique, and he wondered what she thought. She was good at schooling her features. When her eyes rested on his cock, he applied several strokes, running his thumb over the tip each time. Her eyes rounded, and she licked her lips.

The scent of her arousal grew stronger. Behind him on the bed, Maximus groaned indicating he could taste her with his senses, like Gabriel could.

He turned away from her and joined Maximus. No question, Sameya was confused. She perched on the razor sharp edge between desire and sanity. There was nothing sane about the mating desire. If their erotic coupling didn't convince her to join them...he wouldn't give up hope. They needed her, and she needed them. She just didn't know it yet.

As Gabriel reached Maximus, the vampyr sat up and cupped the back of Gabriel's head, drawing him to his mouth. They kissed, tongues grazing and teeth nipping as he trailed his hand across Maximus's chest. Mated for almost a thousand years, they'd luckily not grown tired of one another. Sex was never stale, but exciting and fresh each time.

Maximus's hand slid down his mate's neck to grip his shoulder and flip Gabriel to his back. His vampyr mate straddled his thighs. Using only his fingertips, he circled Gabriel's nipples, drawing them to hard nubs with the teasing touch. Then he bent and licked the taut peaks. With a groan, Gabriel palmed Maximus's head. Teeth scraped his flesh, a nick sharp enough to draw blood and Maximus licked at the red bead.

He heard Sameya's sharp intake of breath and turned his head to consider her. The heavy black kohl smudged about her eyes showcased their amazing shade of mauve. Long sooty lashes completed her irresistible allure. Cheekbones tinged pink had nothing to do with a blush, and her rose-red lips weren't just pouty and kissable, but fuckable, too. The long red and black streaked Goth-like hair added, rather than detracted, from her appeal. Coupled with her heavy breasts, rounded hips and shapely legs, she made for one hell of a sexy creature. And he wanted her very badly.

What of her artifices were real? Or could she construct her appearance dependent upon what drew her victims? Not something he'd ever heard a siren capable of doing, but in the paranormal world anything was possible.

Gabriel tangled his fingers in Maximus's wavy brown hair and motioned for Sameya to join them. She bit her bottom lip, gawking as Maximus moved across Gabriel's torso, ripping moans from him. After a few hesitant steps, she hit the mattress with her thighs, and drew no closer.

Lower across his abdomen, Maximus placed a combination of licks, nips, and kisses. Gabriel pushed his head downward and hissed through his teeth when Maximus tongued the head of his cock. Sameya sat on the edge of the bed and gaped, lips slightly parted, her eyes wide and expressive. Gabriel arched his back, digging his head into the pillow when his vampyr lover swallowed his dick to the back of his throat. Fuck! The piercing in Maximus's tongue slithered along the underside of his cock. Worked up from giving Sameya her first climax, coupled with his lover's expertise at giving head, Gabriel struggled not to ejaculate.

"What—" Sameya cleared her throat, and a blush hit her cheeks when both men peered at her. "What does he...taste like?"

"See for yourself." Maximus shifted to crouch beside Gabriel's hip. He could feel the tension in the vampyr as they waited for her to make a decision.

Sameya blinked as Maximus pumped his palm along Gabriel's shaft, and then placed a lick to the slit.

"We'll taste him together." Maximus held out a hand to her. "I'll teach you how to please him the way he did you."

Gabriel groaned, and Sameya snapped a cautious glance at him. Indecision shined from her eyes.

"Join me, reaper." Maximus tugged on a strand of her hair.

Sameya grabbed his wrist, but instead of knocking his arm aside, she allowed him to lace his fingers with hers and guide her onto the bed. Rising to his knees, the vampyr waited until she reached Gabriel's other hip to tug her forward enough to meet for a kiss over Gabriel's body.

Both naked and lip locked, they were a sight to watch. No resistance from Sameya this time, she fell into the kiss with zest. Her free hand lifted to fist a handful of Maximus's hair. Gabriel's cock twitched, wanting inside her, but she'd obtained her first climax with him. Maximus would be the first to fuck her to orgasm.

Sameya groaned when Maximus departed her mouth and trailed wet kisses down her neck. Relieved she had decided to participate, Gabriel cupped her ass and squeezed.

"Kiss the head of Gabriel's dick with me." Maximus lifted his head from the hollow of her throat. "I'll show you how. Just follow my lead."

Sameya tossed Gabriel a speculative glance, as if she expected him to protest. Maximus palmed the back of her head and tugged her down until she was less than an inch from Gabriel's cock. Her breath fanned against his flesh and inflamed him further. Anticipating the feeling of her virgin mouth on his dick, he held his breath.

On one side of his crown, Maximus mouthed his cock, running his tongue all over the head. "Do this with me on your side."

Gabriel realized he possessed a handful of her hair. He stopped her participation with a slight tug on the ends of the strands. "I won't last long once your mouth touches my dick." Processing, she blinked and exhaled slowly. "If you don't want a mouthful of cum, you'll stop when I tell you. Understand?"

She nodded, adjusted her body to a more advantageous angle. She placed her mouth against the opposite side of his erection from Maximus and mimed the vampyr's actions. Hesitant flicks of her tongue at first, that grew bolder as they continued. Even without the piercing to tantalize, her strokes were divine.

Their oral play matured to a more focused bent several minutes later. The head of his cock disappeared between their mouths, their tongues slithering over him and against one another. Down his length they moved, his crown purpled, veined and throbbing. The soft touch of Sameya's hand cupped his balls as their mouths and tongues moved in unison back up to the tip.

Gabriel clenched his teeth. His toes curled and he breathed through the impending climax.

Maximus lazily tongued back downward before withdrawing from his wet length. "Won't you suck him into your mouth, Sameya?"

He held his breath. Fuck how he wanted to see her lips encircle his engorged shaft. Would his fat cock fit in her mouth?

Only a few seconds of delay after Maximus issued the request, she slipped Gabriel's crown into her wet cavity. Flicks of her tongue had him skirting the threshold of release. Wrapping the sheets around one hand, he twisted her hair in his other one. A broken sigh escaped his lips. She jerked as if surprised by his response.

Maximus palmed the back of her head and added slight pressure. "Don't stop. He likes it."

Gabriel disagreed, rather than like, he.... "Love...it."

He couldn't take his scrutiny off her. Goddamn, the way she moved along his shaft. Not skilled, but not afraid to apply herself either.

"Deeper." Maximus encouraged, pushing her head down, and Gabriel's dick bumped the back of her throat. He groaned as his long-time lover peered at him, a satisfied smile tweaking his lips.

"Release her, Maximus." Gabriel tugged on her hair and met her curious gaze. "Stop. I'm going to blow."

Her violet eyes lightened, and a moment later he was stuffed down her throat again. Maximus chuckled and guided the speed of her blowjob with his hand on the back of her head. Up and down her head bobbed, the head of Gabriel's cock pulsated and couldn't hold back any longer. No more than a dozen dips and he came with a moan, gripping her hair like it was his lifeline to earth. The first jet she swallowed, but she was flicking her tongue around the head of his cock with the second spurt of semen, some going in her mouth and some sticking to her chin.

"Fuck," he groaned when she kept licking him.

Maximus grinned. "Eager to please, isn't she?" He roughly yanked her up to her knees and licked Gabriel's release off her chin before slamming his mouth over hers.

Gabriel sat up and the moment Maximus came up for air, he claimed her for a kiss, his silent way of thanking her for her willingness to please him. He snarled his fingers in her hair and pulled her head back. From the corner of his eye, he spied Maximus fondling her nipples. She had fantastic breasts. Heavier than necessary for the size of her body and large areoles that appealed to him.

Eyes half-mast, she watched them, breathing shallow. Gabriel lowered his head and licked a nipple that Maximus held for him. The vampyr's other hand slid downward across her belly, and he felt her breath hitch only because his mouth was on her breast.

"Spread your legs." Maximus's voice had deepened. Gabriel knew that gruff sound. The vampyr neared his limit of control. "Don't be afraid, *naleah*, I intend you no harm." Gabriel lifted his head to catch Maximus and Sameya locked in an eye-battle while Maximus slid the back of his knuckles across her cheek. "My gift is pleasure. Grant us one month."

Gabriel palmed her lower back, catching a glance of Maximus's finger moving back and forth against her pubic bone. "That's nothing in the scope of our lifetime, baby. Open your legs for Maximus if you will commit thirty days of debauchery"—*and trust building*, but those weren't words he'd utter for fear of scaring her off—"with us."

A long minute of silence passed as she contemplated their request, her gaze flicking back and forth between them. Palms lying flat on the tops of her thighs, she parted them. "I'm sure to regret this."

Chapter Twelve

Maximus wouldn't permit her regret. This decision made her theirs, and he'd fight the gods to keep her, while he claimed her as theirs.

Gabriel sucked on her breasts as Maximus slid two fingers into her pussy, going knuckle deep. "Velvety soft and wet."

So unlike his and Gabriel's hardness. He wanted to be gentle with her, but the dominant vampyr demanded a hard, rough fucking.

Her eyelids fell closed, and her head tilted back as her groan teased the air.

"We're going to make you come, over and over again." Gabriel devoured her mouth after that promise.

Yes, Maximus agreed. Over and over and over and, well…again—beginning now. At the back of her throat, she whimpered as Gabriel pushed a finger into her pussy from between her buttocks. Three fingers thrust inside her, preparing her for Maximus's girth.

Moving in behind her, Gabriel tossed pillows into a heaping mound against the headboard. The tiger kissed her shoulder and peered at Maximus, their fingers moving in tandem. "Fuck her while I hold her, Maximus."

Understanding Gabriel wanted to be as much a part of claiming her as possible, Maximus reached over her shoulder and cupped the back of Gabriel's head. "Yes."

Gabriel reacted, capturing her by the throat with his hand. A tiny squeal emerged from her, and her eyes snapped wide open. Maximus fucked her hard with his fingers, refocusing her sudden distress to carnality as

Gabriel removed his finger from her body. The tiger's long incisors descended and he grazed them along the slim column of her throat. A flash of the white Bengal imprinted over Gabriel's face before vanishing altogether. That quickly, he had himself under control.

"Now." When Gabriel spoke, it sounded off, but with his tiger teeth still evident, Maximus knew how hard they were to talk around thanks to his own set of fangs.

The tiger wrapped his other arm around her waist, and Maximus removed his fingers, intentionally gliding them over her clit. She twitched and bit her bottom lip until it turned white.

"Don't." Maximus tugged on her chin, freeing her lip. "Don't hide your enjoyment from us."

Gabriel pulled her spine flush against his chest and dropped back against the pillows. Using his knees, he wedged them between her legs. He bent his knees, causing her legs to drape over either side of his thighs. Anchoring his feet on the bed, he kept his knees vertical as he spread his legs wide, opening her for Maximus's observation. The hand on her throat slid just below her chin and anchored the back of her head to Gabriel's shoulder.

Violet eyes locked on Maximus as he palmed his cock with slow strokes. His thumb swiped the moisture off the tip, and then slowly circled the ball on the topside of his head. "Do you want me inside you, Sameya?"

A slight movement to her head, but with the way Gabriel held her, she was unable to manage more. Gabriel's gruff command emerged a second later. "Say it."

"Yes." The word was spoken so lightly, Maximus almost missed it completely.

He wanted inside her so bad his fangs ached. Over her shoulder Gabriel's golden eyes watched him. Maximus dropped to his hands between their legs. He sent a fast swipe of his tongue through her open folds, the tip connecting with her clit. A feminine groan emerged, and a male groan followed when he licked Gabriel's balls below her.

Maximus rose to his knees and wiggled closer, until the front of his thighs hit the back of Gabriel's. His erection jutted up through her folds, and he rubbed the head across her clitoris. Sameya's eyes slipped shut on a whimper as he gently pinched her clit with his fingers. "How pretty your pussy would look with your clitoral hood pierced." Her eyelids flew upward. "A piercing for me to play with." He nudged the bottom bead of his barbell over her nub and she arched her hips into the glide.

"Stop talking and fuck me already, vampyr." The husky tenor of her voice betrayed her state of arousal.

How could he refuse a request like that?

Holding the base of his cock, he inched his head inside her. Sameya squirmed and Gabriel splayed his fingers on her belly to hold her motionless. "Remain still."

"Fuck." Maximus grit his teeth. She was so tight and soft, like a silk pussy encasing his crown. If her mouth had felt half this good, no wonder Gabriel had been unable to hold out longer. "Goddamn, you're tight."

"You're killing me, vampyr."

Their gazes locked. He palmed a breast, circling a nipple with his thumb.

Maximus pushed a little further inward, the first of his ladder-back barbells disappearing inside her. "No worse than you're killing me, siren."

Sameya lifted an arm backward to anchor in Gabriel's hair, while scraping the fingernails of her other hand across Maximus's scalp. She wound the digits in his chin-length hair and tugged him down for a kiss.

Her tongue was in his mouth before their lips settled together good. Teeth scraped across his lips, they were hers, not his. She yanked his head back, the sting to his scalp contrary to her reservation earlier.

"Damn you, vampyr, get inside me."

"Watch me enter you," Maximus said. Gabriel released her throat, and she peered between her thighs. He pushed slowly, but steadily, his inches leisurely disappearing into her wet channel. Finally the last of his barbells were in and he thrust hard, burying the remaining length to the hilt. "Sing for me, siren."

Maximus pulled almost all the way out and plunged back in. Sameya sighed, her hips rocking with the movement of his drives into her. Gabriel slid his hand from her abdomen to between her thighs, his fingers on either side of Maximus's cock slipping in and out of her soaked sheath.

Her slick heat grinding down on his cock was as good as being inside Gabriel. Just different.

"Goddamn, you feel so fucking good." He quickened his strokes as Gabriel removed his hand from between their body to stroke and fondle her breasts.

"I didn't know"—eyes wide, her amazement shone from her face—"it could feel this amazing."

A harmonious tune emerged, a tone that could only have come from the Heavens. The call of the mating siren? He'd heard legends of it, but...Maximus peered at Gabriel. He seemed to suffer no ill effect.

"I think she likes us." Gabriel licked her neck; his golden eyes alight with male satisfaction.

Maximus increased the depth of his thrusts, going balls deep inside her. "Sameya is *ours*." The wet strokes of flesh-on-flesh were loud in the room. The tiny noises Sameya made at the back of her throat, coupled with her siren song and Maximus's groans, were the only noises in the room.

Sameya gave him no warning, but suddenly screamed, her pussy clenching on his length as she climaxed. Shuddering, she went limp, her hands falling from both of their heads. But her eyes—fuck him her eyes—remained locked on his throughout her bliss.

Maximus plunged hard, jerking her against Gabriel and eliciting a tiny whimper from her. He went over the edge, moaning as he released inside her. Cock twitching he executed two unhurried thrusts before going motionless. He cupped her cheeks and kissed her gently.

Gabriel palmed his nape and Maximus parted from Sameya's lips to kiss the tiger over her shoulder. The sense of completeness in their life tightened his chest, and Maximus forced back overwhelming emotions. He'd known she'd feel perfect sandwiched between them, but nothing could've prepared him for the reality or the overpowering sentiment that burned his throat.

"I know," Gabriel said against his lips. "I feel it, too."

The tiger always seemed to understand him without him having to clarify anything. Another kiss, harder and chock full of feelings. Maximus was damn glad he had Gabriel with him on the adventure to tame their mate.

Still anchored deep inside her, Maximus levered himself off Sameya just enough she could breathe and lock his gaze on hers. "I release you from your serenade curse."

"Thank you." Sameya sounded breathy. "I'll stay a month." Her eyes said she made no promises after that.

Maximus nodded, grateful she at least afforded them some time. It gave him hope. He slipped his finger beneath the jewel-encrusted collar, intending to remove it as promised if she vowed to stay.

"Don't take it off."

Chapter Thirteen

Maximus stilled at her command and peered at her hard. Distrust blazed from his eyes. Gabriel shifted enough that her torso was angled so he could get a gander of her face. Sameya thought she saw a pattern between the men. The tiger was more eager to trust her than the vampyr, but she had the feeling they'd both fight her tooth and nail to keep her with them.

A riot of emotions didn't just surge through her, but short-circuited everything she'd ever believed and stood for. Freedom from the enslavement of mating had been her single moment in history to evade. Two killer climaxes eradicated her need for liberty, and that terrified her. Finding not one, but two mates and both of them releasing her from the mating serenade...what were the chances of that? Zilch if the other mated sirens were anything to go by.

Sameya owed them the month they'd asked for. It was the least she could do. And...*holy goddess almighty*, she wouldn't refuse the orgasms they'd present to her. No point in denying herself when she had every intention to walk away in a month.

"If things become too intense or...difficult"—she licked her lips, her breath stuttering out as Gabriel's fingertips swirled around a nipple—"I'll be tempted to leave regardless of promises." Confused why she confessed the secrets of her race, she made no attempt to resist the compulsion of honesty. "Sirens covet this secret, and I shouldn't be admitting it, but we aren't bound by our oaths the way the rest of the mystic community are." She could renege anytime she wanted. "It's part of what makes us so good at our jobs."

Maximus ran his finger through the hollow of her throat. "You would grant me the privilege of holding that much power over you?"

"For the month only."

The vampyr flexed his hips and withdrew from her. He dropped onto the bed beside them and rolled to his side to face them, head propped up with his palm. Gabriel repositioned them on their sides, facing Maximus. The tiger remained aligned against her back, his arm beneath her head, and his other arm around her waist, with his hand flattened on her belly. She recognized it as a claim of ownership.

Shifters are so possessive.

The bigger question...why wasn't she shrugging out of it? Cuddling had never been an enjoyable commodity before, but damn everything to hell, she *liked* his possessiveness.

Two frown lines slashed between the vampyr's dark eyebrows. "Why do I get the feeling you're planning on leaving us in a month regardless of how well we work out?"

Sameya executed a one-sided shoulder shrug. "No promises."

She barely restrained the urge to rub the glower off his handsome face. What'd it hurt to admit to herself she was in huge trouble where these two were concerned? But she didn't know enough about them to determine if she liked them or if they would be compatible long-term. Sex wasn't enough to build a relationship on, regardless of how fucking amazing it was.

Maximus sidled closer and ran his fingers through her hair. Forehead still furrowed, he watched as the locks tumbled through his digits. What thoughts ran through his mind?

Behind her, Gabriel wedged his knee between hers and thrust his leg through the opening he'd created.

He buried his nose in her hair, inhaled, and—the sudden purring startled her.

Maximus smiled, eradicating the scowl and softening his features. "Gabriel rarely purrs in his human skin."

She liked the smile on the vampyr's face, and the noise the tiger made had her wanting to curl up between them both. Sheesh, she'd love to keep these men happy. But could she? She'd been alone so long, was it even possible for her to put anyone other than her Empress and herself first.

"Will you permit me to clean you here?" The front of Gabriel's thigh wedged against her pussy and rocked enough it stirred an ache.

The pleasurable throb between her thighs, left over from the orgasms, slowly faded. A soft touch of cloth would probably send her over the edge. Who knew climaxes would make one so sensitive. Add to that the intimacy of another washing her had heat flushing her cheeks. But he'd already had his mouth there, and he sounded as if he'd delight in servicing her. And while she rather liked the stickiness between her thighs, she hadn't even thought about protecting herself from pregnancy. Good thing mystics seldom bred even in best-case scenarios.

"If it will please you, yes." Her voice sounded husky, like she'd risen from sleep.

"Very much." Gabriel rose, removing his arm from beneath her head and leaned over her. He cupped her chin in his palm and turned her head so he could kiss her. Gentle strokes of his tongue and nips to her bottom lip, teasing. "You taste so sweet," he whispered against her mouth. "You're like catnip my cat wants to roll around in and get drunk on."

"Smooth talker." Sameya teased. She trailed a finger over his cheek, the scratchy stubble abrasive against the pad of her index. He'd been clean-shaven earlier in the bar. "You're both a little overwhelming."

"Tell us to back off when you need your space, Sameya." Maximus palmed a breast, his forefinger and thumb pinching a nipple.

She'd try. She really would. But Sameya wasn't known for her patience or levelheadedness. Gabriel grasped her hips, but when she would've looked at him, Maximus dug his hand in her hair. Capturing her attention, he rose up on his elbow and peered down at her, as Gabriel rolled her onto her back.

Hands on her knees, Gabriel spread her legs. "She's glistening with your combined juices."

"There are so many wicked things we want to do to you." The vampyr held her focus, the anticipation in his silver-blue eyes evident.

The tiger swiped is tongue across her pussy and unexpected bliss whiplashed through her body. Eyes going wide, Sameya gasped, jolted as Gabriel's tongue flicked over her clit. The vampyr smiled, slow and wicked. "Didn't you know a cat cleans with its tongue?"

I do now!

"Mmm...." The sound vibrated against her folds as Gabriel pushed her legs wider and adjusted his position to settle more comfortably between her thighs. "I knew your cum mixed with her juices would taste even better."

If at all possible, Maximus's smile grew wider. "Melt into the pleasure, *naleah*."

Staring into his eyes, Sameya whimpered and felt the surge of arousal. Gabriel groaned as she flooded his mouth. Her physical reaction prompted him to spread her lips with one hand and shove two fingers deep into her pussy.

Sameya moaned, her back arching off the bed, as Gabriel anchored his mouth at the core of her body, alternating between lapping at her flesh and sucking on her clitoris.

Tiny hedonistic cries slipped from her lips.

"Goddamn, Maximus, she tastes amazing." Gabriel's words buzzed against her skin.

"Let me sample her." Maximus was already twisting his body around on the bed as he spoke.

With his chest aligned over her belly, his head moved between her thighs. His long hair tickled, causing goose bumps to erupt. Gabriel's soft torment ceased, but his fingers remained in position as Maximus lowered his head to feast.

Sameya quaked as Maximus's tongue slid downward, from her clit to where Gabriel's fingers were moving inside her.

"She's candy to my taste buds." Maximus sucked on her clitoris.

She buried her fingernails into the back of his thighs, squirming into his mouth, but her body trembled for them to advance the exploits further. "No more."

"I want her to come again," Maximus lifted his head, she guessed to glance at Gabriel.

"I can't take more." Combustion was a strong possibility if they didn't cease immediately.

They ignored her. Gabriel fucked her fast with his fingers. "Are you hard yet, Maximus."

The rapid movement of hair tickled her thighs in either a nod or shake of his head. She wasn't sure which one.

"Sixty-nine her. I'll finger-fuck her while you get her off."

"You want me on top or bottom?" Maximus swirled his tongue around her clit.

Sameya moaned and buried her nails further, until blood proceeded down his thigh.

"Bottom. I want her ass up."

"What's this sixty-nine and—" Sameya squealed as Maximus rolled to his back, taking her with him. They ended up with her straddling his face and his very pierced erection bobbing in front of hers. A drop of precum glistened on the fat head. She'd loved the taste of Gabriel on her tongue. Would Maximus's flavor be as delightful?

Fingers tangled in her hair and Gabriel pulled her head back by the strands. Lavender eyes met yellow. "Suck his dick while we make you come hard."

Anticipating having Maximus in her mouth, Sameya licked her lips.

"You okay with this?"

Gabriel's question surprised her. She was more than okay. "Yes."

The tiger released her hair and ran his hand down her back, as Maximus curled his arms around her thighs and gripped her ass with his hands. He spread her cheeks as he laid the first lick to her pussy.

Sameya moaned as she took Maximus's cock into her mouth. He joined her with a groan of his own as she swirled her tongue around his head, using the tip to toy with the Apadravya piercing. Fingers penetrated her and pumped, slow and deep, the sound of moisture loud. Cupping his balls, she sucked Maximus as deep as she could go. On the first choke, she retreated with her eyes watering and focused on the head.

The digits exited her pussy and a moment later a finger pressed against her anus. Sameya squealed around her mouthful of cock.

"Relax." Gabriel ran his hand up and down her spine as he pushed his finger deeper. "Push out as I push in."

Gripping the base of Maximus's erection, she did as Gabriel instructed and he slipped all the way inside her forbidden territory. Maximus sucked hard on her nub and drew her focus off the foreign object in her bottom.

But then Gabriel moved his finger, need spiked hot and fast, nearly crippling her in a mass of melted flesh. It wasn't a climax, but she suspected one approached. Sameya sucked on the cock in her mouth like their lives depended on it. Maximus groaned and laid attention to her clit.

"Push out again," Gabriel said as he eased a second finger into her bottom.

Everything sped up a little then. Digits pumping into her ass, as a tongue sucked and licked on her clit. Each time Sameya thought she'd explode with a climax, Maximus would retreat and thrust his tongue into her pussy. The fingers inside her burned, but felt oh so damned good. The pleasure-pain of the penetration was phenomenal.

"Are you ready to climax, Sameya?" Gabriel jabbed his fingers deep.

"Yes." She sucked Maximus's dick to the back of her throat and moaned as she slid along his cock. "Please, gods, yes."

"She's killing me with her mouth," Maximus said between licks.

"Her mouth is amazing. I want to try her pussy out." Gabriel shifted behind her until she felt his cock butt up against her entrance. With his fingers deep in her bottom, he palmed a hip with his other hand and thrust his dick into her sheath, his balls slapping against her flesh before he stopped.

Sameya screamed around Maximus's erection, quivering as she acclimated to the sudden length filling her. He pulled out, rammed back in. Removing his fingers as he flexed his hips, until only the tips were inside her, he slammed back into her with both at the same time.

Sameya screamed again. Gods the hedonism was too much. Too much to—Maximus came in her mouth with a groan. She plunged him to the back of her throat and swallowed until he offered her no more.

Somehow Gabriel must've sensed Maximus had reached the peak of his release because he curled his hand around her throat and lifted her up on her knees, so her body was angled directly over Maximus's mouth. In rhythm to Gabriel's plunges, his fingers sank into her ass. Maximus worked over her pussy with his tongue as Gabriel pounded into her. She'd feel this claiming later—and that's what it was, as if they wanted to imprint on her, of that she had no doubt.

"Do you like my fingers in your ass while my cock is pounding your pussy?"

Damn, but she did. All she could manage was a nod.

"Say it," the tiger growled.

How close was his Bengal to the surface? Unable to see him she couldn't get a gander. "Yes," the word stuttered out.

Gabriel purred at her admission.

"Don't, Gabriel. You'll regret it." Maximus's lips moved against her clitoris.

Gabriel's fingers exited her ass and clamped on her hip. "She's ours, can't regret that."

What'd he mean by that? He pushed her back down over Maximus and hunched over her. He pistoned into her, a smooth glide of pummeling, so she didn't much care about his meaning.

"Make her come, Maximus, as I claim her." The words were whispered against her ear, as his other hand brushed her hair off her shoulder.

Claim her? He didn't truly mean to claim-claim her did he?

"Wait!" was all she managed to say before his teeth sank into the sensitive curve where her neck met her shoulder.

Sameya jerked, tried to fight back, but Gabriel subdued her by pushing her against Maximus's stomach and holding her there. The vampyr's fingers spread her pussy lips and he feasted on her clit as Gabriel pounded into her, dominating her like the cat he was. The tiger's tongue swished over the spot where his canines were buried into her skin.

Fuck that hurts. But felt oddly euphoric, as well.

With Maximus's mouth clamped on her clit, she came, turning her face into his belly to stifle the sound of her carnal gratification. Gabriel roared like the tiger he was and released inside her, his hot semen filling her until the fluid spilled out of their connection. Maximus made quick work of cleaning it up with his tongue, while his thumb rotated against her clitoris. Biting the vampyr's belly until she tasted blood, she hated them both in that moment, even though she was very much aware she ground herself on Gabriel's cock until she came, once more. Only then did Maximus cease masturbating her with his mouth.

The tiger's fangs retracted, the weird pleasure-pain of it caused her to flinch. Sameya inhaled, biting her bottom lip to the point of pain when Gabriel licked the wound he'd caused.

Fury slammed into her. He had *no* right to claim her. None whatsoever.

Rearing back, she clocked him in the nose with the back of her head and elbowed him in the throat. Gabriel made choking sounds as she scrambled out from between him and Maximus. Sameya launched herself off the bed and swung about to glare at her highhanded mates. Maximus sat, running his fingers through his unruly hair, while Gabriel gasped for breath.

She touched her shoulder where he'd bitten her and the tips of her fingers came away smeared in blood. Hands shaking, she would've leveled Gabriel with a blast of magical fury if not for the magic restricting her. "Tell me you did not mark me, Gabriel."

A wise man would lie through his teeth.

Gabriel at least had the decency to appear shamefaced as he rolled into a sitting position and raked his fingers through his hair. "I'm sorry, Sameya. I had no intention—"

"You lying bastard!"

Whatever expression was on her face, it must've had Maximus worried for Gabriel's safety because he placed himself between them. "You're forbidden to harm Gabriel."

What a fool she'd been to grant them a month and then to divulge the secret that kept Maximus from removing the jewel from around her neck. A foolish and irrational decision and all because of orgasms from her less than upstanding mates. Pleasure turned people rash. Herself included!

"Remove it." Sameya yanked on the collar, giving a mental screech at her helplessness.

"No."

She ground her molars together. "I'll kill you both." Probably just the tiger, but threatening the vamp couldn't actually hurt. And she didn't want him to ever believe she wasn't dangerous.

Maximus came off the bed with his hands held in front of him in a placating gesture. "I know you're angry, but you have to remember shifters lose control of themselves when in the presence of their unmated...mate."

The very reason she despised shifters. "Thanks for reminding me."

Shifters were an unpredictable lot and governed by their emotions. She'd reaped more of them than any other breed in the paranormal world because they'd grown so irrational there was no saving them. That said a lot about a breed.

Gabriel will follow his dead ancestors as soon as I get this fucking choker off my neck. The only decision she had to make was if it'd be a slow or quick death. At the moment, she leaned toward the slower the better.

Fantasizing about exacting vengeance failed to cool her temper. If she didn't remove herself from *the fucker's* proximity soon, she'd start breaking his fingers. And she'd relish his screams while filing down those fucking canines.

Clothes. Focus on locating clothes, girl. Stomping out of the bedroom bare-assed naked wouldn't construct the same impression that being attired would. At least not the impression she wanted to make.

Maximus swiped her garments off the floor. "You're not wearing something I can't pull off without your assistance."

As if she'd let him touch her again. His arrogance was astounding.

She settled her hands on her hips, drawing the vampyr's gaze. Green flared around his irises before dying back to his normal silver-blue. "What would you have me wear, leech?"

"Aside from me?"

"That the best corny line you have?"

Maximus grimaced. "I'm rusty at this flirting stuff. Borrow anything from our closet."

Wear their clothes? She'd rather not, but the alternative wasn't feasible.

Sameya gave the room a quick onceover. Spying the black t-shirt Maximus discarded earlier, she retrieved it. As she stood, she noticed the top hat he'd worn last night when he abducted her.

Had it only been last night?

*Gods save me...*she felt like she'd waged an eternity with them already.

Dragging the cotton shirt over her head, she shoved her arms into the sleeves and was moderately pleased the material covered to just below the curve of her ass. The slashes Gabriel had given the material all centered about her belly. She marched to the dresser, snatched the top hat off of it and plopped it on her head.

Arms crossed over his naked chest, Maximus bit his wide bottom lip, but failed at eliminating the grin. Gabriel leapt off the bed, transforming into tiger mid-jump. Spellbound she watched as the air shimmered about him with twinkles of light before he landed on four feline feet.

Now was not the time to be awed by his transformation. The tiger rubbed against her leg, and she shoved him aside. Or tried given his size.

"He's apologizing." Maximus pulled his leather pants on and buttoned the lower fly—just enough to keep them perched dangerously low on his hips.

Ignoring his sex appeal, she bit out between clenched teeth, "Not forgiven." She pointed at Gabriel. "Stay away." If he knew what was good for him, he'd give her a lot of time to cool off.

She marched out of the room, contemplating the vilest method in which to exact justice on Gabriel.

Chapter Fourteen

Agitated failed to accurately describe her state of mind. Times like these were when she missed having someone to confide in. Anger burned through her breastbone over Gabriel's domineering actions. To try and *mate* her like she was his. Yet...she liked his possessiveness.

A siren tolerating such supremacy made little sense. With her prevailing nature, letting another species manhandle her was absurd.

She touched the weepy wound on her shoulder. The bite tingled in a pleasant way. She should be out for his blood. Instead, she found herself understanding his lack of control.

Tolerant because shifters by nature were emotional creatures, she snorted her disgust. What the hell was wrong with her? She didn't allow individuals to screw her over without repercussions.

Sameya halted, leaned against a wall, and rubbed her face with her palms. Who was she kidding? No one had ever duped her. They were too scared of her to contemplate such an action.

She hadn't borne only the were-tiger's overbearing behavior, but the vampyr's as well. Maximus controlled her with the choker, and they'd both forced her sexually. Most female sirens were involuntarily pushed into sexual submission. If they weren't, none would ever mate because no siren wanted to lose their freedom to their partner.

And both of her mates had released her from their jurisdiction. At least if she decided to remain with them, she wouldn't be a zombie to their demands but would retain her freewill. That was why she'd agreed to stay a month and why she'd given him the lowdown on her ability to renege on a promise.

Shaking her head, Sameya pushed away from the wall and followed the witch's scent to the kitchen. Another woman was seated at the breakfast table with Kat. A shifter, and if her senses were accurate, she was a were-tiger. Maybe from Gabriel's pride? *Just so long as she visits without any expectation from either of my mates, the woman will be safe.*

Sameya refused to contemplate why she was suddenly very territorial of men she had no intention of remaining with at the end of the month. She chalked it up to one more irrational behavior in the long list that was adding up since meeting the guys.

The woman sat with a regal air. Spine straight, shoulders squared, and head tilted so her chin sat high enough she gave the appearance of looking down on someone. Her fashionable blonde hair was sprayed into submission. Did men really prefer a hairstyle they couldn't put their fingers through?

Light blue eyes were direct as the shifter peered at Kat. High cheekbones and a wide sensuous mouth gave the woman a sultry demeanor. She wore a designer light pink silk blouse. A string of pearls circled her slender neck.

Sameya wouldn't be caught dead in pink. Or such refined attire. The pearls weren't her style either. She bet below the view of the table, the pretentious woman wore a matching pencil skirt and pumps.

Stunning. Even with the shifter's hoity-toity demeanor, Sameya felt gaudy next to her.

She sauntered on into the room, catching Kat's attention. The witch gulped and sat a little straighter, while tossing the shifter a nervous peek.

The witch's distress must've warned they weren't alone because the woman turned toward the door. Her cool eyes assessed Sameya's lack of attire, and the other woman sniffled when her gaze snagged on

Sameya's bare legs below the hem of Maximus's shirt. Quickly, her attention shifted upward and caught on the vampyr's top hat she'd crammed on her head. "I didn't realize the boys were entertaining."

Entertaining? She bit back a laugh. Yeah, they'd been amusing her with their cocks and one orgasm after another. Jesus, what amazing things those were. She grew wet thinking about them. Crazy because she'd already had three...or was it four? What was the limit before someone combusted?

In place of her vocal humor, she tendered a smile and pulled out a chair to sit across from the ladies. "What did you think the boys were doing if not entertaining?" Up close the woman's skin was flawless, like pale porcelain. Probably the type of woman Maximus and Gabriel enjoyed more often than not. She tossed Kat a cursory glance and her obvious nervousness told her much. "I mean, you're in their home chatting with Kat instead of them."

Was the shifter a former lover of theirs? Former being the operative word because she wouldn't share them with anyone. Not ever.

This irrational behavior was at odds with her typical rational mindset. She gave a mental sigh and, for the moment, accepted her deranged state of mind.

Was Kat so anxious because the other woman *was* their lover? It wasn't like they'd had time to inform anyone of their newly acquired mate.

The shifter elevated an eyebrow and tucked hair behind an ear with polished pale pink nails. "Little girl, you'll mind your manners in my company."

***

In no position to lecture Gabriel, Maximus ran his palm down his face. "Don't hide behind your pelt for long, Gabriel." He scratched behind the feline's ears. "We have to figure out a way to make this up to her. Maybe feeding her will make her more agreeable."

Gabriel executed a low-throated growl.

"You're right. That's not the way to a woman's heart. I'll *talk* to her instead." A shudder rippled down his spine and caused his stomach to sour. Maximus was a man of action. It was easier to kill something than verbalize his sentiments. "Join us soon. We need to mention Tyron Gryphon's hard-on for her and how we plan to keep her safe."

Gabriel's puffing noise sufficed as his agreement. Maximus went in search of Sameya.

How did one calm an agitated siren? They were lethal in any non-volatile situation, how much more would she be when vexed. Good thing he was immune to her particular brand of charm and that she still wore the collar, otherwise he surmised Gabriel wouldn't have remained unscathed.

He had to figure out a way to explain the impulsiveness of shifters, especially when in the presence of their unmated partner. All without giving the appearance the breed was mentally unstable.

He had no idea how difficult Sameya would be, so he mentally prepared himself for any reaction. She'd spent a long fucking time enjoying her single status, and he could understand why she'd planned to remain unmated. No one would want to lose their freedom to another. But they'd both proven to her that wasn't the type of relationship they wanted from her.

In the right situation, he'd enjoy dominating her—'Spread your legs', 'suck my dick', 'you'll take it all'—but that was the only kind of dominance he craved. And he suspected she'd make the perfect submissive in the bedroom. That was sex. He'd never want to subjugate her personality. Many Doms would enjoy breaking her fiery disposition in and out of the bedroom, but he and Gabriel weren't like that.

Maximus found her in the kitchen, sitting at the table with—*holy fucking Christ*—Gabriel's mom! And then the were-tiger said the worst thing ever..."Little girl, you'll mind your manners."

This could go bad fast. God love her, he adored the woman, but Gabby didn't have the good sense to recognize the more lethal predator. It'd been centuries since the shifters had had to fight for their dominance. Her family's wealth and power gave her a false sense of safety. Because of that prestige in the earthly mystic community, she expected everyone to mollycoddle her. That anticipation wouldn't be forthcoming from Sameya who lived by a very different set of rules in Atlantis, where *she* was at the top of the food chain.

Shit! Not good.

Instead of hostility, Sameya chuckled, shocking Maximus. His gal notched a finger in Gabby's direction, but peered at Kat. "She for real?

Kat squirmed in her seat and sent Maximus an expression that clearly pled for his assistance.

Arching a disapproving eyebrow, Gabby said in her haughtiest tone, "Really, Maximus, dear, your attire isn't appropriate for mixed company."

He peered down. Wearing no shirt, his nipple piercings glinted in the false light. His pants hung low on his hips, exposing the beginning tufts of his pubic hair. He shrugged. "Wasn't expecting company."

"Kat is present!" As a former friends-with-benefits, Kat had seen him dressed in less. "I do hope Gabriel will join us soon *and* be appropriately attired." She sniffed her affront.

God, she was in snooty form tonight. Where the fuck was Gabriel? No one could micromanage the woman quite the way he could.

"I'm sure you've seen him naked, so how would you prefer Maximus to dress?" As Sameya pushed the chair out beside her and patted the seat, Gabby's mouth parted on a scandalized gasp. "Join us, lover."

His gaze snapped to Sameya, but she was busy contemplating his mother-in-law. At what game did his sexy vixen play? Why call him lover in front of the other woman and...*holy shit*! The rest of what she said sank in. She didn't realize this was Gabriel's mother, but thought she was a lover.

Maximus would've laughed if he hadn't caught Sameya's hostile glare. Fuck him, she might not want them, but she was as protective as a shifter.

Gabby fanned her face, her tone high-pitched. "Why on earth would I see Maximus naked?"

Sameya opened her mouth to speak, but Maximus distracted her by catching the back of her neck as he sat beside her. She glanced at him and he explained quickly. "She is Gabriel's mother, Sameya."

"Mother?" His siren gaped at Gabby.

"Sameya, meet Gabby." At her confused expression, he bit his lip to restrain the smile that threatened to flash his fangs. He slithered his fingers through his newly acquired mate's hair. God, he loved the discoloration of her red and black tresses. "Gabby, meet our final mate."

"God in Heaven," Gabby said in her thick Southern drawl. "I can barely sense her power. She's a mere step up from a human. Are you *sure* this is your mate?"

Maximus cringed at his mother-in-law's mystic snobbery. And groaned when he caught the hard glint in Sameya's violet eyes. "You'll mind your manners, Gabby." He hooked a finger in the neckline of his shirt that his mate wore and tugged the material aside, exposing the bite mark Gabriel had given her on her shoulder. It still oozed blood, and he glowered, worried over her body's lack of self-healing. "*Very* sure she's ours. And couldn't be more delighted."

Gabby sniffed, and he was certain she disliked his command for her to mind her manners. "Before she can be presented to the pride, we'll have to clean her up."

Twin black eyebrows smashed together when Sameya frowned. "I beg your pardon?"

With the mood Gabby and his mate were in, this wasn't going to end well.

Maximus tugged his chair a little closer to his mate just in case he needed to grab her before she went after the other woman. "Kat, please locate Gabriel and bring him immediately." With a relieved expression, Kat fled the room.

"It's bad enough her power is so weak." *Shit.* Gabby had her haughty airs on tonight.

"Gabby—"

"I'm speaking, Maximus. It's impolite to interrupt." Apparently someone needed to remind her it was impolite to insult others. Especially when that person was so important to her son's life. "The pride will be appalled someone of his stature has someone as magically inept as this. You know how hard a time they had accepting you." Damn hard, not that Gabby had helped. "I will not have him a laughingstock simply because of your appearance, little girl." She shook her head. "That god awful hair has to go first. Then we'll work on—"

"You crazy bitch. Shut. Up." Sameya pushed to her feet. Maximus sat back, but grasped her hand to keep her close and away from Gabby. But he had no intentions of stopping her from putting her future mother-in-law in her place. It was the only way the shifter woman would ever respect her. "I'm not weak in magic. *You* are. I could manipulate you like a twisty tie if I were so inclined."

"Which you're not motivated to do." Maximus wasn't entirely certain she hadn't already utilized her siren spell against the other woman with the way her jaws flapped in shock.

Sameya didn't spare him a glance, but held Gabby's gape. "I'm a siren, which means you'd be eating your last breath by the time you realized I was there."

"A reaper." His mother-in-law's hand flew to her throat.

His reaper gave Gabby a tight smile. "I would strongly caution against anyone laughing at Gabriel because of me. I'll reap them without a thought."

"Neither will you alter her hair, Mother." Maximus waggled his eyebrows at Gabriel as he sauntered into the room. Sameya stiffened, but otherwise didn't acknowledge his sudden appearance. "Or anything else for that matter. She's perfect the way she is."

The tiger walked straight to their mate, kicked the chair away and aligned his chest with her spine. His arms went around her waist, but their little mate remained inflexible, and Maximus had the feeling she allowed his touch only because of Gabby's presence.

"Congratulate us on finding her. She completes us. And you know how long we've been waiting for her." Gabriel nuzzled her neck, but not the side where he'd bitten her.

Smart move, lover, don't draw attention to your recent mistake.

"Yes. Well...yes." His mother-in-law rose to her feet. She smoothed her skirt even though there wasn't a wrinkle in place. "I should be going. You're newly mated and...." She wouldn't meet their eyes as she cleared her throat.

"You're right," Maximus reclined in his seat, enjoying Gabby's discomfort. "Newly mated pairs are compelled to fuck nonstop."

She flashed him a shocked expression. "Maximus!"

He chuckled and blew her a kiss. "I love you, Gabby."

She walked stiffly around the end of the table and touched his cheek. "I love you, you rascal, even though I abhor those tacky things in your nipples. Won't you consider removing them?"

"I like his piercings." Sameya met the other woman's stare with a challenge in her eyes.

Fuck the siren had his cock twitching again.

"I'll walk you out, Mother." As Gabriel stepped away from Sameya, he held his arm out to his mother and waited until she placed her palm in the crook of his elbow.

"It was a...delight, Sameya." A little too late she remembered her manners. "I'll relate your unique charm to Gabriel's father."

Maximus rolled his eyes.

A saucy grin hit his siren's mouth. "I'm memorable like that."

Gabby opened and closed her mouth a few times, before settling on snapping her teeth together. He didn't think he'd ever seen the woman silenced by anyone before. What a priceless moment. Gabriel shot him an amused grin as they exited the kitchen.

Chapter Fifteen

The instant the door shut, Maximus peeked at Sameya. Her two-toned waist-length hair hugged her curves. His shirt hid those curves, but he knew what lay beneath the garment. When he stripped it off of her later, she would smell like him. That appealed to the possessive vampyr and would please Gabriel, too. "I've never seen anyone put Gabby in her place before."

"Is she always that bitchy?"

"She grows on you."

Sameya made a face. "So does fungus, and I don't like *it*."

He laughed. "She'll be the perfect mother-in-law from here on out."

That title had her fingers touching the shirt where the bite was located.

"The mating-mark will fade." *Eventually.* "You didn't accept it, so it's not permanent."

Sameya crossed her arms in a defensive gesture.

Her silence felt like a bad omen. "I would like to point out that *I* bit you, and you didn't freak out."

"You didn't try to force a mating. He did. If I wasn't wearing this"—she yanked on the gem encrusted collar—"I'd kill him for what he attempted. At the very least, I'd make him miserable."

"He's already miserable."

"Not nearly enough."

Maximus elevated an eyebrow. She might possess a bigger taste for blood than he did, and he survived off the elixir. He rolled out of his chair and moved to the refrigerator. "So, tell me about yourself."

"Like what?" He didn't look her way, but he could hear her confusion.

He snagged the tray of eggs, a packet of diced ham, and a bag of cheese. "I want to know everything." Even the littlest details...like her favorite color. If she owned any pets, what were their names, and their breeds? The name of her best friend? What'd she do for fun? What was her favorite food? "Want to join me for an omelet?" Maximus indicated the items he'd set on the table.

"You eat?"

"Don't you?" At her silence, he peered at her. Eyes narrowed quizzically on the contents scattered across the counter she approached him. "I especially get the munchies after having fantastic sex." Their gazes locked, and she froze like one of his victims in his sights. "For the record, Sameya, what we shared was phenomenal."

She glanced away quickly and shrugged. "I suppose."

Maximus chuckled. "Shame on you for lying."

"In comparison to my other lovers, I guess it was okay." She leaned a hip against the island and watched him as he set a skillet on the stove and sprayed it with non-stick oil.

"You experienced multiple orgasms." From what he'd read, not many women could say that. Neither could they claim to have men that cared about their satisfaction. "Who doesn't think that's phenomenal?"

Using a whisk, he beat eggs in a bowl.

"Those were...disturbing."

The serious note to her voice had his gaze whipping up to meet hers. "How so?"

Sameya shrugged. "You wouldn't understand if I told you."

"Try me." Dumbfounded by her confession, he poured the battered eggs into the skillet. He waited a moment for them to cook before sprinkling cheese and ham in the pan. "You might be surprised by how well I understand."

"It doesn't matter. I'll be gone soon."

Sameya shifted to walk away, and Maximus caught her wrist. "Please, Sameya. Our relationship isn't built on sex with you."

"Yes, it is." A minor twist of her wrist. He understood the hint and released his hold on her. "Neither of you asked if I wanted a liaison with you." It was a lot more than a liaison, but Maximus let it slide. "All I've heard from you both is caveman grunts of mine, mates, mine."

"That was only to prove to you that you're our mate." And it wasn't like she hadn't been doing the same thing with Gabriel's mother before she figured out the woman wasn't one of their former lovers.

"Let's get something straight, vamp. I am *no one's* property."

"Mates are not property, Sameya. For your fellow sirens to enslave theirs, that's...atrocious." He folded the omelet in half over on top of itself and flipped the food. Enslaving a partner was worse than atrocious, but it was the best he could come up with. He really wasn't a man big on communication.

She stared at him as if she were trying to figure him out. He was pretty simple really, but he'd let her discover that on her own.

Keeping his movements measured so as not to alarm her, he casually met her eyes. "I want to know the woman you are. Inside and out intimately. What makes you laugh? What makes you cry? What—"

"I don't cry."

She almost had earlier when he'd been undressing her, but he wouldn't remind her of that. "What is your favorite food? I'm a chef. I want to cook what you love."

A tiny smile tweaked the right corner of her mouth. "I don't eat. Or drink for that matter."

"Hmm...." Interesting. He'd heard stories *timerelics* no longer required nourishment, but he'd, also, believed them myths. He retrieved a plastic container off the counter and popped the lid. Washed strawberries created hills and valleys within the dish. "Allow me to tempt you to indulge."

Holding the fruit up by the top, he rested a forearm on the counter and leaned toward her. Her gaze riveted to his mouth, while her tongue swiped across her blood red ones.

Didn't like orgasms? *Pfft*...he suspected she liked them more than she'd admit, but since she couldn't lie, there *was* something about them that bothered her. The quick lick to her lips however, signified her desire to be kissed. Even if unknowingly, she invited his attention.

Maximus ran the pebbled tip of the strawberry along her bottom lip. Her otherworldly purple eyes brightened, and her lips parted. An open solicitation, but he suspected she held no knowledge of the temptation she projected. Declining her offer equated to self-mutilation, and he felt it in the longing of his cock.

He slid the fat, succulent base between her lips and pushed the fruit inward. Sameya surprised him by sucking on the strawberry. His dick reacted, becoming harder and pressing uncomfortably against the leather.

"Bite." The one word was all he could push past his lips at that moment.

No arguments forthcoming, she obeyed, her teeth slicing off the tip of the strawberry. Sameya chewed, her eyes widening. "Mmm...."

Maximus smiled, using his thumb to wipe off a spot of juice from the corner of her mouth. "Strawberry." He sucked his pad and held up the remainder of the fruit. He popped the rest of the strawberry into his mouth. In a silent offer for her to help herself to the fruit, he pushed the bowl closer to her and was delighted when she selected another one. "Why are orgasms disturbing, Sameya?"

The second strawberry halted centimeters from her mouth. Tentatively, she met his gaze and shrugged as she swallowed what was in her mouth.

"All women enjoy them." At least all the ones he'd been with had.

"You would have me believe you're that familiar with women?" She munched on the fruit pinned between her fingertips.

Maximus plucked the remainder of the strawberry from her hand and tossed it in his mouth.

"Hey!"

He flashed her a wicked grin. "Why wouldn't I have knowledge of women?"

"You're with Gabriel. Shifters are possessive."

"True, but you thought Gabby was our lover."

She shrugged. "She seemed like yours and Gabriel's type."

Maximus chuckled. "Far from it." He slid the omelet onto a plate and proceeded to make another. "I'd never been with a man before Gabriel came along. Mating doesn't mean instant love or trust, but it's a bonding of the souls. We took our mating slow, and before we mated, we'd fallen in love with one another."

The typical mating ritual was frenzied, and so out of control, the parties rarely knew what was going on until it was over. But a shifter and vampyr together was taboo, so they'd taken it slow to make sure they weren't reading the signs wrong. Since nature didn't put together what couldn't procreate, they'd known a female would someday enter their lives. Maximus had expected a shifter female, because to add a third species to their tri-union was so forbidden, it rather worried him. But already his protective instincts were honed razor sharp toward Sameya.

In time he hoped she'd love them, but they didn't have time for that. "I would die for Gabriel and would kill without regret for him. I feel the same for you."

She looked away. Why'd that make her uncomfortable? Maximus cupped her chin in his palm and turned her to face him. "We both delight in the softness of a woman, listening to her soft cries as we give her pleasure. We've shared many women together in our bed, but we have never invited another man into our relationship." To fuck another male would've been cheating. He ran his fingertips along her eyebrows when they arched a little higher. "Now that we've located you, there won't be another woman." *Even if she leaves us.* Such injustice in that truth.

Fingertip running the length of the round bowl filled with strawberries, she watched him. If the frown furrowing her forehead was any indication, her thoughts were troublesome.

Maximus lowered his hand, but maintained eye contact. Waiting for whatever she had to say...if she ever spoke. When she did, it wasn't what he was expecting.

"My power is cerebral." Sirens controlled others with their mind. He comprehended that. "I lose control of that function when I...climax."

She sounded as uncomfortable with the word as she was with the defenselessness she suffered from having one. "You believe that makes you vulnerable?"

"I know it does." She pulled his shirt to the side exposing the marks Gabriel had given her. They still seeped blood. "Had I owned my faculties, this wouldn't have happened. I should've fought him harder, but I was so lost to the feel of him inside me and you doing...your thing."

"Can't you self-heal?"

"No. But I don't need to if my cognitive abilities aren't compromised."

Without any thought, Maximus shifted closer and licked Gabriel's mating marks. A tremor ricocheted through her, as her tiny gasp of surprise painted the air. Shifting to the end of the island, Maximus palmed her nape and pulled her against him as he tongued the puncture wounds.

The taste of her blood lured him to bite over the lesions Gabriel gave her. Worse, he wanted to sink his fangs into her as he thrust his dick into her wet sheath. He'd withheld his need earlier for fear of scaring her off.

The taste of her essence dissipated, the injuries healed by his saliva. Maximus slid his tongue up her throat, and she angled her head exposing her jugular to him. Even if it wasn't intentional, his vampyr interpreted it as a sign of trust. His fangs hit his lips, and he scraped them back and forth along her neck leaving red lines, but taking care not to break her skin. Her pulse visibly escalated. He sucked on the rapid tap, caught it between his teeth and flattened his tongue over the steady thud, relishing the feel against his over-sensitive senses.

One of her hands came to rest on his hip. The other cupped the back of his head. She seemed to understand his need to claim her like this because she melted into the pose, her breathing steady as he inhaled her scent.

He and Gabriel would always protect her. Her vulnerability was unacceptable to them. How could he make her understand that?

Fingertips dragging down her spine, they traipsed through the cheeks of her ass and teased across her pussy, wet and sticky from hers and Gabriel's release.

He thrust two fingers into her.

"Maximus!"

"You want me," he said without releasing his hold on her pulse.

"Yes." Her husky voice had him pushing his fingers deep. She whimpered for him. "But I don't like it."

Physically she liked it, but mentally, she was a bit reticent. "And Gabriel?"

"The same."

His fingers plunged in and out of her, and she tilted her pelvis back to deepen his penetration. She had no idea how natural she was at sex. "Will you stop me from taking you once more?"

"N-no."

Just as Maximus suspected, she was incapable of resisting them as they were her. The mating call was as impossible to oppose as her siren song. A good thing since during the beginning of any mating, they'd be driven to have sex often.

He released her throat, withdrew his digits from her body, and lifted her onto the counter. In the doorway, he spied Gabriel leaning against the doorjamb. The tiger nodded for Maximus to proceed. He combed his fingers through her hair and kissed her before assisting her to lean back.

"Stay on your elbows and watch me." He captured her calf between his hands and guided her foot up to anchor on his shoulder.

"W-what about Gabriel?"

"You want him here?"

"It feels wrong that he's not."

A good sign their unmated female wanted them both even though she was angry with one. Kissing her ankle, Maximus glanced at Gabriel. "What say you, Gabriel? You going to join us?"

Sameya twisted enough so she could angle her head to get a glimpse of the tiger.

"I'm sorry," he said as he ambled toward them. "I shouldn't have bit you, Sameya. I wasn't thinking clearly."

"Don't do it again." Gabriel stopped on the other side of the island and wrapped his arms around her waist, nuzzling his face against her neck.

"I still get to bite, but I promise not to mark unless you give me permission." A vampyr bite was different than a shifter's. The only time a shifter breed bit was to give the mating mark...or to reclaim his partner.

"Make sure you don't mark me, Maximus." Sameya lifted an arm and cupped the back of the tiger's head. "I have no idea why I'm forgiving you so easily, Gabriel. But I don't want to be angry with you."

Gabriel lifted his head enough to peer at her face. "You're vulnerability is our problem, too." How long had he been listening to their conversation? The tiger rubbed his nose against hers. "To lose you would kill us both."

"You don't know me well enough to feel that way." She bit her bottom lip as Gabriel inched Maximus's black shirt upward, exposing her belly.

Maximus captured her face between his hands and stared into her eyes. "Our souls are connected, we *would* be devastated to lose you. And if you think walking away from us in a month is going to be easy, you're deluding yourself."

"We will make it as hard on you as possible." Gabriel flicked a finger over one of her cotton-covered nipples. "We won't play fair."

"Not when we're playing for keeps." Maximus lifted her off the counter, and she wrapped her legs around his waist. "Gabriel can't assist very well from across the counter. Will you bring the strawberries, Gabriel?"

Maximus carried her to the table and placed her on it. With a hand on her back, he slowly guided her to lie back. Once she lay flat, with her butt on the edge of the surface, he clamped her arms over her head and held them there with a hand on her wrists.

The sound of the stainless steal omelet pan scrubbing against the stove caused him to look around and catch Gabriel removing it from the burner. The clicks of knobs being turned indicated Maximus had forgotten to turn off the eyes, as well. Distracted by Sameya, he'd forgotten about the omelet and only now caught a whiff of burnt food.

He refocused on Sameya, and a moment later, Gabriel placed the bowl of fruit on the table near Sameya's hip. Maximus slid his palms down her arms before selecting a plump strawberry from the dishware, as Gabriel ratcheted up the shirt in tiny increments. Only an inch of flesh exposed at a time. Giving her no forewarning, Maximus flicked the stubbly fruit through the folds of her pussy.

A sharp inhale kissed the air. Back and forth he moved the fruit, coating it in her and Gabriel's juices, as the tiger continued the slow upward drag of the garment.

The fabric caught on her right nipple, but gave free with a pop, exposing the pebbled nub. Gabriel crooned his appreciation with "Mmm," as he swiped a strawberry from the bowl. He bit off one end and soaked her nipple with the juice. A moment later, Gabriel sucked on her breast, repeating the process with the other mound.

Maximus pushed the fruit into her pussy and grew harder watching it disappear within her. He added a second and then a third and rotated his thumb against her opening. The fourth one he used against her clit as he tongued at the fruit buried inside her.

Sameya rocked against his mouth, her moans and whimpers making him harder. Gabriel purred as he suckled at her breasts, using the strawberry to heighten her experience. With her hands clamped on the tiger's head, she was in a constant state of movement...arching her back to thrust her breasts into Gabriel's mouth, while rocking her hips into Maximus's tongue.

Maximus spread her vaginal lips with his fingers and buried his tongue deep into her, retrieving one of the strawberries. She sighed as the fruit slid out of her. Using only his teeth and mouth, he captured it between his fangs. Around the nectar, he said, "Gabriel."

The tiger lifted his head with a soft growl of dissatisfaction at being interrupted, his eyes glowing tiger-bright. Gabriel and Maximus met in the middle, kissing as they shared the strawberry. The sweet taste of fruit and Sameya's arousal burst on his tongue as they kissed. Gabriel tangled his fingers in Maximus's hair, and the tiger's purr grew louder. When they broke apart, Maximus dragged his fangs across Gabriel's bottom lip.

Sameya's, "I envy that strawberry," snapped them out of their lull. Gabriel chuckled as Maximus settled into a chair and buried his face between her legs.

Chapter Sixteen

Sameya was certain she would fragment into a billion pieces any moment. These men were intense, more than she could've ever hoped to anticipate. This much ecstacy couldn't be possible. Couldn't be realistic in a normal setting. At least none of the mated female sirens she knew seemed happy.

The vampyr's tongue flicked inside her, coaxing another strawberry out of her, while Gabriel alternated between laving and suckling her breasts. The tiger's hands were all over her, cupping one breast and caressing her body with the other.

She cried out as the fruit dragged along her clit. So slow, with just enough pressure to make her entire body quiver, but not enough to force her climax. In a bad, bad way, she wanted to come. She loved and hated those orgasms.

She was *not* the after-sex snack she'd envisioned Maximus imbibing on. With his tongue swirling on her clit and his fingers extracting the fruit from her body, she inched closer to shattering. Another flick and her insides vibrated for the climax, only to have Maximus pull back at the critical moment. Orgasm dying, her tears of frustration shocked her. She never cried. Ever. But she needed what he was denying her.

"Maximus, please," she whispered, rolling her head from side-to-side.

"Be patient." She could hear Maximus shuffling, but couldn't determine what action he performed.

Gabriel removed her hands from his head and abruptly stood. Confused by his sudden departure, she reached for him, but he stepped out of her grasp.

"Gab—"

Maximus captured her hips and tugged. Feeling as gooey as melted butter, she slid off the table and straight into the vampyr's arms. His cock impaled her so deep they were pelvis to pelvis in a second. Sameya cried out at the rapid penetration. Maximus groaned.

The exquisite bliss of having him inside her turned her world foggy and she struggled to pull herself back from the chasm of carnality. But the effort was useless.

Gooseflesh scattered across her body as Gabriel yanked the T-shirt over her head. The tiger palmed the back of her head and cupped her chin with his other hand. He kissed her, thrusting his tongue into her mouth.

"I'll be right back," he said against her lips and then released her. She collapsed against Maximus, praying he'd begin to thrust forthwith. Praying he'd give her one of those dreaded orgasms very, *very* soon.

No such luck. He tangled his hand in her hair and drew her head back so he could examine her. "Tell me what you want, Sameya."

"Let me come." That request should've horrified her, but being exposed in their presence felt natural.

"I don't think so." He licked a nipple and rolled it between his teeth.

Sameya grabbed a handful of his chocolate hair and yanked on the strands. His eyes flashed green and a slow playful grin tilted the corners of his mouth. "Maximus! No more dawdling. Please, no more."

"This what you want, *naleah*?" He slid his hand between their bodies and placed the pad of his thumb against her clit. He circled the sensitive nub in soft strokes.

"Yes," she breathed, allowing her head to fall back. That was exactly what she needed. A little faster maybe, that would get her what she wanted quicker.

The table was abruptly shoved toward the window, and her eyes snapped open to catch a glimpse of Gabriel moving in behind her. Wherever he'd gone, it hadn't taken long. Maximus cupped her cheek regaining her concentration as Gabriel kissed and licked down her spine.

"I'd be a bad mate if I forced orgasms on you." Maximus's touch left her clitoris. "Don't you agree, Gabriel?"

"Quite right, Maximus." Gabriel's lips moved against the flesh of her lower back.

Sameya's eyes widened. They meant to amp her up and leave her hanging? How...cruel. Admitting she disliked the climaxes he gave her must've offended him more than she'd anticipated. That hadn't been her intention, but she understood how he could've misinterpreted her meaning.

Maximus leaned back, resting his shoulders against the wooden chair. "You're welcome to *use* me until you come."

The challenge in his eyes said he didn't think she'd do it. The very idea was...arousing. She clenched her feminine muscles and thought he ground his teeth together.

Sameya placed her hands on the back of the chair on either side of the vampyr's head. She lifted herself up and lowered back down. Pelvis-to-pelvis, she rotated her hips and whimpered as her clit scrubbed against him and his length shifted inside her.

"Faster, Sameya." Maximus pinched a nipple.

"I'm doing this my way."

Gabriel caught her hips, held her motionless, and put his lips against her ear. Even though the tiger spoke, it was the vampyr who held her attention. "You'll do it *our* way or we'll both leave you unsatisfied. Now...." He shifted, a hand curled around her throat and his fingers trailed down her spine and between her butt cheeks. "I'm going to slide a vibrator into here"—he nudged her anus with a fingertip—"and then you're going to do exactly as Maximus says. Agreed?"

She tried to nod.

"Say the words." The tiger persisted.

"Yes."

"You're going to come so hard, you might wish afterward you hadn't agreed."

Sameya whimpered at Maximus's statement. She couldn't imagine a climax bigger than the ones they'd already given her.

Gabriel held her steady by her throat and handed some items to Maximus over her shoulder. "Let her watch you lube up the dildo I'm going to put in her ass."

The vampyr's fierce gaze held hers as he swung the toy upward into her view. Pink, sparkly, maybe five inches long and wider in the middle.

Gods, it was huge. Gabriel's penetration with his fingers earlier were the first she'd ever experienced in that forbidden spot. There was no way that thing would fit inside her.

Maximus sucked on the item they planned to put inside her. A popping sound rent the air when it exited his mouth. "It's not as big as you're thinking it is." He pressed a button at the base and the sex toy made a whirring sound. "Less than an inch in diameter, Sameya."

That was supposed to mean something to her? And make her feel better?

Maximus ran the vibrator across her cheek. "That's low speed." Twice more he pressed the base. "High."

"Do you want to stop?" So focused on Maximus, Gabriel's softly spoken words against her ear caused her to jerk. "Say the word and we'll discontinue our play."

"I'm...g-good." She wasn't so sure, but she knew she had no desire to stop them. In the month she'd promised them, she'd embrace all the carnal delights they offered her.

Maximus shut off the dildo, popped the lid on the lube and spread a thick line of clear gel along the toy. After squirting a sizeable dollop on Gabriel's fingers,

Maximus handed the shifter the lubricant, before smearing the emollient all over the vibrator.

"We bought it especially for you." The tiger nuzzled the base of her ear.

When had they found the time since Maximus *venomed* her? Deciding the answer didn't matter she withheld the query.

"There'll be some burn." Maximus warned. "Relax and push down as Gabriel pushes it in. The pain will fade quickly."

What was she getting into? Way over her head already and she didn't have the good sense to call a halt to—slippery fingers probed her back entrance and she squealed.

"Easy, baby, we're getting you good and wet so the butt plug will go in easier."

"It's exciting her. She's creaming all over my cock." If not for the blaze of the vampyr's green eyes, Maximus's matter-of-fact statement would've led her to believe he felt nothing. But she'd learned when the vampyr showed in his eyes, his emotions ran high.

"Mmm...good to know." Gabriel's finger plunged deep into her bottom, and Maximus groaned. A second finger entered her, burning as he worked them languidly.

"I wish you could feel the way she's squeezing my dick while you're doing that. Between her cunt tightening up and the feel of your fingers, I might blow just sitting here."

"Don't be juvenile, Maximus." The teasing note to Gabriel's voice evoked a chuckle from Maximus. Sameya had no idea what they were talking about or what could be funny. Especially when she prophesied she'd combust any second.

Gabriel's probing terminated and he removed the butt plug from the vampyr's hold. "Ready, Sameya?"

As ready as she'd ever be. "Yes."

Gabriel released her throat and Maximus pulled her against his chest, wrapping his arms around her. His heart beat against her ear, his breathing a steady puff against her hair. She heard Gabriel slouch to his knees and then felt him spreading her butt cheeks. That he saw her so intimately exposed and that she allowed him to play with her so familiarly burned her cheeks with...what? Definitely not mortification. If anything, she anticipated this new encounter.

I have no will to impede what's about to happen. I want this experience with them.

The tapered tip pierced into her rectum without incident, and she focused on the odd sensation of the toy penetrating her. She winced and tried to shift away at the sudden sting.

"Relax." Gabriel rubbed the base of her spine. "Push down against it."

As Maximus kissed her forehead, she made a tentative push. She gasped, curling her fingers into fists on Maximus's chest. "That hurts."

"It burns," the vampyr corrected, his chest rumbling beneath her ear. "We've both experienced it. It gets easier."

Did she want this to get easier? Gabriel must've pushed the button on the butt plug because it suddenly whirred to life. *That* felt good. Sameya moaned and pushed harder against the sex-toy.

"Good, baby, almost at the widest part." Gabriel rubbed her flesh where the toy probed.

"I'm going to come." And she very much feared she would. The burn coupled with the vibrations and Maximus's cock as deep as he could go inside her, made for a heady combination of pleasure.

Maximus and Gabriel both chuckled.

"Not yet, *naleah*." Somehow Maximus squeezed his arm between them and pinched her clitoris. Hard. Her approaching orgasm evaporated.

Not fair. So not fair.

Wrapping her hair around his hand, Maximus pulled her head back. "Submit to the rest of the invasion while we watch."

Gabriel shifted to crouch at their side. He added a notch of pressure to the toy, and it slid all the way in, the burning vibration delicious. Her gasp rent the air, and a trembling started in her legs. A heap of limp, useless flesh, if it wasn't for Maximus she wouldn't be upright in his lap.

"Look at her face, so beautiful wearing that expression of ecstasy." Gabriel fiddled with the dildo. "It's not coming out."

But she was coming. Soon. Any second.

"Fuck, she just got impossibly fucking tight." Maximus paused, his gaze running all over her face. "Sameya, don't come."

"Can't stop…can't stop…."

Gabriel pinched her clit this time. Sameya cried, tears hitting her cheeks, so lost in the haze of bliss that threatened to drag her under, her vision grew fuzzy. Their words sounded far, far away.

"I'll put this on her to keep her from coming." Gabriel held up a clamp-like apparatus. She had no idea what it was.

"Please," she whispered.

His response, he fastened the object over her clit.

Maximus licked the tears from her cheeks. "Fuck me, Sameya."

More tears fell as the ecstasy grew intense, but no orgasm arrived. She felt so stuffed, but wanted and needed more. Maybe she could obtain release if she started to move. Holding his vampyr-green scrutiny, she white-knuckled the back of the chair and lifted herself, riding his cock slowly. Maximus's piercings scrubbed along her channel, the Apadravya speared through the head of his dick, hit that magical spot deep within her.

"Baby, you're going to come so hard it's going to blow your mind." Gabriel stroked his erection, running his thumb along the head.

That would happen quicker without the gadget hooked to her privates. "I can remove this, then?"

"No." Maximus caught her wrists seconds before she touched the thingy that killed her climax. Sameya groaned her disapproval as he pulled her arms behind her and clamped them with a hand at the small of her back. "Can you help me suck Gabriel as you ride me?"

Glancing between them, and desperate to reach an orgasm, she quickened her thrusts. "I'll try."

"Slow down, *naleah*." Maximus's free hand landed on her hip and decelerated her pace. "Don't want you coming too soon."

She slammed down on him. "I do."

"Stuff her mouth with your dick. That should slow her down." To spite Maximus, she ground down on him.

"I love how her eyes glow, expressing how much she enjoys it." Gabriel crowded their space, pulled her hair into a ponytail and turned her head to face him. Holding the base of his erection, he tapped the crown against her mouth. "Open up, baby."

Sameya met his golden eyes and parted her lips. Without forewarning, Gabriel thrust to the back of her throat. She gagged and wanting a little control, struggled against Maximus's hold on her wrists. His grip tightened as Gabriel withdrew enough she could catch her breath. She jerked her head, hoping to dislodge Gabriel's hold on her hair.

"Nuh-uh, baby." He cupped her cheek with his other hand. "Submit to us. We are in control of your pleasure. Just...submit."

"You won't regret it," the vampyr said.

Sameya breathed hard through her nose, not certain she wanted to give them that much power over her.

Gaze intense, Gabriel thrust back into her mouth, but not far enough to gag her. "Keep your eyes open and on mine."

Her eyelids lifted, and she dropped down on Maximus's cock. With her sights locked on Gabriel, he set a steady pace fucking her mouth.

"So fucking hot watching my dick slide between those lips."

"Suck a little harder." The hand Maximus maintained on her hip, kept the movement of her hips at a languid pace, just enough to keep her skirting the threshold of release. "Good girl."

Gabriel's grip tightened in her hair, and he groaned. "Goddamn, what a good girl."

"That's hot, *naleah*. You sucking his dick while fucking mine. Do you like us inside you?"

Gabriel pulled out of her mouth so she could answer Maximus's question, his grip on her hair unyielding. "Do you?"

"Yes." As much as she wanted her freedom, she wasn't confident she could walk away from these men. And not because of the sex...but because of the way they treated her. Like she was *everything* to them. She'd never been anything to anyone.

Maximus smiled as Gabriel altered his position so the vampyr could take over the blowjob. Sameya rode Maximus, keeping the stride unhurried, while watching him work over Gabriel's cock. Sometimes he licked to the base, tongued the balls, to trail the tip back up to the crown and suck Gabriel deep into his mouth, cheeks hollowing. The oral fuck would speed up and cause Gabriel to moan and jerk. Right when she'd think he was going to climax, Maximus would slow the pace. Other times he'd take Gabriel so deep she could see the imprint of his erection widening Maximus's throat.

The vampyr licked precum off the slit on the head of the tiger's dick. "He's going to blow any moment."

"Let me finish him." That request shocked her. She'd had no intention of saying it.

Each time they come inside me, they're marking me as theirs. All of Atlantis would smell them on her when she returned.

Gabriel twisted about and was in her mouth before she could barely blink. "Maximus, command her to relax her throat. I want to get as deep as possible inside her mouth."

"Relax, Sameya." Maximus quickened her movements on him and she held her breath as her pussy throbbed.

Weird how the collar forced her compliance and Gabriel was going down her throat without her gagging.

"Goddamn. Goddamn." Gabriel twisted her hair until her scalp stung. He made tiny jabs into her throat, but never left the depth of her mouth.

Maximus ran his fingers along the lump in her neck.

"Stop touching us there, Maximus. Feels too good to come just yet."

The vampyr used his thumb to stroke the outline of Gabriel's cock on her neck. "Hum, Sameya."

Excited by Gabriel's loss of control, Sameya stared at the tiger and hummed. A strangled noise left his throat, and the white Bengal tiger imprinted over his skin for a flash of a second. His grip on her hair intensified as he palmed the back of her head. Gabriel lost control and fucked her mouth and throat, driving her face into his abdomen with the strength of his thrusts. The frenzy couldn't have lasted longer than a minute when he came; pulling back to fill her mouth with cum rather than shoot it down her throat.

"Don't swallow." His voice sounded guttural, as he made small jabbing motions into her mouth.

When he exited from her, Maximus slammed his lips over hers. Their wet, cum-sloppy kiss had her grinding down on his cock. Tongues meeting and tangling, one of the men removed the apparatus off her clit. Sameya moaned as the first small wave of rapture deluged her body. The vibrations in her ass increased as if it'd been punched to high speed. Maximus groaned into her mouth, she guessed he felt the dildo's higher speed, also.

The vampyr jerked his head back to lean against the back of the chair. With their eyes locked, he released her hands. "Rub your clit if you want to come with me."

Sameya positioned one hand on the chair beside his head and the other over her nub. She flattened her feet on the floor and lifted herself up and dropped down on his length without any control to her descent. Each drop jabbed his Apadravya against her G-spot. Fingers circling fast along her clitoris, her breathing escalated, as did his.

Suddenly she didn't want any of their lovemaking to end, but knew he'd come without her if she didn't join him. The feel of him inside her pussy and the dildo in her ass, stuffed her so full, she never wanted this to end.

Maximus came, his cock jerking inside her, the hot spurt of liquid filling her. "Don't stop!" He gasped. "Take your pleasure," the words were barely more than grunts.

Whimpers left her lips like desperate pleas to the climax goddess. Gabriel knelt and fucked her with the dildo as she rode Maximus. The third thrust of the object in her ass did it for her. Throwing her head back, she came with a scream, riding Maximus through the radical bliss. Nearing the end, Gabriel shoved the vibrator into her and she came again, harder this time.

Maximus captured her face between his hands. "Yes! So perfect."

A starburst of light overcame her vision, and her brain ceased to process anything but the ecstasy.

"Shit!" She heard Gabriel snarl. And she didn't think it was in a good way. Sameya tried to focus her body off the climax, but her brain refused to fire-up.

A heavy thump hit the floor followed by more snarling.

Maximus tensed beneath her, his hands tightening on her hips. "Motherfucker—" He twitched beneath her.

Sameya dragged in a labored breath; her body shivered with short-circuits of convulsions, reminding her body of the intense bliss it'd experienced moments before. Even though a sense of dread overcame her, she couldn't get her brain to cooperate.

In tiger form, she caught sight of Gabriel leaping at a man she didn't recognize. A female held a blade to Maximus's neck, a thin line of blood already trickling down his skin. Whatever the chick had used on him, he was out.

"Think of mind-fucking me and I'll slice his throat." The unknown female offered her a sick and twisted smile.

Yanked off Maximus from behind, she hit the marble floor, her elbows and knees protesting the violence. The pain unimportant as she tried to serenade them, but not even a small warble emerged as she tried to push her magic out of her over-stimulated brain.

She blinked up into the smiling face of a male she'd never seen before. "Got you, bitch."

He sprayed something into her face. Sameya cried out and swatted at her stinging eyes. She reacted with a serenade that worked this time. But instead of the song controlling them, it echoed in her head. Pain shot through her limbs, overriding all enjoyment. Grasping her temples Sameya curled into a fetal position.

Moments later velvety blackness overrode all of her senses.

Chapter Seventeen

In his tiger skin, Gabriel paced a small path in front of the locked steel door. Too angry to shift, he issued random growls of fury. His right shoulder continued to bleed, but it'd heal soon. While the ache was tolerable in shifter form, and he'd endured worse injuries, he worried about his mates.

Maximus remained unconscious, sprawled on the concrete floor. They'd taken him quickly, and rather easily, with a knick of wormwood to the throat. Wormwood was next to impossible to find, and he'd never seen any himself—until tonight. Many believed the worms that burrowed through and lived in the wood excreted a substance that was toxic to vampyrs and not the timber itself. Legend revealed the only place it could be found was in Atlantis. That particular wood was the one thing guaranteed to take a vampyr down.

Manacles made of the lumber circled Maximus's wrists and neck, preventing him from rousing. Gabriel hoped his spouse awakened before dying.

He had no idea where Sameya was located. Gabriel had tried to get to her when he spied Tyrone Gryphon, but the bastard had subdued her with ease by spraying something in her face. And she'd been practically depleted from the orgasms they'd forced on her. She'd said they weakened her, and he'd arrogantly thought they were safe in their magically locked-tight home.

Gabriel snarled. They forced danger on her every time they made love to her. The idea of what Gryphon could do to her turned his stomach sour. Anger leached through his tiger, and he heaved himself against the door with a roar. The barrier didn't dent. Had it been anything but steel—his weakness—he'd have torn down the barrier.

"Gabriel?" At the sound of Maximus's scratchy voice, he swung about. "What the hell happened?"

Maximus pushed up into a seated position and slouched against the wall. Breathing shallow, and his skin pallid, the vampyr's predicament was gloomy. Chuffing two heavy breaths, neither calming Gabriel, he shifted, wincing as he altered into his human skin. Injuries always hurt worse in mortal form.

"Tyron Gryphon happened." Gabriel put his hand through his hair and related the events, as he knew them. He'd taken down ten of Gryphon's minions. Ripped the throats out of two of them. The remaining bastards had managed to restrain him. His only consolation was that they all wore various lacerations. None of them had come away from the scuffle unscathed. "I don't know what he used on Sameya, but she went down quickly after he sprayed it in her face." He turned and rammed his fist against the door. Knuckles splitting, they dripped blood on the floor. "We've got to find a way out of here. She's alone without us to—"

"Stop." Maximus curled his fingers around the wormwood collar. Seeing his mate's flesh bubble around the restraint, Gabriel fisted his hands as his claws burst through his fingertips. He ignored the punctures they created in his palm, focusing instead on what his lover said. "Sameya's strong and smart. Don't count her out."

"I'm not." Gabriel prowled back to Maximus and knelt in front of him. "Thinking of the things Gryphon could do to her without us there to protect her...it drives my cat crazy."

"I know." Maximus scratched at the flesh blistered on his wrists.

"I already tried to remove these." Gabriel indicated the wormwood restraints encircling Maximus's wrists and neck.

The vampyr nodded, but changed the subject. "What about Kat?"

"I have no idea." He hadn't even thought of her. What type of friend did that make him? "The last time I saw her was when I left the kitchen to get the box of toys. She was playing the X-box, and I cautioned her to stay out of the kitchen unless she wanted an eyeful."

"Gryphon obviously knows our vulnerabilities." Maximus tapped a finger against a wrist restraint and motioned to the steel cage they were housed inside. Steel was the only thing that could contain a shifter. "How did he learn Sameya's weakness? We don't know what he sprayed in her face. How did he even know she was with us?"

"I don't know." Not liking Maximus's labored breaths, Gabriel sat down and pulled him against his chest. "My best guess is he had the house bugged." He ran his fingers through the chocolate strands of his mate's shoulder length hair. "I'm going to kill him, Maximus."

"If he's left a single mark on Sameya, he suffers first."

Gabriel could get on board with that. They sat for a while in silence. Maximus lying on his side, with his head reclined on Gabriel's legs.

"You think we pushed her too hard in the kitchen, Maximus?" He couldn't stop thinking about the things they'd done to her. The things she'd allowed them to do to her. Nary a complaint from her, and he'd sensed her reticence with the butt plug. He'd also tasted the spice of her excitement.

"She needed to know what we're about if she's going to make an informed decision whether to remain with us." Maximus went into a coughing fit that racked him harder than a grand-mal seizure. Wormwood sickness worked rapidly and was lethal ninety percent of the time if not countered almost immediately. Gabriel prayed for a miracle from every god he knew about. "We can't pretend to be something we're not."

He wanted to tell Maximus to conserve his energy and stop talking, but that felt like giving up. "But we could've taken it slow. We don't have to fuck her together before the month's out."

"Don't go soft, Gabriel." The vampyr squeezed his thigh, his grip so slight it was obvious his strength waned. Panic clogged Gabriel's chest with a hard knot, but Maximus continued to talk. "The monsters in us need to take her that way to make her ours. She needs to know what it's like, to determine if it's something she can handle." A weary sigh rattled from his mate's lungs and Gabriel resisted embracing him tighter, as if that'd dampen the danger of the wormwood. "We both know not all women are capable of accepting our demands in the bedroom without the double penetration. Sameya seemed to handle us fine. Better than fine. That woman gives as good as she takes."

"Maybe. I don't know." He trailed his fingertips over Maximus's cool brow. His lowering body temperature a bad symptom. "She was scared of us in the beginning."

"I wouldn't have classified her as scared." Maximus licked parched lips that were cracking as Gabriel watched. His long-time mate was losing strength faster than he'd like. "She was determined to remain alone and have nothing to do with us. But scared...."

"She was scared, Maximus. We forced ourselves on her." Yet he felt no regret about that. Probably because coercing a mate was a common denominator among the mystics and shifters.

"She was frightened that we're her mates, but not afraid of us."

Gabriel nodded. Maximus spoke true. Sure of her capabilities, Sameya was too arrogant to be fearful of anyone. Which brought to mind the predicament they were in. "We didn't even protect her when she's at her weakest, why would she remain with us? I wouldn't."

"I...don't know. We can hire security and get Kat's coven to drench the house in wards."

"If Kat's alive." Gabriel grimaced over those words. To give the thought life unsettled him.

"Before we can worry about any of that, we have to get out of here." Maximus's eyelids drooped, and his mouth sagged to one side.

"You okay?" Gabriel nudged his shoulder.

"Feel wi—wa—*weird*." His vampyr smacked his lips. "Tung...pheel...phat."

Tongue feel fat, Gabriel interpreted Maximus's slurred words. At least that's what he thought he said.

Maximus went into a very real grand-mal seizure, eyes rolling into his head, foaming at the mouth and his entire body jerking.

Gabriel went feral, his cat roaring their grief.

***

Sameya's head pounded like a heavy metal drummer resided within. Throat dry, ears ringing, and eyes scratchy, she blinked several times before finally elevating her eyelids enough to peer about. The over bright room caused her to cringe and made her head hurt worse.

Where the hell was she?

"Thank the Blessed Mother you're okay."

She turned her head in the direction of the voice. A tall woman with long brown hair, and teal eyes stared at her. She seemed familiar in an irritating sort of way. They weren't friends, Sameya knew that much.

"How does your head feel?"

Sameya caught the woman's wrist before her fingers could graze her forehead.

Kat. She recalled the other woman now. Maximus and Gabriel's witch. The one who'd collared her.

"I don't like to be touched." Frowning at the iron cuff on her wrist, she released Kat and lifted her other arm. Another one on the other wrist, both etched with Atlantian magical symbols. Memories scrambled back into her head so fast she grimaced at the sudden ambush. She had no idea who her attacker was, but there was one thing she was very certain of...he was a fool to come after her, even if he *had* executed his attack brilliantly.

He will pay. Once I find him.

Rolling to her side, she sat and scooted to the edge of the bed. Still naked with the dildo in her ass and vibrating, she should've been embarrassed, but instead fury clambered along her spine. She'd locate the nearest bathroom or closet and shut off the sex-toy, but weirdly she preferred one of her men remove the gadget.

My men? I've officially lost my mind. They're not my men. She threw her legs over the side of the mattress. She really should remove the object rather than save the honors for Gabriel or Maximus. Survival was priority number one, and she had no clue if she could walk with the toy stuffed up her ass.

"Take it slow. You've been out for an entire day."

Sameya looked over her shoulder at the other woman. Seriously? In what universe had she been thrown where a witch mothered her?

However, the solemn lines etched onto Kat's forehead suggested her concern was sincere. That fretfulness was a novelty in Sameya's world where no one worried about her. Ever. Unless they feared she planned to reap them.

"Are Maximus and Gabriel alive?"

"They were when we were brought here. Gabriel was injured. Maximus shackled in wormwood."

Wormwood. Not good. He wouldn't sicken and die as fast as a young vampyr would, but even the oldest and strongest of them would fall quickly to that particular lumber.

"What'd he spray in my face?" It still reeked whatever it was.

First on the agenda...locate a washcloth and scrub this shit off my skin.

"It smells like rose petals."

Not expecting an answer, she elevated her eyebrows at the witch. Curious how the attacker discovered that in aerosol format, rose petals act as a cerebral flat liner to a siren. Only another siren could've fed her assailant that information.

"They're my best friends, and I failed them." Kat stared at her hands as she twisted her fingers together. "My magic should've protected us from an infiltration. I didn't even know these goons were there until it was too late."

"So you're to blame? Good to know." Sameya stood, finding her legs surprisingly steady. Walking didn't shift the gadget in her bottom or hinder her movement either. Another plus in her favor.

"Yes," Kat said in a very small voice. "I've brought shame to my coven."

"You're an idiot."

Kat's head snapped back, her eyes wide with surprise.

"Whoever's magic this is, it's stronger than yours. He is to blame. Your pity-party is counter-productive." She tested a small serenade and was delighted when it didn't rebound in her head. Serenading herself was an experience she never wanted to repeat. "Why aren't you wearing iron fetters?" Other than the bump on the witch's forehead, she appeared relatively unharmed.

"No need for shackles when his magic does the job easy enough." A displeased scowl settled on Kat's face.

"Get over yourself." Sameya despised fragile women. And she hadn't suspected the other woman would be a weak link. Most witches weren't. "You might be strong for your age, but even I have no problem swiping through your magic. That spell you had around the house wouldn't have contained me for two minutes."

"Yet, the magic in the collar I created keeps you trapped to the men."

Sameya grinned. She could work with cocky. "That's different. It's mixed with Maximus's power." *He is damn strong, not to mention persuasive.* And she was feeling a whole lot of protectiveness knowing her mates were somewhere and in danger. "Vampyrs are unaffected by my siren spell. That means so is his magic."

The bedroom door opened. Kat's shoulders snapped straight, and her glare waylaid the entrance. Patience taxed, Sameya watched as a soldier entered. She'd recognize the arrogance of a leader anywhere, and this man wasn't wearing it in his demeanor.

"Good to see you're awake, Sameya."

Interesting that he knew her name when she had no idea who commanded him. She inclined her head. "Wish I could say the same." Since he wasn't the leader of this expedition, she didn't bother asking for his name.

His gaze traveled the length of her naked body, his eyes darkening. "You brought this on yourself." He clucked his tongue at her.

Typical henchmen style to lay the blame on others.

The stranger made a 'come here' motion with his hand. "Gryphon wants to see you."

"Gryphon?" Hadn't Gabriel said that name when she'd first met him?

"Your captor and new master."

Imbecile. No one mastered her. "We must not keep his highness waiting. But...." She trailed a fingertip around her bellybutton, drawing his focus. "You'll understand if I demand some clothing first."

He held up the bag he carried in his left hand. "Of course, Sameya. Gryphon sends you attire. I doubt they're what you'd prefer, but slaves aren't allotted finer wear."

"You think I'm a slave?"

He touched the iron shackles on one of her wrists before offering her the bag of clothing. "Those were specifically made for you. Iron laced with magic."

Atlantian magical inscriptions that can subdue a younger siren, but not one of my advanced age. Proof the one she sought was younger than her and wasn't aware of her immunity. The siren responsible for her predicament would suffer.

Gryphon's guard stepped closer, peering down at her. She hoped he didn't think he cowed her with the way he towered over her. "He's promised to give you to me when he's finished with you. A reward for helping bring you to justice."

If not for his seriousness, she would've laughed. She kept her head bowed and tried to humble her voice. "Lucky you." If *she* were lucky, he'd think her intimidated.

"Very lucky." One of his fingers flicked a nipple. Sameya knocked his hand aside. His long fingernails gouged into her neck and he shoved her to her knees, but only because she allowed his attack. No need to alert him to her vigor just yet.

Kat gasped.

A browbeaten appearance served her purpose. Hands tangled in her hair, he smashed her face into his soft crotch. Anger spiked at being manhandled, and she ground her teeth to keep from biting into the delicate flesh.

"I hope he keeps one of your mates alive long enough for me to fuck you in his presence. Probably the tiger. I'm sad to say the vampyr is almost gone."

Yeah, he looked and sounded as heartbroken by Maximus's nearing demise as she would be about his death later. Behind her, Kat's breath hitched with obvious tears. Sameya guessed the other woman wept for Maximus.

If either one of her mates were harmed they'd all *live* to regret it for a very long time.

"On your feet, slut. Master has a show for you." He jerked her to her feet, his nails drawing blood. "Not the first blood you'll shed for me." He licked the substance off his fingers. "I like my women to endure pain for a long time. But not as much as Gryphon does. You'll be pleased when he finally tires of you."

Such arrogance to deem her defeated.

Sameya ignored the stinging of her flesh as she pulled the iron-laced dress over her head. Fools. The entire lot of them. It'd take more than a little bit of iron and a blast of rose petals to trounce her.

The garb barely covered her bottom, but the low cut of the material in the front almost had her breasts spilling over the fabric. He hooked a chain to a loop on her wrist-cuffs and led her from the room. Like a goddamn dog. The offenses against them were mounting.

Chapter Eighteen

Sameya entered the chamber with the guard guiding her with his iron leash. The room housed a single rectangular table that could've fit twenty guests but only two chairs were in place. A domineering male sat in a chair at the head of the table. She'd bet this was the leader of the gang…and wouldn't you know it, he was a griffin. Probably why he'd chosen the name Gryphon, but that was assuming they were one and the same.

The man was strong and advanced in years, but he'd be easy to sway with her serenade. And not because he was overweight, but one brush of his power against hers and she knew she'd outgun him without much effort.

His beady-eyed gaze traversed her body, making her feel soiled and in need of a long hot shower. He patted the spot next to him, while tapping his belly with the pudgy fingers of his other hand. "Won't you join me, Sameya?"

As if he truly believed she had a choice. Arrogant creatures and their idiocy! She would enjoy exposing his error. The guard led her to the male, whom she presumed was Gryphon, and handed the length of chain to the man.

"Sit."

"Are you Gryphon?"

"Yes." He yanked, and she went to the floor in front of him, her knees protesting the impact with the marble floor. "But I prefer Master. At least for a time. After I tire of you, Mondo here"—he flicked a hand with long fingernails at the guard who'd walked her in—"will have the privilege of owning you."

"You're confident of that outcome."

"I know your secret weaknesses, siren. Rose petals and iron." He gulped a finger of liquor from a glass, his lewd gaze navigating her body once more. "Did you remove the dildo in your ass?"

She ground her teeth together. "No."

"I fingered you after you were down." Bile hit the back of her throat. Violated when she couldn't defend herself...he was a sick and twisted bastard. She'd make sure he writhed in agony for that affront. "You're soft. I'll enjoy feasting on your pain."

Griffin's ate the agony of their victims. Everything began to slowly come together. Sameya was a powerhouse of magic, a *timerelic* of power that'd survived countless generations, the rise and fall of nations, all of that meant she'd last longer than his average prey.

"Another siren gave up our secrets to get me out of the way?"

Gryphon offered no reply, but she needed none. He trailed a finger down her neck, and she flinched away. "I have a bit of sport for us to watch before I dine on you."

At least twenty henchmen entered the room in a single file. They must expect a lot of trouble out of her...or someone. Dread morphed through her.

Gabriel was wheeled in first, trapped in a steel enclosure in his tiger form. He could barely move. Their eyes met and he snarled, ramming the lock with a shoulder, knocking the crate about. The men pushing his crate were caught off guard and tumbled to the floor amid hollers and screams to get him under control. Gabriel continued to ram the door, but it didn't budge.

A curtain in the corner of the room was yanked down, exposing Maximus. Naked and bound to a cross, his back was littered with oozing lacerations. The bearer of that whip lifted a wormwood tipped flog and laid another set of wounds across the vampyr's back. Maximus jerked, but only a groan came from him. Knowing he suffered caused her fingertips to sizzle and a buzzing to echo in her ears.

Sameya drenched the room in a serenade so potent it would've killed a young mystic. As a result, several of Gryphon's henchmen dropped where they stood, dead before they hit the floor. The one who wielded the cat-o'-nine-tails plummeted to the floor with a startled yelp after she pointed at him. She turned toward Mondo, who was on his knees at the door sobbing. She'd met children with more bravery. "Bring me the witch immediately."

The remaining men were reaped without a glance in their direction, the thuds of their dead bodies hitting the floor like dominoes.

"How? You're in iron. And the Atlantian symbols etched in them are strong enchantments." Nothing Gryphon could do now except follow her commands, and she could see the resignation in his eyes. He'd already accepted his death.

"Catch up on your history, Gryphon." She smacked his cheek. "Or get a siren old enough to know the truth of a *timerelic*'s vulnerabilities. I'm too old for the iron to bother me. As for the inscriptions…they're *my* spell." Which meant someone high up in E'Neskha's organization was responsible for this treachery because none but the most trusted were aware of the etchings. "The spell can't be used against me."

As she released the cuffs from her wrists, she half-ran, half-walked toward her men. "Open the door," she instructed the only other remaining survivor in the room.

The lock disengaged. Gabriel knocked the guard down and shifted out of his skin in a sparkling array of lights. In the next breath, he had her in a bear hug that choked her with tears at his obvious emotion.

"I'm okay," she said as he placed kisses along her face and patted her down at the same time. She captured his hands and brought them to her mouth. She kissed his blood-caked knuckles. "Gabriel, I'm okay."

He crushed her against him, claiming her mouth in a kiss that could've torched Texas with the heat coming off it. When the lip-lock ended, he whispered against her ear, "I want to mark you so bad, my tiger is almost feral with the need."

"Gabriel, you've got to get it together. Maximus needs us."

"I know." He kissed her temple. "I know."

And just that quickly, he snapped into command mode. Sameya cracked the wormwood manacles on Maximus's wrist and neck. Working together, she and Gabriel untied their vampyr and looped his arms over their shoulders.

Kat entered the room with Mondo trailing her.

"Blessed Mother!" She rushed toward them. "He needs blood to heal properly."

"I'll sit over there"—Gabriel nodded at the chair near Gryphon, who watched everything with wide-eyed acceptance—"and you both help him straddle me so he can imbibe directly from my vein."

"You've already lost a lot of blood, Gabriel. I can sense the tiredness of your tiger."

Sameya didn't comprehend the problem. "I can command someone to offer their vein."

"He's too far gone." Kat stared her straight in the eyes. "The only thing that'll bring Maximus back is the blood and connection of a mate."

She peered at Gabriel over Maximus's lolling head. "Will my blood work even though we're not mated?"

"A mate is a mate, but you'll have to open yourself to him and...imitate the mating." She could tell by the challenge in Gabriel's eyes he didn't think she'd do it. And asking her to take this step was a huge sacrifice. It'd be the start of a real mating, a blending of their souls, just without the marking. What did a physical mark matter when her soul would be forever connected to him?

In the end, there was no choice. She couldn't allow him to die. The idea of losing him terrified her, and she wouldn't even contemplate the meaning of that at the moment. "I'll do it. Sit him down in the chair. I'll straddle him."

"He might resist at first, Sameya." Gabriel gently settled Maximus into the chair beside Gryphon. "He has his pride, and forcing you into a mating isn't what either of us wants."

"I'm rather persistent when I want to be." She straddled the vampyr's thighs and clasped his head between her hands, drawing his mouth to her throat.

"What about your serenade. How far does it reach?" Gabriel smoothed his fingers through her hair. She comprehended he needed to touch her, to soothe his tiger.

"Everyone in this home attached to Gryphon is under my command."

"Will your control weaken if you do?"

How much blood did Maximus need? "No."

"I'll watch your back anyway." He kissed her forehead. "I love you, Sameya."

Startled, she blinked at him. She opened her mouth to reply but nothing came out. What'd she say to that? She knew nothing about the emotion. She'd loved no one in her life. She hadn't even known her parents.

Instead of replying to Gabriel's confession, she focused on helping Maximus.

"You'll bite me, Maximus." She bit his ear hard enough to garner his attention. "If you don't bite me, I'll leave you at the end of the month. I swear it on Empress E'Neskha."

"Not...leave," he muttered against her throat.

"Then take me, vampyr."

The scrap of his fangs against her throat made her moan. Funny she was excited about this. His tongue swabbed her pulse and he groaned, his hands moving to her hips, his grip tighter than she anticipated.

"Damn you, bite me now."

Cupping her ass, he lifted her slightly as he buried his fangs into her throat. Sameya gasped at the rush of sensation. The suckles against her throat were like sucks to her clit. Maximus pulled her hips down and thrust his upward, impaling her. Her hand tightened in his hair and he held her motionless as he ingested her blood.

"I didn't warn you of that on purpose." Gabriel flicked his knuckles along her cheek. "Afraid you'd change your mind with the others present."

She'd forgotten about everyone else. Damn these men had a way of making her forget her surroundings.

Then she felt it, the mental link with him, like a lock clicking into place. Maximus's thoughts weren't open to her, but his emotions were raw. Fear that she'd leave him. Joy at finding her. Satisfaction with the way she responded to them. Protective instincts. Devotion to her and Gabriel, he'd never stray. If he tried, she'd know.

His fangs left her throat and he embraced her, holding her motionless against him as he worked on regulating his breathing. After a long while, Maximus finally looked at her, his mouth parted and his fangs streaked with her blood. He licked her throat before lifting her off his cock and settling her on her feet.

Confused, she stared at him. Her throat tingled where he'd bitten her and she was a hair's breadth away from coming.

"I won't mate you like this." Wincing, he retracted his fangs.

Why did she feel like he'd rejected her?

"It's not personal, Sameya. You know I'd—"

"I know, Maximus." Not hanging around to hear any more, she pointed at Gryphon. "Follow me."

As Gryphon slowly rose from his seat, Gabriel offered his wrist to Maximus. "Take some from me, you stubborn-ass fool."

"I'm good."

"Take his blood, Maximus." On the heels of rejecting her, his hardheadedness pissed her off. "Your magic is down. You need it."

"I'm good."

Sameya hooked her fingers beneath the collar Maximus put around her neck less than a day ago. A small twist and the choker burst into dust. Alarm widening his eyes, Gabriel stepped toward her. She held out her hand to halt his step. "I'm not walking away. At least not yet."

"Sameya." Panic flared on her vampyr's sallow features. He attempted to rise, but his arms shook so badly his ass never left the seat.

"Your magic is *down*, Maximus. Take what Gabriel is offering or I *walk*." Dismissing her men, she grabbed a fistful of Gryphon's shirt and tugged him to the cage. "Inside you bastard."

"It's steel." Gryphon trembled, horror glazing his eyes.

"Yes. And it'll burn like hell, too, but it's not half the horror you committed against Maximus or, I'm certain, you planned to do to me. So consider yourself lucky I'm not torturing you as retribution." The griffin wanted her, so he'd brutalized her mates. For what reason? To make her suffer? That couldn't be the reason, or not entirely because he'd nearly killed Maximus without her present to witness the atrocity.

Chapter Nineteen

Gabriel wanted out of this home, but Maximus needed to rejuvenate a little before they could depart. Sameya might be in control of the situation now, but he remained on alert.

"Is Maximus improving?" Sameya asked when he entered Gryphon's kitchen. She was seated at the table with a map spread out before her, her long hair tangled across her back and the iron dress. The slinky dress was sexy on her, but the garment's intentions were heinous.

"He's resting, but much improved. Why haven't you changed clothes?" With nothing better to do, he opened the refrigerator and studied the contents.

"Kat took a vehicle and went to get me something decent to wear."

Decent was Sameya naked, legs spread and either his or Maximus's dick stuffed inside her. Shutting the refrigerator, he turned and leaned against it. "What are you doing?"

"I found this in Gryphon's study. It's a map of Atlantis, along with blueprints of the palace, with the weaknesses highlighted. I'm assuming they're possible entry points for when the rebels plan to overthrow Empress E'Neskha."

He joined her at the table and studied the map and schematics for a coup. "She sent you to earth for a purpose, didn't she?"

Sameya nodded. "We know there is a rebellion brewing. There was Intel someone on the outside is working with Atlantians. I couldn't figure out why, but now I think I get it. The Intel was to drive me out of

Atlantis and further weaken Empress E'Neskha. If Gryphon managed to defeat me, that would be a major victory for the rebellion."

What she said frightened him. It meant she was in even greater peril than Tyrone Gryphon had presented. Gabriel jerked her up upright. "Sameya, the danger you place yourself in terrifies me."

"I'm old, Gabriel. Very old. I'm good at reaping, and protecting my Empress. You worry for no reason."

"Gryphon endangered you!" When he realized his fingertips had turned white where he held her arms, he relaxed his grip.

"I was never in any real danger. Only you and Maximus were."

"We must protect you, Sameya. It's our job as your mates."

She smiled; her eyes alight as she pulled him down to kiss him softly on the lips. "Gabriel, that's a two-way job. As your mate, I must protect you and Maximus."

He growled at her. "Aren't you cantankerous tonight."

No doubt, he was short-tempered. He'd almost lost Maximus and Sameya had saved them all. For an alpha tiger that warred with his primal need to guard his mates. "Bend over the table."

"I beg your pardon?"

Gabriel ran his thumb back and forth across her bottom lip. "I'll remove the butt plug."

"Oh."

"Unless someone removed it already." He'd kill the motherfucker who touched her so intimately.

"No." Sameya licked her lips and ogled at his mouth. "It's still...in place."

"If you're still horny from Maximus's brief fucking, I can finish you."

Her gaze slashed to his, and he almost laughed at her shock.

"Without Maximus?"

"I finished him off while I put him to bed."

"Without *me*." The corners of her eyes crinkled as she bit her lip. He didn't think she realized how exposed her emotions were at the moment.

"Are you jealous?" Gabriel curled an arm around her waist and drew her closer. The way she felt against him was perfect. "You really have no need to feel insecure. He didn't want to leave you earlier."

She nuzzled her face against his chest. "Who fucked who?"

"I sucked him. He crashed asleep afterward." Lips skimming across her temple, he ran a hand down her spine. "Release my slacks, and I'll give you a quickie. We both need it, Sameya. It'll calm us a little." God knew his tiger was wild inside him and claiming her would go a long way in calming his beast, even if it was bad timing. They'd been taken because she couldn't defend herself after climaxing.

"I hope no one walks in," she said as she unfastened his pants.

Gabriel enjoyed being watched.

"Or danger approaches again like last time." She closed her eyes and released a slow breath. "I coated the room in a serenade. That should protect us for a short time."

"I'll make it fast, but damn good." Gripping her ass with both of his hands, he lifted her and she wrapped her legs around his waist. He lowered her down on his cock and had her anchored against the refrigerator before he was completely seated inside her.

"Fuck, Maximus is right. You're ridiculously tight with the dildo in you."

"Feels good."

His dick jerked. "It'll feel better when it's both of us inside you."

He reached around and clicked the button on the toy to the highest speed. She moaned, her cunt clenching around him, while the vibrations tickled the underside of his cock.

Taking a moment to enjoy being inside her wet sheath, he kissed her as the sex-toy whirred away inside her.

"I can taste Maximus on your lips," she said against his mouth, her fingers on his jaw.

She tried to shift her hips against him, but the way he held her, she was incapable of movement. Just the way he wanted her.

"I'm not ready to move yet, Sameya. I won't last long."

She wound her fingers in his hair and jerked his head back to meet her gaze. "Gabriel, fuck me. Hard enough I'll feel it later and have a reminder you and Maximus are alive."

"Oh, baby." He lifted a hand off her ass and palmed her cheek. "I'm sorry you were frightened and that we didn't protect you as we should've."

"Talk later. Fuck me now."

He smiled, liking her in this mode. He placed his hand back on her butt and spread her cheeks. Flexing his hip, he pulled all the way out of her and slammed back inside to the hilt. He repeated the motions, fucking her hard, rocking the refrigerator with his drives. It was the first time he'd taken her face-to-face and there was a lot to be said for this position. He could see her face, watch her eyes dilate, and he'd get the satisfaction of watching her come while he was in her.

Gripping his shoulders tight, Sameya whimpered and moaned for him, her pussy squeezing him until he feared he'd blow before she came. Another hard thrust, bottoming out inside her, and she climaxed with a cry, throwing her head back against the appliance. Her entire body vibrated with the release, and he groaned at the way her cunt squeezed his cock through her orgasm.

Her eyes were closed when he rammed home and joined her, releasing deep into her womb. He nuzzled her neck. The mini twitches plaguing her body testifying to the enormity of her pleasure.

He kissed her cheeks and nose. As he carried her to the table, he dragged his chin along her jaw. He settled her on her feet, turned her to face the map spread on the table, and then pushed her over onto it. He kissed one butt-cheek and bit the other.

Gaze honed on her ass, he spread her cheeks and watched as he slowly removed the sex-toy from her bottom. She whimpered as the widest part exited her tight forbidden territory.

He pushed the dildo back inside her and it penetrated her with ease. She moaned, her fingers balling the map into her fists. He fucked her a few more times with the toy. "Your body has adjusted easily to the dildo. You'll enjoy the fullness even better when it's us inside you."

Gabriel went to his knees and licked her folds as he pumped the toy into her. She quivered, the sounds of her enjoyment exquisite.

"Do you like the way the toy feels as I fuck you with it, Sameya?"

"Yes." Her voice was husky and he wanted to bury his tongue inside her pussy and fuck her with the vibrator until she came again. "I...." She panted, her hips flexing in tiny little jerks.

"Go on." He flicked the tip of his tongue across her clit.

"I enjoy everything you and Maximus do to me," she said in a rush.

Why'd she hesitate to confess that? Because she didn't want to admit how they made her feel? Her reservations remained too elevated for his peace of mind.

He removed the toy, and she whimpered when it left her body for good.

Unable to resist the inclination, he licked her anus and she cried out as he continued to rim her with his tongue. She was so sensitive. Everywhere they touched excited her. *She* excited him.

She was aroused again, and he knew he could take her once more. Instead, he slithered his tongue from her rosebud, through her folds, tasting his semen on her. He licked and rotated around her clitoris, and Sameya groaned when he suckled on her sweet nub.

Abruptly he left her, rose to his feet, and stepped away from her as he pocketed the toy. He ran his palm over his mouth. "I'm going to check on Maximus."

Her rapid breathing halted as she realized he was leaving her. Smiling, he walked out of the kitchen. A sexually frustrated mate was not a bad thing. He'd witnessed her expression when Maximus wouldn't complete the mating. He suspected she felt rejected, but that wasn't what had gone on. Maximus wanted her to crave them and their pairing. A forced mating could result in regret and resentment. A nightmare ending. It wouldn't be the first time something like that happened.

She fancied them, while struggling to maintain control of her future. Nothing would be gained by her reserved disposition. She couldn't have them without committing to the relationship. One way or another, a decision must be made. He and Maximus wouldn't settle for a half-assed mating with her. It was an all or nothing situation.

***

Sameya peeled herself off the table in slow increments. The sweet friction of movement tantalized, but not enough to get her off. A frustrated groan exited her throat.

Why'd Gabriel leave her clinging to the edge of a climax? Better yet, *why* had she allowed him to fuck her and weaken her with an orgasm? They were in their enemy's house for goodness sake because of that siren flaw!

Her reaction to them was insane. If she could have them filling her and pounding into her twenty-four-seven, she'd jump at the chance. Sex with them was that damn good.

Wetness hit her thighs. Gabriel's semen. She sighed. She had to leave them. No other option presented itself. Those fantastic climaxes rendered her vulnerable, which meant she couldn't protect them either. That fact was made all the more evident by Gryphon's abduction of them. He'd almost killed Maximus. That terrified her more than anything else. She hadn't worried so much about herself because by the time she came-to, she was healed and ready to kick ass in reaper style. But Gryphon—the bastard—would've succeeded in murdering Maximus if not for the return of her siren abilities.

Being associated with her brought danger to their doorstep. For their safety, she must reject the mating. Enemies came with her job description, and her mates deserved more than a lifetime of looking over their shoulders.

She strolled to the sink, wet a paper towel and pressed it between her thighs. The coldness did nothing to alleviate her arousal, but was only effective in wiping away Gabriel's seed. She shook her head. What messed up children they'd have if they were lucky enough to conceive. Sirens never mated outside their species. She wasn't even sure what magic a half-vampyr-siren or half-siren-were-tiger-shifter would possess. Would the half-breed be able to shift or drink blood? Would it receive any of her siren skills?

Idiotic, fanciful thoughts. She wouldn't have children with either of these men. Nature didn't crossbreed species. Never had to her knowledge...but she couldn't discount their ability to do the one thing no one but her mate could do. They gave her climaxes.

"Hey, I hope these do." Kat entered the kitchen and Sameya was thankful for the interruption. And that she hadn't entered five minutes ago.

The witch tossed the bag on the counter and Sameya opened it to withdraw a pair of jeans, and a black T-shirt that said 'Sin like you're drunk on Micah Kool-Aid'. Whoever the hell Micah was, she didn't know. No undergarments were provided, so she yanked off the dress she'd been given to wear. The cotton of the T-shirt was soft, but it lacked the scent of her mates.

Next came the jeans. They were snug and when she moved, they scrubbed against her clit.

Fuck!

Her hormones were out of control, along with her sensitivity to sensation. She'd never been like this before. Was it because she'd found her mates and participated in their perverted sexual activities? Would it ever get better or was she stuck like this forever?

"Thanks for the clothes." She swallowed, fighting back the acute arousal as she walked toward Kat.

"I saw you and Gabriel." The witch made an apologetic face, and Sameya groaned. "So I went to see Maximus while I waited."

"I'm sorry you saw that." She rubbed her temples. "I tried to tell him anyone could walk in at any time." Not that she'd done anything to resist, instead she'd released his pants for him.

The other woman's amused chuckle caught her attention. Sameya elevated her eyebrows waiting for the witch to explain. "Gabriel has a voyeur fetish. He likes for people to watch. No doubt he'd have preferred I observe rather than leave."

Sameya shook her head. What a strange world she'd walked into. Atlantis was so much easier.

"You want to talk about them?"

"No." Girlfriends talked and Kat was their friend, not hers.

"Nothing you say will reach their ears. I pinky swear." Kat grinned and made a crossing motion over her heart with her pinky finger.

Unsure what 'pinky swear' meant or why the other woman made the motions over her chest, she guessed it was a vow of some sort. "No. I'm not comfortable with your offer."

Kat shrugged. "The offer stands anytime you need it. I've known the guys a long time, and I want to be your friend."

"You ever sleep with them?"

The witch's eyes rounded. "Well...um..."

Gritting her teeth, Sameya slashed her hand through the air in a 'stop' fashion. "Answer enough. Because you fucked them, I can never be your friend."

Knowing her men had been inside this woman made her want to claw her heart out and then reap the bitch. Which made no sense considering she planned to leave them.

"It was a long time ago, Sameya."

"It doesn't matter."

"Of course it does. I see the hurt in your eyes."

"It. Does. Not. Matter." She rose to her feet, intending to walk away.

Kat caught her wrist. "I'll erase myself from their life. That should make things easier for you."

Was she for real? She heard the respect in her mates' voices for this woman. She was their friend, no way would she ask them to forfeit Kat. There was nothing fair about that. "I would never hurt them that way."

The witch released her hold on Sameya's wrist. "Yet you have no problems rejecting their mating. That'll damage them beyond repair. They'll survive my withdrawal better."

"I'm protecting them by leaving them."

"No." Kat shook her head. "It's for your safety. You're scared to let anyone into that cold, dead heart of yours." The other woman pushed to her feet and looked down on her. In that moment, Sameya hated being short. "I pity your loneliness and inability to open your heart to love. I never want to know what it's like to *fear* that much. Gabriel and Maximus are the best men I know. Gentlemen. Honorable.

Goodhearted. Passionate. And they would do anything for you; worship you, love you, while asking nothing in return. I *wish* they were my mates."

"I'm not afraid of letting them in." But was that true? She'd never avoided anything except finding her mate. To discover she had two, both outside her species, well...that did kind of terrify her.

"Oh, you're running scared. And they have too much honor to keep you against your will." The witch made a lopsided grimace. "You can have all the power in the world, but allowing fear to defeat you...what a shame."

Incapable of listening further, Sameya snatched the map off the table, spun on her heels and marched from the room. She didn't miss the smirk the witch tossed her before she managed her exit.

No one in Atlantis would look at her that way, at least not in her presence. But as much as she was heartsick for her homeland, she didn't miss it the way she should. She was lonely there.

She entered the dining hall where she'd left Gryphon housed within the steel cage. Where he'd staged his whipping of Maximus. The bastard! He enjoyed inflicting misery and death on those who didn't deserve it.

As she walked toward the enclosure that contained Gryphon, she couldn't help but compare Atlantis to her gilded cage. She had men here that wanted her. There wouldn't be a single soul in her homeland that would miss her.

Gryphon scuttled to the corner of the cage and watched her warily. He had every right to fear her. She wanted to seek revenge against him for what he'd done to her men. She could make death painful, or leave him catatonic in a state of unending agony. But she'd do nothing until her Empress granted her permission. And they needed answers about the others that were involved in his terrorism.

"I need information about the coup you plan."

He hesitated. Was he shocked by an Atlantian's knowledge? "I don't know what you're talking about."

"Right. We can do this the easy way or the hard way." She could rape his mind with her siren song and glean every minute detail he knew. But it was extremely painful for the recipient. "I'm partial to the hard way."

He must've recognized the anticipatory gleam in her eyes. "I'll tell you everything you want to know."

"Nah...I've changed my mind."

She struck with her song, and he jerked in the cage. Digging through the first layer of his mental locks, Gryphon went into a seizure of sorts. The crate rattled as he flopped about inside and foamed at the mouth. Compassion low, she ripped through the remaining bolts like a scalpel sliced through flesh. His back bowed, and he shrieked. The evil of the man had Sameya stumbling backward. Like the icky texture of grease his wickedness left her feeling dirty, and she doubted a long, hot shower would suffice to clean away the taint of his misdeeds.

Snapshots of his vile exploits flickered through her mind. The families he'd destroyed. The multitude of children he'd culled to satisfy his pedophile fetish.

She wanted to kill him in honor of the innocent. It'd be easy to snap his mind and take his life. She was already in his head, but Empress E'Neskha worked with a different justice.

Visions of all the women he'd raped, abused and tortured for his revolting amusement sifted through her. There were thousands of them, and he'd grown fat feasting off their agony.

Sameya cringed, tears burning her sinuses.

So much power at his disposal and while he could find sustenance elsewhere, he'd chosen to dominate the less fortunate because he could and because he enjoyed inflicting harm.

Appalling behavior that spanned centuries. This was not the mind of a decent man, but a psychopath who would never stop leaving a trail of dead bodies.

Gryphon twisted in his cage, pleading with her to stop. Yet, he'd gotten off when others begged him for mercy. She showed him the same generosity he gave to them and burrowed deeper into his revolting mind.

His shrieks became her balm, a minimal type of justice.

But no matter how hard she worked to ferret out his cohort in Atlantis, the image and name grayed in her mind. A powerful mystic to dim her ability.

Hugging her waist, she wept and sent out a slew of magical daggers to ravage his mind. Unfortunately they wouldn't leave him permanently damaged, but he'd suffer until her Empress arrived.

Maximus was suddenly there in front of her on his knees, crushing her against his chest. The warmth of Gabriel hit her spine and the Sameya-sandwich comforted her in ways nothing else could've.

Pulling out of Gryphon's mind, she felt dirty, but she clung to Maximus, allowing the tears to fall. Someone should cry for the nameless that'd fallen to Gryphon's depravity.

"*Naleah*, I could feel your anguish across the house. Talk to us." Maximus pressed kisses to the top of her head, while Gabriel pressed his face in the curve of her neck and shoulder, his warm breath relaxing her marginally.

"He's so depraved," she whispered against his chest.

"Were you in his head?" Gabriel rubbed a hand up and down her spine.

"Yes." She pulled back a little from Maximus. He maintained his grip on her hips, but allowed her the space to peer at him and glance over her shoulder at Gabriel. "I needed information on those who intend to overthrow Empress E'Neskha. He didn't offer it freely, so I carved it from him."

"You're scary, baby, and sexier because of it." Her tiger kissed her cheek.

Sameya offered a faint smile. "You're pretty talented yourself, Gabriel." Had a killer tongue and a fantastic thrust.

"You shaved at least a century's worth of years off my life." Maximus's grip tightening on her hips relayed his anxiety.

Poking him in the gut, she teased, "Drama king."

Her vampyr kissed her forehead. "Lean on us, and trust us to aid you. That's what we're here for, *naleah*."

Sameya skimmed her fingertips along his jaw. "I'm fifty-two thousand, one-hundred thirteen years old. I've never leaned on anyone in my life." Not even her parents because they'd died shortly after her one-hundredth year. And sirens weren't the cajoling sort, especially not with someone as powerful as she.

The guys allowed her to stand and extricate herself from their sandwich. Her brain kept skipping over what Maximus had said...that he'd felt her anguish. *How*? She shouldn't be an open book to anyone.

They both remained on their knees, their bodies facing one another but gazing up at her. Sameya trailed a finger across Maximus's jaw. "You're feeling better?"

"Yes, Gabriel took care of me."

In more ways than one, even though she doubted that's what Maximus meant. First with his blood and by finishing him off when Maximus had shunned her passion. Those moments should've been hers, but were stolen from her. Not filched by Gabriel, but because she refused to make a pact to join their lives.

"Good," she said through a throat thick with emotion. She had no desire to leave these men, but she couldn't walk away from her duties to her Empress. It was better if she began to distance herself from them now, because she'd been playing a very dangerous game with them.

Maximus's gaze flicked over her shoulder. He nabbed Gabriel by the arm and the men rose together. Sameya turned and discovered her Empress had entered the room. It was as if her thoughts had brought the royal woman to her.

Going to her knees, she bowed her head and placed her arm above her head, exposing her forearm. "Empress E'Neskha, my service to thee alone."

Chapter Twenty

Stunned by Sameya's deference to the Empress, Maximus assessed the other woman, curious if she deserved his beloved's devotion. The ruler of Atlantis was so tiny he suspected a breeze would blow her away. Thick aqua streaks highlighted the woman's white-blonde hair and framed her oval face with hard ringlets. Light orange eyes focused solely on Sameya. The woman's expression was one of fondness and respect. For such a countenance to be turned upon his mate made him proud.

"You know I don't like it when you do that." E'Neskha touched Sameya's shoulder and her soft voice carried further than he'd anticipated. "Rise, Sameya." As his woman elevated to her feet, the Empress gave them a direct stare. "You two are?"

"Maximus." He clapped Gabriel on the shoulder. "My mate."

"Gabriel." The tiger executed a small wave with two fingers.

"Friends of yours?" The Empress angled her head to keep her focus in Sameya's direction, but Maximus knew she'd be able to see any movement from either of them out of the corner of her eye.

Their siren sent them a precautionary glance. "Um...yes, you could say that."

So, she wouldn't claim them. Not that Maximus was surprised, but he'd hoped.

E'Neskha approached them and offered her hand. "A pleasure to make your acquaintance."

Gabriel kissed her knuckles like they remained in the Victorian era. "The pleasure is mine."

Maximus had no idea what was considered appropriate in this situation, but there was no way he would prostrate before her as Sameya had. He settled on a slight head bow. "An honor."

She perused them both, as if trying to determine something of significance.

"Empress, where are your guards?" Sameya touched E'Neskha's shoulder. "You're in grave danger."

"My sentinels were attacked his morning." The Empress might've responded to Sameya, but she was busy contemplating him and Gabriel. "I didn't receive your message until seconds before I arrived here. We were busy defending the palace."

"Damnit!" Their siren began to pace a furious path, her steps a rapid *patpatpat*, her hands moving in agitation as she talked. "I knew I shouldn't have allowed you to talk me into departing Atlantis. Less than a week and everything's gone to shit and fast."

Fuck, she was adorable when flustered. But... "A week? Gabriel and I have been hunting you for six months."

"Not hunting me." Still pacing, his woman made a face at him as if he was off his rocker.

"Wild goose chase." Maximus directed the comment at Gabriel, but pondered Sameya, his hands fisting at his sides. What had been Gryphon's purpose in sending them after her when she'd been inaccessible until seven days ago? The man had endangered his mates and nearly killed him and all for what reason?

The Atlantian ruler ignored his comment and glowered at Sameya. "Your mission here was important. We needed to ferret out the infidel. You're the best at what you do, not to mention you're the only one I trust implicitly."

That snapped her out of her pacing. "I'm responsible for your welfare. If something happened to you, Empress, I would never forgive myself." Maximus didn't want anything happening to *his* siren, he could live with the Empress' harm. Eyebrows drawn together, Sameya faced them, not making them wait long to hear what was on her mind. "You said six months, Maximus?"

He nodded, but Gabriel was the one to respond. "Every lead turned up a dead end until you showed up in *Dirty Liquor* the night we met."

"I was there for the elf. The one I reaped."

"I remember." The tiger crossed his arms over his chest. "I also remember you showed zero recognition when I mentioned Tyron Gryphon's name. I've had my suspicions since."

"Why didn't you say something?" A little forewarning would've been nice, and Maximus had no idea why his lover hadn't spoken up sooner.

Gabriel shrugged. "Distractions got in the way. Starting with you *venomeing* Sameya and everything that occurred after."

"I'm not following." The elfin like leader peered between the three of them.

"We'd been led to believe the elf had vital information on the rebellion." Sameya rubbed her forehead. "He knew nothing more than our griffin over there." She motioned to Tyron Gryphon. "Which leads me to believe the griffin is as big a pawn in this takeover as the elf. Both were used to draw me out, to render you vulnerable, Empress, and to distract me with the two of them."

Disliking the way the events had spiraled out of control so far, Maximus massaged his nape. "Could this individual be taking over Atlantis now that you're both out of it?"

E'Neskha shook her head. "No. When I departed, I'd serenaded the entire population. Everyone is asleep."

"Is that possible?" Gabriel said exactly what Maximus was thinking.

"She's the best. It's very doable," Sameya confirmed.

"Okay." Maximus put his fingers through his hair. "Let's start with who gave you the false Intel that instigated your departure?"

"Lucius." His feisty little mate sent her Empress a pointed stare.

The other woman paled. "He...." She shook her two-toned blonde and aqua head. "He couldn't be involved. Lucius was injured in the attack and might not survive. Crushed rose petals in aerosol form were sprayed in his face to neutralize him. He was then electrocuted and shot in the chest."

"The rose petals are what Gryphon sprayed in my face, as well."

And no one but a siren knew of their weaknesses, he and Gabriel hadn't even known of the rose petals until now. "If Gryphon was working for him, that would explain how he knew your weakness, Sameya."

"E'Neskha, the only siren with the ability to identify another siren's mate—aside from the parties involved—is Lucius. He knew the mating compulsion would weaken me. They attacked at my weakest moment."

The Empress clasped her hands between her breasts, and tears welled in her eerie colored yes. "You're wrong. I cannot believe he would do this. And you're not mated!"

In denial! Maximus allowed Sameya to handle the situation.

"He taunted more than once how he'd like to see me fall to my alpha mate, E'Neskha."

"You two never got along. Have you found your mate? Is that part of all of this?" The Atlantian leader shot a cagey glance at him and Gabriel.

"I wouldn't sleep with Lucius even after he tried to force me. When I kicked his ass, it made things worse." Maximus's fangs hit his bottom lip and the tiger beside him executed a low grumble of displeasure in the back of his throat. Sameya ignored them. "One day he'd tease that my mate was a vampyr. The next day a shifter. I thought he was being a jackass like always, but...*he knew*, E'Neskha. I'm certain of it. Even you cannot deny he resents my position with you."

"Sameya, he is my baby brother," the words were nothing more than a whisper. The horror etched onto the woman's face said it all. Confirmed betrayal would rip her soul apart.

"I'm sorry. I wish I could come to another conclusion. But the facts are mounting against him. I raped Tyrone Gryphon's memories, and confirmed, as we suspected, the traitor resides in Atlantis. But only fuzzy images of the infidel remain in his head." She motioned toward Gryphon to indicate whose head she referred to. "Adjusting memories is one of Lucius' gifts. No other. Maybe he adjusted your memory with his power so you'd think he was injured when he really wasn't. It'd further his cause." Seemed plausible to Maximus. For the first time, Sameya offered solace and placed her palm on her leader's shoulder. "If it's any consolation, I don't believe he'd harm you. Me, yes, but not you."

Silence lapsed between them as they stared at one another. Maximus wished he grasped the inner workings of a woman's mind, but he couldn't glean what these two were thinking.

"For good or bad, E'Neskha, we must return to Atlantis and—"

"I'm returning forthwith. I'll confront Lucius." The Empress sniffled, and Sameya nodded.

"You know he won't confess his deeds, but I'll join you."

"We're coming with you." Sameya jerked to face Maximus, while her Empress swiveled toward them, her gaze shrewd. Before his siren could argue, he said, "No way are we letting you out of our sight with your life in jeopardy."

"Get over yourself, Maximus. I can take care of myself."

"Made all the more obvious by our recent capture." He made a show of flashing his fangs. Gabriel would've understood it was his silent way of saying 'that's the end of the conversation'. Sameya's violet eyes flared, and her jaw hardened in a clear sign of mutiny. "We need to be there to assist should your secret be turned against you once more."

"A nick of wormwood brought you down, Maximus. How's that helping?" Ouch. She hit below the belt with that one.

"It took ten of them to bring me down." Gabriel stalked to Sameya and got in her face. "You're not going without us."

"Don't get cocky, shifter. With my choker gone, I could serenade you easily. The weakest siren in Atlantis could. Turned against me, you're a whole shitload of help!"

A rumbling came from deep within Gabriel's throat.

In case she didn't get the hint, Maximus said, "So you know, you've pissed him off."

"Which one of them is your mate, Sameya?" The Empress peered between the three of them, her interest obvious in the fine lines fanning from the corners of her eyes. "You said Lucius teased you about a vampyr and a shifter, so which one of them weakened you enough Lucius' men could bring you down?"

Sameya cast a nervous peek at them, then squared her shoulders and said, "Both."

Eyes widening, the leader's mouth parted. "Mated to a shifter and a vampyr?"

"Yes." Sameya dragged the word out. "I've not committed to remain with them." She glanced between him and Gabriel. "And they *know* that."

"Nonsense." Empress E'Neskha's chin notched higher. "Only a fool turns down the blessing of multiple mates, even if they are outside your race."

Maximus grinned at Sameya. Oh, how he suddenly adored her Empress.

"But—"

"No buts." The Empress interrupted his woman. "They'll return to Atlantis with us."

"Thank you. I owe you." Gabriel chucked their mate's chin while speaking to the Atlantian leader. "I'm glad to know your Empress is sensible, especially when you're not."

"All I ask is that you protect Sameya," E'Neskha said.

That went without saying.

"This will only incite the propaganda against you." Sameya rubbed her forehead. "Those who want you out of your seat of power will use this to demonstrate how you're changing Atlantis. Not for the good either because no one likes foreigners within."

"What of the witch over there?" Sameya glanced at Kat when E'Neskha asked about her. Maximus had almost forgotten she was present.

Sameya was the one who responded to the leader's question. "That's their familiar."

"Friend," Maximus corrected.

"She does magic for you for free. In our world, that's a familiar." She narrowed her gaze on the witch in question. "E'Neskha, I do have an idea that might rattle Lucius enough to make a mistake, but you'll have to hold off on confronting him, and I can't tell you what the idea is because I need your surprise to be genuine. I'll need to bring the witch with me to set the plan in motion."

A brief nod from the leader. "Granted."

"No one said anything about Kat coming." Maximus shook his head. Placing their friend in danger wasn't part of any deal.

"Too bad." Sameya tossed him a flat smile. "The witch tags along, or none of you are part of my plan."

"See it done within the next hour. I'll be expecting you in the *Hall* forthwith." With a softly spoken word Maximus didn't catch, the Empress vanished into a green mist that evaporated with her departure.

As Maximus attempted to figure out how the hell the other woman disappeared, Sameya turned to the tiger and became all business. "Gabriel, while in Atlantis, you'll need to shift to your fur and remain that way when you're not in my quarters. A siren won't try to serenade a real tiger, and I'd prefer no one know you're a shifter. Things will go smoother if everyone believes you're an authentic tiger. Safer that way."

"Done. But so long as you understand I will guard you with my life, and I'll kill anything that even thinks of harming one hair on your head."

Her expression softened. "Ditto, tiger."

"Sameya, about Kat—"

"Don't." She swiped her hand through the air, cutting Maximus off. He adored her bossiness, but not her willingness to endanger herself. "The witch is strong enough to hinder a few sirens. They won't expect her to retaliate if they believe she's been serenaded. Any surprise we can get against Lucius is welcome."

"You're endangering Kat's life." That wasn't something Maximus would tolerate. The fact she was so cavalier about her own life bothered him.

Stubbornness set in her jaw, defiance flashed in her violet eyes. Before she spoke, he knew she wouldn't back down. "Your choice, leech." They were back to name-calling, and he bit back a grin. "She comes or you don't."

"What's my role to be?"

"You'll be exactly what you are." He elevated an eyebrow, not seeing how this helped her position. "But you'll be collared so everyone will think you're charmed. I'll lead you about with a leash." Her eyes were positively alive with the idea, probably anticipating a little payback. "Kat and Gabriel will be leashed, as well."

Maximus would follow her anywhere, do anything for her...but he'd never been collared like one of the subs at the local BDSM establishment. Yeah, he'd put one on her and a few other women over the years. The idea of one snapping about his throat though, that was an uncomfortable thought. "It's only for show? And only outside your bedroom?"

A black eyebrow elevated. "Worried I'll use it against you the way you did me, Maximus?"

"Frankly, yes."

"So little faith." She made a *tsking* sound. "The collar won't really be charmed. You'll be pretending. I would never do that to you."

Subtle, but he got her point. He'd charmed her to his will without regret, but when the tables were turned hers was for pretend...and for a higher purpose. "Very well. I consent to being 'charmed' by you."

The fucking truth because he'd never allowed anyone to parade him around like a Goddamn pet before. Pride rebelled against the notion, but he'd degrade himself in front of others for her or Gabriel. If it meant keeping her safe, he'd do just about anything.

Chapter Twenty-One

Kat infused magic into the collar Maximus would wear. Just enough mojo that anyone would believe Sameya had actually charmed a vampyr since she couldn't serenade one, but not enough to force him to do her bidding if he wasn't so inclined.

Black, just like the clothes he wore, she ran her fingers over the soft leather as she peered up at him. "If there was any other way, I'd—"

Maximus dragged her against his chest and devoured her mouth in a hot, wet kiss. With his tongue in her mouth curling around hers, he palmed her thigh, slid his hand to the back of her knee, and hooked her leg around his hip. His erection pressed against her pussy, and she moaned into his mouth. The collar all but forgotten, she slid her fingers into his hair and clung to him.

She groaned a protest when he ended the embrace. With his mouth skimming hers and kissing the corners of her lips, he said, "Do it now before I change my mind."

Sameya blinked, having trouble adjusting from arousal to reality.

"The collar, *naleah*. My vampyr is protesting, so put it on me immediately."

Kissing him, she shifted her hands out of his hair and touched the ends of the leather together. The magic imbued into the object did the rest, fusing it into one cohesive piece. She hooked her finger in the ring at the front of the collar. "Thank you."

"Don't thank me yet." Bright green flashed in his eyes, evidence of the vampyr's wariness. "I'm contemplating how hard I'm going to fuck you when Gabriel and I have you alone again. If I should dominate you, make you beg for release, or if I should allow you to come at all."

A tiny gasp parted her lips. He went on, describing what he intended.

"I'll peel your clothes off your body. Give me permission now to disrobe you."

She bit her bottom lip, uncertain if she should grant his wish. What he described, along with the visions of losing control with him, might send a thrill through her belly, but that was fantasy. The reality might be different...particularly if he found a way to stop her from climaxing.

His voice lowered, turned darker. "Sameya, grant me permission."

While she'd retrieved her clothing, they'd packed a bag and Kat had created collars for the three of them. Her attire couldn't be removed without her consent. "Per-permission...granted."

"Afraid I'll abuse my power, *naleah*?" Maximus ran his thumb back and forth along her jaw, his contemplation intense.

"A little."

He leaned forward, nipping her lobe with his fangs. Then he pressed his lips against her ear and whispered so no one else could hear. "Once naked, I'll bend you over, have you spread your legs so I can dine on your pussy and ass. Then I'll ram my cock inside you so hard you'll scream. Should I let you climax?" She would've nodded, but he fisted her hair, halting her movement. "I'll have to consider if you've earned the right to come or if I should punish you because you insist on endangering your goddamn life."

Appalled he'd prefer she not aid her Empress, Sameya jerked backward, but he held her tight.

"As difficult as your request is for me, I submit to you now." He pulled back enough to catch her gaze. "But later you *must* submit to me."

"Gods, Maximus." She shivered and he smiled, one that suggested he knew how aroused she'd become by his proposal. Would she really allow him to do all that he said? Certainly not!

Rattled by what he'd detailed and her body's reaction, she faced Gabriel quickly. The knowing lopsided grin he wore hinted he'd heard Maximus. He confirmed it with, "If he doesn't let you come, maybe I will." She inhaled slowly as he stepped closer, his turn to whisper in her ear. "Or maybe I'll settle for finger-fucking you while he eats your pussy."

Wetness surged between her thighs. "Gabriel."

He kissed her hard before shifting into tiger. She ran her fingers through his fur. The soft rumble of a purr sounded in the room. She kissed his head as she fastened the collar on his neck. Then she snapped the leash on the hook.

Facing Maximus with his leash, she squirmed under his studious regard. He caught her wrist and tugged her arm upward toward the O-ring. Metal binged against metal, but latched with ease. The witch was already collared and leashed.

Looping her fingers through the handles of the three leashes, she called up the portal mist. Using a smidge of magic, the cage housing Gryphon elevated off the floor. He gripped the bars as she thrust the stainless steel into the opening, and then she guided Gabriel, Maximus, and Kat into Atlantis.

A small vestibule led to the doorways of the *Hall* where she knew she'd find Empress E'Neskha. The guards positioned on either side of the doors wouldn't refuse her entry even if their nervous glances at those in her company hinted they'd like to. Vampyrs weren't allowed in Atlantis because of their superiority over most species and a siren's inability to serenade them. Kept Atlantis safer that way. The way Maximus's fangs protruded over his bottom lip left little doubt as to his ancestry. Gabriel caused little commotion and Kat even less.

She motioned for the guards to guide the crate holding Gryphon. As she approached the doors, they opened. Empress E'Neskha was receiving court. Perfect since it allowed for a bigger audience for what would transpire. And Sameya would bet it was why she held court.

Positioned at a higher elevation than everyone in the *Hall*, the leader peered down at her. Lucius was at her side; his slack-jawed gape directed toward Sameya drawing a lopsided smile from her. She bet he didn't expect her to enter the building, much less arrive with one of her mates in tow. And with the way he peered at Maximus, she had no doubt he recognized the vampyr.

Silence descended in a rush, rippling through the crowd like a wave. E'Neskha rose from her throne as those in residence turned toward Sameya. Only after she and her group came to a stop a few feet away from the steps leading to the Empress did Sameya speak.

"Good to see you're well, Lucius."

"Why wouldn't I be?" Pompous bastard elevated his eyebrows and stared down his nose at her.

"I'd heard you were injured in a raid. I was worried your sister would be distraught."

"But not you."

As an answer she smiled. Using the side of her foot, she kicked the cage holding Gryphon and turned her attention toward her leader. "One of the traitors set to destroy you, Empress."

"Impressive work. Quicker than I anticipated, as well." E'Neskha descended the stairs, her spine straight and her shoulders squared.

"I would request a private audience with you to give you the name of the traitor in Atlantis." If she wasn't mistaken, Lucius' breath hitched. She offered him a lopsided grin. "You will want to join us for that meeting, Lucius."

He bristled and said in his haughtiest voice, "You do not tell me what to do, siren."

"If Sameya wants you to join us, Lucius, then you'll be at that meeting." E'Neskha had always trusted her strategy and played along with Sameya now. "And the others with you?"

"A gift for you." She offered the leash strapped to Kat to her leader. The witch snapped a surprised glance in her direction, but offered no objection. E'Neskha didn't bat an eyelash in shock, but cooperated, her eyes alighting with genuine delight. "A witch with magical promise, Empress. Easily serenaded, but I grant you permission to override my sway and handle her however you desire."

Kat walked toward E'Neskha in a drone-like state as the Atlantis ruler slowly tugged her leash forward. "I shall treasure her. Thank you." The Atlantian fingered the witch's cheek, her dark hair, and then pulled the taller woman down so they were nose-to-nose. "What trick shall I have you perform first?"

"Whatever pleases you the most." Sameya had to give Kat points, she played the serenaded part well.

"What of the vampyr?" E'Neskha tugged down on Kat's collar. "Sit, my pet."

As Kat sunk to recline at the Empress' feet, Sameya replied, "My new plaything." She grinned, knowing Maximus wouldn't like her statement. "He's charmed, and as docile as a well-fed pussy-cat."

"Does he bite?"

Often. "Only if I want him to."

The fair-haired ruler peered at Gabriel, who suddenly began to purr, startling the crowd. E'Neskha chuckled. "You always did have a taste for the exotic, Sameya."

"They'll go nicely with my brownie and my pair of Zion."

"Indeed." She palmed the witch's head. "Join me for dinner in three hours, Sameya. Bring your new acquisitions. We'll discuss the other details you've learned then."

Sameya inclined her head and bowed low. As she rose, E'Neskha said, "That you captured my foe reconfirms why I maintain you as my royal guard. You will be rewarded well."

"Your satisfaction is reward enough." She led her men from the room, noting the curious stares and those deep in hushed whispers. She was certain at least one of E'Neskha's enemies witnessed the exchange.

The walk to her room was short, as she was positioned near her Empress for maximum protection. Magically sensing her as she drew near, her door vaporized long enough for them to enter her abode. As soon as they stepped through, the opening became solid once more.

Releasing her mates' leashes, she had little time to prepare for her Zion's greetings. Huge paranormal canine's loped into the room, tails wagging and tongues lolling. She went to her knees and wrapped her arms around their necks.

"My boys. My sweet, sweet boys, oh, how I've missed you." Wet licks to her neck and face. She giggled as they overbalanced her, and without clinging to their necks she'd have tumbled to the floor. One week out of Atlantis and she'd missed them dreadfully.

"A dog lover," Gabriel said with much disgust in his voice.

Swiveling in her crouched position, she studied her tiger. Naked from his shift back into human his tattoos were stark against his muscled flesh. "Particular cats have their appeal."

His golden eyes grew hot at that confession.

Chapter Twenty-Two

As she rose, she motioned to the dogs that stood waist high. "Meet my long-time companions, Nero and Thrax. You two"—she rubbed the heads of the canines—"these are my...mates."

Maximus's perusal was so concentrated she shifted from foot to foot. He unhooked the leash from his collar and tossed it on the sofa with a hard fling. Silence extended between them as he approached and offered his hand for the dogs to sniff. In her personal space, he hooked a finger into the waistband of her Basilisk pants and simply stared at her as she waited for him to react.

Nervous beneath his quietness and stern regard, Sameya cleared her throat. "I know you like to cook, so I had Dart stock my cabinets and icebox. If you prefer something else, Dart will get it for you."

"Who is Dart?" Gabriel strolled closer, his body language more playful compared to Maximus's serious one.

"My brownie."

Maximus arched a dark eyebrow. "As in the tiny species that enjoys cleaning one's house."

"Yes. More or less. She does many other things than just clean. I keep her well stocked with liquor. Tequila's her favorite."

Gabriel chuckled. "A drunk fairy. That must be entertaining."

Sameya shrugged. She'd never seen Dart intoxicated, so she had no idea if the brownie could become inebriated.

Maximus yanked on her pants, and she stumbled into him. A hand to the back of her neck steadied her, and he massaged her flesh. "I want these off. Now."

"N-now isn't the best time for...p-play." But by the goddess her belly burned in anticipation. "After our meeting with E'Neskha is the best time. You'll have as long as you n-need." Maybe it was best to get it over with fast.

"How considerate. She's thinking of our timeframe, Gabriel." He shot the other man an ironic glance.

"I believe she's a little nervous, Maximus."

Of course she was nervous. Her vampyr had detailed what he'd do to her later for collaring him.

Her tiger moved in behind her, his palms landing on her shoulders to glide down her arms and circle her wrists. He pulled them behind her back and held them imprisoned at the base of her spine. "I probably would be, too, with the way your vampyr is gazing at her. Like you might eat her." She didn't think Gabriel meant the sexual variety. "Maybe you should clarify why she deserves discipline."

Discipline? Wait a minute! That she wouldn't tolerate. "I'm not a child. I'm an adult who has the freedom to do as I please. If being mated means I have to answer to either of you, you're dead wrong!"

"I'm angry with you." Maximus knelt in front of her and quickly pulled off a boot.

"What have you to be angry about?" For the life of her she couldn't figure out why he would be mad.

The second shoe followed the first, and he rose before her. His thumbs hooked between her flesh and pants on either side. "The hostility in that room was tangible. Thick. More than one wants your Empress out of her seat. And you can bet your ass you are the hot focus of an assassination attempt."

"Felt like half the congregation had a death wish for her," Gabriel added against her ear. "As a shifter, I sense things like that more acutely. I pinpointed at least two dozen who followed you out of the *Hall* with hatred in their eyes."

"Want to tell me why they'd make a go at you if your Empress is the best siren?" Talking around his fangs seemed a touch difficult, and Maximus's words were over accentuated.

"She might be the best at sleep serenades, but she's not the most powerful."

Gabriel pushed her hair over her shoulder and nipped her earlobe. "Let me guess, you are the most powerful."

"Yes," she whispered as he sucked her lobe into his mouth.

"Which makes you the most likely siren to take your Empress' seat should something happen to her." She should've known a shifter would be good at strategy. "And the first they want to remove from the equation in such an event."

"Yes, but I don't want it."

"Either way that puts you in severe danger." Maximus dragged her pants off quickly. "That you willingly endanger your life so casually pisses me the fuck off."

"And me." Although the serenity of Gabriel's voice could've deceived her.

Maximus surprised her when he ripped her corset off. "Maximus!"

His hand clamped around her throat, pressing her head against Gabriel's chest. "Foolishness, Sameya. My vampyr won't permit me to let that go without some form of repercussions. Maybe if I make you beg and scream, I'll satisfy my beast. I have no idea."

"I haven't granted you permission to punish me in *any* way. I do what I must for my Empress. You would do the same."

As she was getting good and worked up, Gabriel palmed her mouth, silencing her. Maximus tightened his hold on her neck, garnering her full attention. "Your loyalty to your Empress is commendable, but we're convinced she's not worth *you* dying for."

A moment after her vampyr's final word, her tiger demonstrated how big a brute he could be. In a series of effortless moves, he spun her around, and tossed her over his shoulder. The impact against her belly startled her for a moment.

"Put me down! Damn you—" Her tiger smacked her ass. "Ow!" In retaliation, Sameya swatted his backside. A lot of good it did her because her revenge made them both chuckle.

Upside down she twisted enough to catch sight of Maximus opening her bedroom door.

Just as she drew air into her lungs to start screaming about how she'd get even for their highhanded behavior, they were inside her bedroom with the door slamming shut. Gabriel tossed her onto the mattress, and she bounced as she swatted hair out of her eyes.

Maximus rummaged through his overnight bag he'd packed earlier and she'd delivered before their arrival. No idea what he was looking for, she didn't much care either.

She went to sit up, but Gabriel pressed his hand against her collarbone and commanded, "Don't move."

The nerve of her guys! She whacked his touch aside. "Goddamn it, you two—"

Maximus yanked her into a sitting position, his roughness cutting off her dialogue. He wrenched her hands together behind her back, and cold metal hit her flesh, making a clicking sound as her wrists were ensnared in cool manacles.

Did he just handcuff me? They were taking things too damn far.

Fury had her serenade tingling at the base of her skull. She struggled to withhold the magic while testing the constraints of the steel. When the cuffs held tight, she glared at Maximus. "You *handcuffed* me?"

"So it would seem," Maximus said cool as ice.

"You have no right!"

"We have every right." The vampyr tied her hair back with something she never got a glimpse of.

"You're safety is priority number one to us." Gabriel spoke as she peered up at him. "That we value your life more than you do, infuriates us both."

"How barbaric! I'm a siren with—"

Gabriel gagged her with something that reminded her of a rubber ball. She screeched, but he calmly secured it behind her head. Next came something soft over her eyes, darkness descended as the tiger blindfolded her. She twisted and jerked at the handcuffs again, but like before, they held.

A fist wrapped around the ponytail, holding her head motionless. Fangs pierced her neck and she cried out in euphoria, as Maximus sucked and licked until she grew lightheaded with rapture.

His incisors withdrew from her flesh. "I can't decide which tastes better, your blood or your pussy." He slid his tongue along the wounds, healing them, and she shivered her delight. "You're at our mercy, Sameya. How does that feel?"

Their domineering conduct wouldn't help their bid for her to remain with them. If anything, it'd harm their—

She squealed when she was suddenly flipped her face down on the mattress.

"All this bluster, Sameya, when you could halt it by serenading Gabriel and forcing him to stop me," Maximus said, his British accent thicker than normal. Palms landed on the back of her thighs and dragged upward across her bottom and higher, along her back, until Maximus leaned over her, his mouth against her ear. "Want to know what I think?" He didn't wait for her to answer. "I think you want it rough, so you can use that against us later as a lame ass excuse not to remain with us. But guess what, *naleah*...I bet you're wet with anticipation."

Maximus abruptly shifted away and one of them pressed a finger inside her. Her surprised hiss died against the gag.

"She's wet, Maximus." So it was Gabriel who penetrated her, not the vampyr. "Got anything to say in defense to what Maximus said, baby?"

Not one thing came to mind since he was dead-on accurate. And she was gagged, so it wasn't like she could say anything anyway.

"You've been bad, *naleah*, and bad mates must be chastised." Maximus swirled his tongue at the base of her spine, his fangs indenting her skin. "Be a good girl and submit to us, Sameya. Grant us permission to use you however we want. I promise I'll let you come if you do." His speech vibrated against her spine and sent goosebumps along her skin, and her pussy throbbed to be claimed by them. He licked up her spine, his incisors grazing her. "Make a fist for yes."

Was he crazy? Submit for protecting her Empress when that was her fucking job? They were straight from the dark ages with their idiotic thought process. That they saw her as some feeble woman who needed their protection was galling. She was a reaper for Christ's sake!

But she couldn't stop thinking *she* was the crazy one for not making that fist for yes. Her men aroused her with just words. Hadn't they already used her however they wanted? And she'd enjoyed every second of their claiming.

The smack to her butt cheek startled her with a crack of flesh meeting flesh. Squealing, she jerked at the impact and instinctively tried to rub the sting out her backside. Hands bound, all her movement gained her was a firm hand between her shoulder blades. Another whack. Harder this time and delivered to the other cheek. She screamed at him to stop, but with the ball-gag, nothing but agitated squawking emerged.

"Answer my question. One fist for no, and two for yes." Maximus palmed her burning flesh and caressed as if to eradicate the stinging—at least she thought it was Maximus touching her.

Her vulnerability suddenly walloped her. Naked, handcuffed and gagged, her ass exposed to them both. Defenseless...if she didn't engage the serenade. Was this how those she reaped felt in their final moments?

Yeah, she could serenade Gabriel and force him to stop their deranged idea of punishment. But...something held her back. They were acting barbaric, but a part of her comprehended their annoyance. She'd be furious if either of them placed their lives in danger.

In the end, submitting to them wasn't that difficult. She balled both hands into fists.

"You won't regret surrendering, Sameya." The delight in her vampyr's voice warmed her and already made her happy she'd pleased him.

One of them went to their knees between her legs and spread them. He gripped her thighs with his hands and pulled her up to her knees. Torso on the mattress, she imagined how exposed she was to them.

"Pretty, wet pussy." Gabriel kissed her butt cheek, his prickly jaw identifying him. Without any forewarning, fingers thrust into her wet channel. Relaxing her hands, she groaned against the gag. "She's squeezing my fingers, Maximus."

"I like watching her take us." The vampyr's breath puffed against her bottom.

Gabriel pumped his digits into her fast and hard. The slippery sound of her arousal grew louder in the room as her sighs lengthened. Maximus's longish hair tickled her thighs seconds before his tongue slipped over her pussy. Her muffled squeal bled into exhalations of bliss as he worked over her sensitive flesh. In no time, she came with a moan, her body trembling with her release.

"My turn," Gabriel said.

A moment later, she was flipped onto her back. Hands cupped her ass and lifted the weight of her body off her cuffed hands. Gabriel's mouth buried between her thighs—the shorter hair gave away his identity—and his tongue claimed her intimately. On the heels of her release, she was overly sensitive and she cried out at the extreme sensation. Thanks to the contraption in her mouth, the sound had little impact. She would've pushed Gabriel away had she possessed control of her hands and would've begged him to stop had she not been gagged.

"Is that too intense, *naleah*?" Maximus ran his fingers through her hair, and with the other hand he played with her nipples. She turned toward the sound of his voice, and hoping he'd make the tiger stop, she nodded quickly. "That's part of your punishment. Embrace it." He shifted closer to her head, gripped her hair hard enough her scalp stung. "Suck my dick, mate."

Not accustomed to being referred to as 'mate', it took her half a dozen seconds to realize he was talking to her. He didn't wait for her to agree, just angled her upward by the back of her head and guided her toward him.

The gag was removed, and Sameya whimpered as Gabriel's tongue thrust into her cunt. Maximus's cock butted against her mouth, the wetness of precum moistening her lips. "Open up and let me fuck your pretty red mouth."

Unfamiliar with giving blowjobs, she wanted him to take it slow and thought it best to tell him. "Maximus—"

His thumb landed on her lips. "Shh...don't talk." Following the downward tugging on her chin, she opened for him and he slid his cock inside, all the way to the back of her mouth. A throaty hiss emerged from him. Funny how she could identify Maximus by sound and knew it was him and not Gabriel. Not being able to see either of them strangely heightened her libido. She licked the underside of his dick. "Yes," his lisp was more evident than before, and she imagined his fangs had descended completely.

As Gabriel feasted on her pussy, Maximus fucked her mouth, gagging her more than once. With each thrust to the back of her throat, she relaxed a little more and permitted him to plunge as deep as he could, until her face was buried in his pelvis.

"Fuck that's hot watching you take my dick."

Lost to the hedonism of their claiming, she soon couldn't tell where her moans and whimpers started and Maximus's ended.

Gabriel gave up on the teasing play and settled to sucking on her clit in earnest. Chronic groans ripped from her as her body vibrated from the severe pleasure-pain of his oral attention.

"Going to come, *naleah*." Maximus's voice was a mixture of pants and lisps. Damn she wanted to see his face, but she could imagine the softness of his features as he neared climax.

As the tiger sucked, he flicked his tongue across her clitoris and she squealed, her pussy vibrating to be filled. Her cry was all Maximus needed, a second later he filled her mouth with hot spurts of cum. She swallowed, but he continued to fuck her. His thick release spilled out coating the edges of her mouth and chin.

With one last groan, Maximus pulled out of her. "You're so messy." She could feel the moisture on her face where his seed had overflowed.

She tried to rock her hips against Gabriel's mouth, but the way he clutched her, she couldn't move. Gabriel released his suction, licked a few times and drew her clit back into his mouth.

Sameya cried out, and Maximus swiped his release off her chin with his tongue and kiss her, fucking her mouth like he'd raid and conquer her. She feared they'd conquer her heart, she'd lose herself, and become a shell of the woman she'd been.

"She's been very good, Gabriel," Maximus said, placing kisses to each corner of her mouth. Fingers entered her pussy, and she cried out. "I knew you'd like that."

Her tiger began to purr. The vibration was like a mini-vibrator against her nub, coupled with the repetitive licks and sucks it was almost more than she could tolerate. Heat curled in her belly, spread through her limbs, and a gush of moisture exited her body as Maximus pumped his digits into her. Her back bowed, and she came with a scream that burned her throat.

Suddenly the fingers were gone and her world shifted. A moment later she was straddling one of their thighs and a mouth descended upon hers. Gabriel. Unlike Maximus, he kissed slowly, took his time exploring her. That she could taste her release on his tongue aroused her despite her two orgasms.

That meant her vampyr crowded her back placing warm, moist kisses against her nape, each wispy touch like a shot of lust. He removed the blindfold, but she kept her eyes closed.

Gabriel adjusted her hips and dropped her onto his cock without any warning whatsoever. She whimpered against his mouth as her tiger impaled her as deep as he could go. A hand on her ponytail wrenched her head back by the strands, severing her kiss with Gabriel, and her eyes snapped wide open at the sudden sting. Maximus twisted her head, and she stared into his eyes as Gabriel's cock flexed deep inside her.

The vampyr ran his finger along her cheek. "Hold off your climax as long as you can."

Like she could come again after those two amazing orgasms. "Okay." She could pretend if he could.

He chuckled. "Liar."

Her tiger lay back on the bed and drew her down on top of him. He wrapped his arms around her waist to keep her snuggled against him, as he flexed his hips sliding in and out of her in rapid succession.

Enjoying the feel of his cock, their combined heavy breathing ticked long minutes off the clock. She could sense Maximus watching them as his hands roamed across her backside, cupping her ass.

Gabriel flipped her to her back and positioned her legs over his shoulders. Gripping her hips in both hands, he yanked her toward his body as he thrust hard into her. She groaned, her back arching off the bed. He fucked her hard, without mercy, her cuffed hands taking the brunt of her weight. Caught between pleasure and pain, she fought for release, but it hung suspended on the edge.

Flesh slapped together so loud it drowned out her whimpers and mewls. With his gaze locked on hers, they were united as one through more than body.

"You're close, Gabriel?" Maximus's question startled her.

"Yes." Gabriel didn't lose the force of his drive or eye contact with her.

By the gods, will I be able to let them go?

"Drop her legs off your shoulders so I can get you both there together." At Maximus's instruction, Gabriel rolled his shoulders and her legs slid down his arm to catch in the crook of his elbows.

Her tiger's inspection shifted to where they were connected. When the vampyr's fingers found her clit and rubbed, she cried out, her skin prickling in anticipation of ecstasy.

A long keening came from her lips as her torso twisted on the bed. She couldn't climax again, not this soon. Too soon! Her flesh felt hot and sensitized to just the cool circulating air.

If possible Gabriel's drives became more pronounced and Maximus flicked his fingers faster, adding pressure. Her toes curled and she tensed as warmth snaked through her body. Her fingers tingled and she pulsed where Gabriel pounded into her.

The climax wasn't mild by any standard and startled her with its suddenness. She screamed, bowing off the bed and then dropping limp on the duvet, whimpering as her body twitched. Blackness inked around the perimeter of her vision as Gabriel continued to pound into her and Maximus sustained his strokes against her flesh, moving quicker as she jerked and bucked beneath the tiger.

Gabriel rammed into her, dropped his head backward and came with a tiger's roar. So loud her eardrums vibrated.

"Maximus, please...." She would've twisted away had she been capable of the feat. The vampyr continued to circle her clitoris, ignoring her plea.

Gabriel pulled out of her as he hooked his hands behind the back of her knees and pushed her legs toward her body, tilting her so her pelvis faced the ceiling. Pussy exposed to them, they watched as Maximus worked his thumb over the greedy clit that felt as if it twitched and ached for him.

"We're going to watch you come again, Sameya."

"Can't," she whispered, her body so fiery she felt as if flames consumed her.

"I wish you could see your cum soaked pussy the way we can. So fucking hot."

"Very hot," Maximus agreed with Gabriel.

Their crudeness shouldn't be stimulating, but it was.

No warning, Maximus lowered his head and sucked on her clit. She cried out, clenching her hands into fists. Then Gabriel claimed a turn and they went back and forth, sucking and licking on her clit until she trembled with her need to orgasm. With Maximus sucking and laving on her nub, she came so hard white light burst in her vision. Groaning, her body trembled. Finally he showed her mercy and sat back on his heels. But Gabriel felt inclined to swipe his tongue through her folds half a dozen times, each flick against her clit made her jerk and groan.

Eyes closed, breathing shallow, and her limbs useless appendages, she lay there unable to move. Her men lay down on either side of her.

"I want to put a plug in your ass, Sameya." Maximus licked the sweat from the hollow of her throat.

Gabriel adjusted her onto her side and released her from the handcuffs. He hooked her leg over his thighs and thrust two fingers into her pussy, slow and easy, playing in their sticky release. So sensitive, she lurched, but allowed him the liberty.

"Are you asking permission, Maximus?" Her scratchy voice evidenced the cries that'd been forced from her. They'd kill her at this rate.

"Yes." He nuzzled his nose against hers. "Next time we fuck you, I want us both to claim you at the same time. The plug will help prepare you."

Gabriel penetrated her anus with the fingers that'd been inside her wet sheath. Breathing halted, she accepted the slight burning, but again allowed the invasion.

"I permit it." How could she not when the idea of being claimed by them both—to be theirs completely, seeking gratification in unison—elevated her pulse?

Maximus smiled as he slid fingers down between her breasts, across her belly and lower until his fingers penetrated her pussy. In harmony, they fucked her pussy and ass, their movements growing bolder, deeper, and more forceful as her bliss expanded. Moments before she crashed into another orgasm, they both added a third digit. She climaxed in a blinding rush. They finger-fucked her through the release until she was spent.

"I will never get tired of watching her get off or helping her get there." Maximus licked a nipple.

"Me either." Gabriel kissed the back of her neck.

She wasn't entirely sure she'd ever tire of the ecstasy either. They *would* kill her. "Love it, too," her words were slurred as she drifted to sleep.

Chapter Twenty-Three

Gabriel nuzzled her neck, while the fingers on her hip made a swishing motion. "I think we wore her out."

Maximus smiled, tenderness in his eyes as he peered at their woman. "Yeah. We lucked out with her as a mate. She's pretty fucking amazing."

Gabriel hadn't expected her to be so damned faultless when they located her. Well, as perfect as she could be with her independent streak. But he even found that trait equal parts sexy and annoying.

"They'll come for her first, Gabriel." Worry crinkled the edges of the vampyr's eyes.

"It's what she wants." He'd gleaned her tactic from the moment she boldly swaggered into the *Hall* and handed Kat off to E'Neskha. Hell, if he were going after his enemy, he'd do the same. Remove the strongest link first. Sameya was without a doubt the greatest complication for those that wanted the Empress out of office.

"Fuck!" Maximus ran a hand down his face. With a sigh, he traipsed a finger along her jaw. Sameya sighed, and Maximus inched closer to her until she was sandwiched between them. "Having her vulnerable to us like that...*fuck*!" The vampyr met his gaze over her shoulder. "Her lying between us like this makes my cock twitchy to be inside her again."

"I share your misery." With her ass nestled against his crotch, his desire to fuck her once more grew.

Maximus kissed her forehead. "Goddamn if she doesn't have us turned inside out."

"Indeed." Gabriel slid his hand off her hip and cupped a breast. When there was no response, he decided she truly was sleeping. Although how she managed to snooze at a time like this was beyond his comprehension. "I'll sleep in my tiger just in case."

"Those Zion dogs of hers—what were their names? Nero and Anthrax?" He shook his head. "Nero and *Thrax*. They're a smart breed and protective. They should be cautioned about the danger she's in."

Gabriel had thought the breed extinct. But to find two in his mate's care wasn't all that shocking. "I can communicate with them while I'm in my fur."

"I don't know much about brownies, so I have no idea if they can be of use?"

"No clue." Gabriel wished he knew, but his knowledge of the creatures was extremely limited. "Won't hurt to talk with it anyway." If they could locate the fairy. "One of us should be with Sameya at all times."

"Agreed. We must assume they'll use all her weaknesses against her."

He'd never heard of crushed rose petals before, but he made a future mental note not to send her a dozen roses. "Kat needs to visit her quarters to make sure there is no magical eavesdropping."

They should've thought of that sooner, frankly.

"Goddamn." Maximus made a frustrated face. "We should've considered that earlier."

"Yes." Nothing could be done about that at this late date. "I've been thinking. We'll have to alter a few things now that Sameya is in our life. Figuring out where we're going to live for starters." He doubted they'd be welcome indefinitely in Atlantis.

"What makes you think she's going to stay with us?"

"The alternative is unthinkable." The very possibility clenched his gut. "When we were separated from her and Gryphon had her, my tiger was crazy with the possibilities. I've never been so out of control. I've already fallen for her."

Maximus nodded. "What's not to love? Never thought I'd fall for a sassy-mouthed, pig-headed reaper. But now that I have, I cannot imagine anyone else filling her shoes."

"She's perfect for us. We can*not* lose her."

His vampyr lover cupped his cheek. "No one says we have to let her go."

"We're not holding her captive."

His mate chuckled, flashing his fangs. "Not what I meant, although I do kind of like the idea."

"Your vampyr would." They were so dissimilar. Their very natures conflicted.

"What I meant was, just because she says no to us doesn't mean we have to give up. We have an eternity to woo her, lover. She can't resist us forever. Not with the way we make her feel."

"If she hides here, we're screwed."

"Nah." Maximus's thumb dragged across Gabriel's bottom lip. "I have a feeling her Empress will assist us if Sameya decides to be hardheaded."

"If she doesn't get overthrown first."

"Good point."

Gabriel buried his nose in Sameya's hair and inhaled. "We should rest with her during the interim. That'll keep us in tiptop shape and refreshed enough to battle whatever might come at her."

But the "Sameya" that was called from the doorway halted any of that. The men looked at one another.

"I got this." Maximus drew on his leather pants, secured them and exited the bedroom.

***

The Empress and Kat were present when Maximus departed the bedroom. Fear cramped his gut. If they could enter her chambers this easily, it would be far too simple for her enemies to invade her personal space, also.

The Zions—Nero and Thrax—greeted the leader, and she caressed them both in a fond manner. He hoped they wouldn't greet anyone else in such an exuberant fashion.

"I need to speak with Sameya." The Empress' current fashion wasn't as strict as when she'd been receiving in the *Hall*. Loose fitting, green harem type pants and a white shirt made of the same filmy material covered her slender frame.

"Sameya's unavailable. You okay, Kat?" He met his friend's eyes. She didn't seem injured or compromised.

"Yes. E'Neskha has been a polite hostess."

The siren smiled, but the affectation seemed insincere. "I appreciate your assistance with my issue, Maximus, but I must speak with Sameya."

"She's sleeping." Gabriel strolled toward them, hands stuffed into his pockets. His best guess, the tiger had heard the Empress, and instead of chancing Sameya waking, he'd ventured out to aid Maximus. "She's still recouping from the rose petals sprayed into her face. Surely her Empress can understand she needs some time."

A two-toned aqua and blonde eyebrow elevated. "Gentlemen, your protective instincts are commendable, but these are dangerous times. You'll either wake Sameya or I'll do it myself."

Gabriel came to stand beside him, shoulder-to-shoulder. United they'd take on the Empress if needed. No desire for that outcome to occur, Maximus attempted a different tactic. "How long have you been the Empress of Atlantis?"

The woman stuttered a moment over the sudden change in topic. "A little over fifty thousand years."

Wow! That was a long damn time to rule a kingdom. "Sameya's been with you all that time?"

"Yes. She's three years my senior, so we were raised together. My parents welcomed her into our home and raised her as their own when her parents died." She tossed her hair over her shoulder. "I think of her like a sister and friend. She's the only one I trust implicitly. A good thing with my brother's treachery."

Maximus crossed his arms over his chest. "Why doesn't your brother feel the same way about Sameya if you were raised together?"

"We were grown when Lucius was born. He's resented her for many a century now."

Gabriel rolled on the balls of his feet. "How will you proceed?"

"I—" Using her fingertips, E'Neskha rubbed at the frown lines slashing across her forehead. "I have no idea. That's what I need to discuss with Sameya."

Maximus stared at her. She'd been ruling for so long, why was it hard to make a decision now? "Sameya will die if she continues to support you. I suspect you'll both die." He blew out a long, worried breath. "There were too many against you in the *Hall* today. The hostility was enormous. This isn't a small, one-manned operation, but rather a contingent of Atlantians united in opposition."

"You were able to feel their animosity?"

"Yes."

"I did as well," Gabriel said.

"I'd feared as much." The Atlantis ruler sounded melancholic, and her features sagged as if she'd burst into tears any moment. "I'll allot you more time with Sameya. Decisions can hold for a short time, but please have her join me the moment she wakes."

Gabriel nodded, while Maximus pondered the leader. She offered a small, tired smile that never reached her eyes. She departed, leaving Maximus wondering what the hell went through her head.

Two hours later Maximus pulled on a pair of black boxer briefs and sauntered into Sameya's kitchen. Sunlight flooded the room through a huge set of windows that overlooked an impressive oceanic landscape.

Does darkness ever fall? Since his arrival, the sun had hung high in the sky.

Shaking off the weirdness of the days here, he rummaged through her cabinets until he located a canister of coffee. After prepping the coffee pot, he waited. Tapping his foot as he watched it drip...drip...*driiiip*...much too slowly.

His body hinted the hour was much later than he thought. Late enough he was long past due for a shot of caffeine.

"Those opposed to E'Neskha will come for Sameya soon."

The squeaky voice startled him, and Maximus jerked at the intrusion. Spinning about, he found a creature not more than a foot tall. She stood on the counter top, staring at him with her arms crossed over her flat chest. Pointy eared, with cherubic features and white hair that trailed behind her on the counter.

"Those against her Empress will come for her," the tiny fey reiterated.

He noted she called E'Neskha, Sameya's Empress and not hers. "I'm aware. Are you the brownie?"

"Name's Dart. Feel free to use it. Are you a blood sucker?"

"Yep. Call me Maximus."

Her sparkling rainbow eyes studied him. "I can see why she likes you. You're more than a one-nighter?"

"Mates."

White eyebrows elevated. "And the other fellow?"

"Mate also."

Both eyebrows ratcheted higher. "What do you plan to do about the threat against her?"

The changes in topic made his head swim. "Get her the hell out of Atlantis if possible."

Dart sat on the edge of the counter, her legs dangling over the side. She looked like a doll a child would play with. He'd seen newborns bigger than her. "You'll protect her."

Insulted he allowed his vampyr to show in his eyes. "She's my goddamn mate." *Of course I'll protect her.*

She held up a doll-sized hand. "No disrespect meant, bloodsucker. How far will you go to keep her safe?"

Fascinated he peered at her. A brownie cleaned homes and according to Sameya served as her jack-of-all-trades if the stocked cabinets were any indication. As tiny as she was, he imagined she often went unnoticed. "What are you suggesting?"

Her legs swished back and forth. In a swirling array of sparkling lights, a box of dog treats appeared in her hand. She tossed two toward the Zions that'd crept up behind him. "Would you kill the Empress to save Sameya?"

"Are you part of the revolution?" He watched her closely, opening his senses, but couldn't detect any guile.

Dart rolled her eyes. "Why would I bother? No one governs a brownie."

The coffee pot beeped indicating it'd finished brewing. *Finally*! Opening cabinets in search of a mug, he said, "You work for Sameya. Isn't that something like being governed?"

"Here." She thrust a mug toward him; it's bulk huge against her tiny frame. *It's a wonder she can lift it.*

He hadn't seen her move, nor had he witnessed any of that sparkly magic, so he had no idea how or when she'd come by the cup. Neither did he care at the moment. He needed caffeine, so he accepted the dishware.

"Sameya compensates me with fine, *fine* tequila. And...I guess I sort of like her. A little." She moved like a jaguar on speed. Going onto her tippy-toes, she got in his face as best she could. "You tell her that and I'll bite your fucking leg off!"

Maximus laughed, startled by her vehemence. Like his gal a little? He didn't think so. Dart wanted to appear aloof, but her emotions were high. At the brownie's glare over his amusement, he cleared his throat and forced a straight-faced mien. "You're serious?"

"Dead."

"Bite my leg off, hmm?" He stepped aside and poured his mug full of coffee. *Bite my leg, indeed*! Even crazier the little brownie thought that'd actually cow him. "Your secret is safe." And in order to say that with a straight face, *he* had to bite the inside of his mouth. "As for the Empress, I'd kill her in a heartbeat if I thought it'd save Sameya."

"I like you." Dart sauntered away, her little feet stuffed into itty-bitty stilettos made a tapping sound against the marble. Maybe she wasn't as tall as he'd originally suspected. "We'll get along just fine."

"Do you know who leads the upheaval?"

"Yeah. There's a list of names of the militants." She pointed at the table as a sheet of paper magically appeared.

"Are you coming with us when we leave?" Maximus sipped his coffee, studying her over the rim of his mug. Presumptuous of him to assume Sameya would leave Atlantis, but at this point he couldn't foresee any other way to keep her alive.

"What's in it for me?" She swiveled to get a gander of him over her shoulder.

"Anything you want."

"*Anything*?" Her eyes grew round, and her features softened.

"Within reason, and so long as I can get my hands on it without endangering life or limb."

"Reese Cups. I want a big bag of them once a month."

What a bizarre request! "Reese Cups?" She had to be yanking his chain. Tequila was her vice from Sameya, and from him she wanted sweets?

She nodded and licked her light pink lips as if she could taste them now. "The miniature kind...so I won't get drunk as fast."

Drunk? That was what the liquor was for. Maybe she was like the ogre. Tea was their form of spirits.

But when had she tasted a Reese Cup? She lived in Atlantis, and the best he could tell the inhabitants did not trade with the earthy realm? Maximus did not ask. "Agreed. Any other housing requirements?"

"How big is your domain?"

He shrugged. "Six thousand square feet. Give or take."

She clapped her hands together, her eyes swirling brighter. "My dream home to clean! I'll happily join you all."

He'd gladly let her clean since he despised the chore.

The brownie leapt off the counter and skipped across the floor and out of sight. Maximus shook his head. What a weird conversation and even stranger creature.

Refilling his mug, he turned to stare out the window. Fluffy clouds dotted the sky, while greenery and an explosion of color suggested Atlantis were smack dab in the middle of spring. If they followed the earth's orbit, that wasn't possible. They should be at the end of summer.

A short while later, the door to Sameya's bedroom opened and closed. He turned to see his woman strolling toward him, fingers rubbing the sleep from one eye. After the Empress' visit, Gabriel had shifted into his tiger and curled up to sleep beside their mate.

"Morning. Afternoon. Evening. I have no idea what time of day it is."

Smiling, she stopped in front of him and peered up. "It's evening."

The sleepy tone to her voice reminded him of the way she sounded after climaxing.

She wrapped her arms around his waist and cuddled against his chest. Stunned it took him a moment to process the shock of her embrace before he set his coffee aside and returned her hug. He rubbed his cheek against the top of her head. "Something wrong, *naleah?*"

"No, I wanted to be close to you. Do you prefer I not hug you?"

"Touch me however you want whenever you want." Maximus ran a palm down her spine. That she felt comfortable enough to embrace him fed his optimism.

"I'm not certain I can walk away from you and Gabriel."

He squeezed her tighter. "Good."

Sameya tilted her head back to peer at him. "It's not the sex. Even though it *is* amazing."

Maximus grinned. "I know."

"I feel connected to you both in a way I cannot explain." She buried her face against his chest and breathed deeply. "Your scent…it's like an elixir. I love the unique blend of man and vampyr." She ran a fingertip along his jaw. "Gabriel's the same way. And snuggling with his cat, having him purr while I pet him." She shook her head. "I cannot explain this response I'm feeling here." She touched the spot over her heart. "I barely know either of you, but I trust you both as if I've known you all my life. It's like you're both connected to me on a molecular level."

"We *are* joined on a molecular level." He buried the fingers of one hand in her hair and clamped his other hand on her hip. "Our bond will become stronger when we officially mate. I've heard stories that some who are mated can talk telepathically. Others can sense the emotions of their mate. Very similar to earlier when I could sense your anguish when you were mind-fucking Gryphon."

Staring at his mouth, she nodded. "I'm afraid for your safety. Yet, I'm sensing neither of you will leave if I ask it."

"See, you're already sensing our emotions." He flashed her a wicked grin, exposing his teeth.

She reached up and ran her thumb along one fang. "Vampyr, I need you to mark me as yours."

Anticipation had his heart ramming against his ribs. "I do that here."

Watching her expression, he slid his hand down her hip and across her thigh, until he could trail his fingers along the artery on the inside of her leg, inches below her pussy.

"Will you fuck me, too?"

He wasn't sure if it was a request or an inquiry. "Yes, but only with Gabriel present."

She shivered as he trailed his fingertips across the outer edges of her cunt. "I want that, Maximus. Gabriel should mark me harder than he has already. Permanently."

"Do you know what you're getting into?" It'd be a full-blown mating. They couldn't allow her to depart after that, not without sending them both into a depression. It'd be like her dying.

"I—yes." She cuddled against him once more, her face buried against his chest, her breath puffing on his skin. "The idea of walking out of your lives makes me sick to my stomach."

"I'm glad to hear it." Not that it made her nauseous, but that she'd accepted her attraction to the mating magnetism. He and Gabriel had been mindless when they'd initiated their mating dance. It wasn't any easier with Sameya, they'd both been struggling not to fuck her and mark her until she was exhausted. Respecting her decision was difficult, worse than a case of blue balls, but so worth the effort if she became theirs in the end.

Chapter Twenty-four

Sameya never wanted to leave his arms, but choices were limited. She had an Empress to save before she could get on with her life with her men. Of course she had no clear concept of how that would happen. They couldn't remain in Atlantis, and the idea of leaving...well, it was better to be with them surrounded by the pestilence called humanity than alone without them in her homeland.

Nero and Thrax would come with her. Of that she had no doubt. They could pass as some mixed breed Mastiff or Great Dane. Only a wee bit bigger than their human counterparts, and a whole hell of a lot more dangerous, but provided she wasn't endangered they were nothing more than big lap babies.

Dart was a different matter altogether. She'd invite the brownie to tag along, but she couldn't guess what her response would be.

She'd woken curled up against her tiger, his purring soft, but expressing his contentment. As she'd put her fingers through his fur and scratched near his ear, his purr had grown louder. He'd tilted his head and licked her arm. A nuzzle like a man would've done. In that moment, she'd realized they meant too much to her to kick them out of her life. They were as much hers as they claimed she was theirs.

Leaving Gabriel asleep, she'd found Maximus wearing a puzzled expression, while sipping coffee and staring out her window. And she'd been struck all over again by how much they'd come to mean to her in such a short amount of time.

Without thinking, she'd walked straight to him and hugged him. Not the touchy-feely type, her response had surprised her as much as it obviously had him. He'd taken several seconds before returning her embrace. At first she'd worried she'd made a mistake. Cats were affectionate by nature, but she had no idea the norm for a vampyr.

Loving the feel of him, Sameya dragged her cheek against his bare chest. She kissed him, and then licked the spot.

Maximus's hand tightened in her hair. "Sameya." His gruff voice hinted how close to the edge she pushed him.

Why the control? "Don't you want to fuck me?"

"Of course, I do, but it's been less than three hours since we disciplined you last." His hand shifted and ran along the curve of her ass, fingertips swiping through the crevice.

"Mmm...I think I like being disciplined."

He chuckled. "I do have a toy to place somewhere intimately." Holding eye contact, he trailed his jaw along her cheek. His voice deepened to a level that buzzed directly across her clit. "To prepare you for later."

She couldn't wait. "When I return from my meeting with E'Neskha."

"No, before. With every move you make, I want you to think of us while you're with her."

"That's so...kinky."

He flashed a wicked grin. "Think I can make you come with just the toy in your ass?"

"You could blow on my clit and make me come."

Maximus grinned. "You're too easy. You've got to make us work for your pleasure sometime."

Why on earth would she want that? "Not anytime soon."

She squealed in surprise when he swept her into his arms. He nipped her ear as he strode to the bedroom. Almost as quickly as he'd picked her up, he settled her on her feet at the end of her bed. "Clothes off. Go to the center of your bed, and face the wall on your knees."

"Bossy," she teased with a grin as she wiggled out of her clothes and climbed onto the bed.

Gabriel lifted his head off the pillow, blinking as he peered at them in tiger form.

"Spread your legs." She could hear Maximus fumbling around in one of their overnight bags.

Sameya widened her stance, not the easiest thing to do on her knees in the middle of a soft mattress. The cat shifted closer, knocking her off balance. With a hand on his back, she caught herself from tipping over. A gasp wrenched from her lungs as he placed an abrasive feline lick between her legs.

"Cats like cream," Maximus said against her ear, surprising her with his nearness. "Do you like the way his tiger tongue feels against your pussy?"

"Gods, yes."

The laps grew more pronounced, dragging from her entrance and up across her clit in a languid glide. Maximus curled his hand around her throat and pulled her spine snug against his chest. "Has a much different feel than his human one, huh?"

She could only manage a nod.

"Want him to make you come like this while I put the dildo in your ass?"

Such crassness and yet the visual they inspired turned her on even more. She nodded again.

"Say it." Maximus demanded as Gabriel crouched, removing his tongue from her folds. The vampyr pushed the toy into her pussy and twirled it. "Tell us what you want, Sameya. And who you want to do what."

"I want your tiger to make me come, Gabriel." A hard jab of the toy inside her and her breathing stuttered. "M-Maximus, I want you to fuck me with the toy."

"Where?"

"In my ass. Please."

Maximus sank his fangs into the curve between shoulder and neck. She gasped at the sudden possession by him. Moving his fingertips from her neck to beneath her chin, he tilted her head back against his shoulder. Frozen in that position, with his gentle sucks against her skin, he removed the toy from her body and slid it backward to the tight ring of her bottom.

Gabriel's purr wasn't unexpected. The vibration of the noise against her pussy when his tongue returned to her folds was a shock. She moaned and Maximus thrust the toy partway into her. Her gasp halted the plug's intrusion.

"Relax," he said around his fangs buried in her throat. He wiggled the item in her bottom before fucking her with half the gadget. There was no vibration with this one like with the last. It didn't matter she still found enjoyment in the slight sting.

Maximus sucked. Gabriel licked. The plug went all the way in and she winced at the burning fullness. The pain coupled with the pleasure, nearly crippled her. Without the man behind her, she'd be flat on her face.

She rocked her hips against the vampyr's hand and the tiger's oral. Taking the hint, Maximus fucked her with the sex-toy until she was unable to breathe through the intensity of the sensation. Eyes wide, she managed to angle her head enough to lock gazes with Maximus's.

Sameya lifted an arm and grabbed a fistful of the vampyr's hair, as her other hand buried in the fur of Gabriel's head. She came with a scream, her entire body shaking, and her knees wobbling. Maximus lifted his head, licked her wounds and buried the toy as far as it would go.

The feline between her legs issued one final stroke, then reclined on his back and shifted into man. He reached up and pulled her down, out of Maximus's hold, and kissed her. Even on the man, she could taste herself.

Knees beneath her, and ass up, exposed to the air and Maximus, he tongued around the toy, adjusting the object slightly. She groaned into the tiger's mouth.

"I want to suck both of you until you come in my mouth," she said in-between kisses. It was another way they could mark her. But she wanted the rest, the final mating. She needed it. "Please."

Sameya pushed back on her heels as Maximus tapped the plug, and it began to whir with vibrations in her ass, proving it came to life like the other. How would she concentrate?

"Want our dicks in your mouth?" Maximus kissed her.

"Yes." She nipped his bottom lip hard enough to sting. "Now off the bed and give me what I want."

Since he'd just shifted from tiger, Gabriel was already nude. Going to the edge of the bed, she gripped the base of his cock and swirled her tongue around his fat, uncut crown, as Maximus quickly removed his pants. Gabriel groaned as she sucked on his head and stroked the vampyr's erection with her other hand.

Moving to Maximus's dick, she took him all the way to the back of her throat without preamble, the Apadravya piercing cool against her tongue. The ladder-backs going unnoticed against the top of her mouth. He gasped as she swished her tongue back and forth along the underside on her way back to the tip of his length. Both uncircumcised, she gently pulled back the foreskin on each and alternated between them, sucking on their exposed heads. They kissed each other and groaned as she worked them over with her mouth.

"Fuck! Goddamn, Sameya!" Maximus clenched her head between both his hands. "I need to fuck your mouth. Hard and out of control because that's the way you make me feel."

That's the way *they* made *her* feel.

As a response, she flattened her tongue and slid it along the base of his dick. Taking him down her throat sufficed as all the encouragement he needed. He held her head motionless, as he assumed control, driving his cock into her throat over and over again. The scrapes of his piercings surprisingly non-abrasive.

She looked up as he fucked her. With his hand in Maximus's hair, Gabriel kissed him and then they both watched him thrust between her lips over and over again, each plunge deeper and coming faster than the last. He sank deep, until her nose was flush against his pelvis. Gabriel's thumb stroked her neck and along Maximus's cock buried in her windpipe. His first twitch of his climax erupted. On his pull out, he spilled his seed on her tongue. She sucked him back into her mouth, swishing her tongue along the sensitive head. His groan and quivering pleasing her.

Swallowing, she smiled at him and placed a kiss against the slit.

"You should be proud of yourself." Maximus palmed her cheek. "That was fantastic."

She moved on to Gabriel's length, tonguing his balls before sucking him into her mouth. Long slow strokes across his hard flesh. There was power in knowing she controlled their release. And now she felt like playing, so she licked down his erection, and lavished attention to his balls. She flicked her tongue over him on the way up to the head again. His repeated grunts and groans incentive to continue toying with him.

Maximus shifted them so she sat in his lap. He pushed her legs over the outside of his thighs and spread his legs wide. Cool air kissed her exposed pussy and then his fingers found her.

She moaned around Gabriel's dick stuffed in her mouth. The cat gave her little time to prepare. Helpless and embracing the vulnerability, he fucked her the same way Maximus had, balls deep down her throat, as the vampyr fucked her with his fingers, his thumb grazing her clit.

Trapped between them, she became a useless lump of flesh, experiencing sensation after sensation. She stared at Gabriel through watery eyes, swishing her tongue along his length as he thrust into her mouth. She came, crying out as his cock surged down her throat.

"Fuck," Gabriel groaned, fisting her hair he held her head motionless as he fucked her throat and climaxed within seconds of hers. His dick twitched in its narrow confines. He pulled out of her mouth. "Did I hurt you, Sameya?"

"No." Her voice sounded raspy.

Maximus shifted to the center of the bed, spooning her with his fingers still buried inside her. "Rest for a spell."

"Did you forget something, vampyr?" She dragged a nail over his hand, as Gabriel leapt onto the bed and shifted back into his cat. He settled down beside her.

"No." Maximus nuzzled the back of her neck. "My fingers remain inside you while we sleep."

"Gods, the things you two do to me." And she loved every second of it.

In response, the vampyr bit her nape, but not enough to draw blood. "We're only getting started."

Gods have mercy.

Chapter Twenty-five

Sameya's boots clicked against the marble as she strode toward the Empress.

"I'm surprised Gabriel and Maximus allowed your departure." E'Neskha's amusement was evident in the slight upturn of her lips.

A distraction in sexual play wouldn't halt Sameya's agenda. She *would* put the revolt to rest. Sameya flashed her leader a grin. "They were asleep."

"That's an intense duo you have."

"It's not like I picked them." Nature selected the best for each individual, nothing random about it. "Had they been awake, I'm sure they'd be shadowing me."

The other woman laughed. "They'll be agitated when they discover you missing."

Sameya shrugged. Once they found her note detailing where she'd gone, she figured that agitation would turn to ire. Better her mates discover her independence now rather than later.

"You'll remain with them?" Her Empress motioned to the seat opposite the table where she sat. The Atlantis leader offered her no refreshment, because neither partook of nourishment.

Sitting, she gingerly crossed a leg over the other and tried to ignore the vibration of the dildo in her ass. "Yes. I cannot see a future without them."

"Then why are you waiting to mate them?"

She glanced about, finding none other present. "Where's their witch?"

"Kat is elsewhere." E'Neskha leaned forward. "Be your blunt self. No others are present."

"They've been determined to win me over since I wouldn't commit to them." Sameya tapped a fingernail against the tabletop. "I enjoy their efforts, don't want them to end."

The other woman glanced over Sameya's shoulder. "The orgasms are all they're touted to be?"

"Better. So much better. Which one of them is behind me?"

"Both." Maximus answered for her Empress, his fingers curling around the back of her neck.

Gabriel shifted into mankind, but just barely. His white Bengal remained imprinted over his human form. "Goddamn it, Sameya!" The feline snarled and flickered bright. "You fucking promised to keep us informed!"

Maybe they were a little more agitated than she'd anticipated. "I left a note."

"A *note*!" He morphed back into the tiger and paced in front of her, tail swishing, fangs bared in an unceasing low-throated growl.

The grip on her neck tightened as the vampyr's other hand threaded in her hair and tipped her head back to meet his furious green gaze. "You should've *told* us where you were going so we could've joined you. Fucking protected you." He released her and crammed his fingers through his overlong hair. "Do you know how terrified we were when we discovered you gone?"

"Newsflash, Maximus. I want them to come for me. It's the only way I can draw them out."

Gabriel roared and tackled her and the chair to the floor in one easy leap. In the next breath, he had her neck between his jaws in a death-grip—well, what should've been the beginnings of a death-choke. While not in any real danger, it was effective at displaying his temper.

"Gabriel says no," Maximus said, his tone too mild for Gabriel's evident wrath. He stared her in the eyes, his vampyr on display.

"My goddess." E'Neskha giggled, a high-pitched trill of awe. "I'd always heard shifters were easily agitated, and ruled by their emotions. Does he realize she could neutralize him with a single thought?"

"He knows." The vampyr maintained his focus on Sameya. "Our stubborn mate needs to learn her place in our life."

Her place? If he meant at the sidelines while they went head on into danger, then they both needed a reality check. "I *know* my place, vampyr, it's as your equal. Damn sure not so much as half an inch behind either of you." The tiger growled against her flesh. She wrapped her fingers around his ears and wrenched them until he chuffed. "The sooner you both realize I'll never allow you to coddle and protect me, the better." The cat remained in position, making puffing noises of disapproval, his whiskers tickling her. "Get over it, Gabriel. Just so you know, the next time you put your teeth on my neck either use them or be prepared for me to serenade you."

A lick to her skin was his response. Gooseflesh paraded across her body.

"Don't you dare distract me with your tongue." His tongue was wicked good at distraction. Releasing her neck, he settled on top of her and licked the indentions his canines had created. "Shit, you're heavy like this." When he began to purr, while delivering small flicks of his tongue against her skin, she attempted a different tactic. "You want to fuck me ever again, you'll get off me."

That delivered the outcome she sought. He moved backward a fraction, enough that she could sit up, but not sufficient enough to sit up straight without bumping her head into his feline jaw. "Really? This is ridiculous. Your hovering is getting on my last fucking nerve."

"Your life will never get boring with these two around," E'Neskha said.

She can say that again.

Sameya rolled to her feet, and Gabriel morphed into man. Her Empress' eyes widened, and only then did Sameya realize he hadn't reappeared with his clothing on. Yeah, the tiger was well endowed, but thankfully her leader remained mute about the obvious.

Shifters and their lack of modesty. Sameya rolled her eyes.

She dusted the back of her pants off, not that there was ever a spot of dirt in the palace. "Now that we've settled our domestic dispute, can we get back to business?"

Maximus leveled a glare on E'Neskha and opened his mouth to speak, but Lucius presented himself instead. "I'd no idea the tiger at your side was your other mate, Sameya. I figured you'd done away with him. Your duplicity astounds me."

Her Empress shot her a nervous glance. Sameya stiffened at the sight of E'Neskha's brother. "Lucius...." The tiger at her side issued a low-throated growl when she identified the male. She clasped his wrist in her hand and shot a thread of serenade into him. "Sorry," she muttered when she looked at him and his eyes widened at what she'd done. The only reason for the song was to keep Lucius from getting to him first, and he wouldn't be able to override hers. Since she offered no commands to the song, Gabriel was free to act as he chose.

She eyed the male siren. "I figured you'd have taken the cowardly way out and be running by now."

"Why on earth would I do that?" Lucius cocked his blond and aqua head to the side as if contemplating her.

"We both know why, *you traitor*." To pretend he wasn't the instigator of the rebellion against his sister was an insult to her intelligence.

The arrogant bastard smirked. "You know me better than that, Sameya."

Gabriel effected some more low-throated growling. She didn't chance a glance in Maximus's direction, but she wouldn't be surprised if his fangs overlapped his bottom lip.

"I'm considering relinquishing my status as Empress." E'Neskha reclined in her seat, but for all the effort she put into a casual pose, it failed wide of the mark, her tense shoulders giving her away.

"If she does, I'll be making a bid for her position."

Sameya ignored Lucius, her focus centered on her leader. Why would she contemplate something like that? They'd spent over fifty thousand years maintaining the safety and well being of Atlantis. To give it up on a whim, because it *had* to be an impulse, otherwise her possible resignation made little sense. Surrendering wasn't in her personality, and she would never give up on her people merely to spare a battle. Not if it were in their best interest. "Why?"

"As if that's any of your business." Lucius sniffed haughtily as he approached. "You're overstepping your boundaries."

"And you're getting on my nerves."

"I think it's time to concede, Sameya." E'Neskha shrugged, sending her brother a disillusioned glance. "We discussed it once before and—"

"Discussed it two thousand years ago. To forfeit when it's revealed Lucius is the turncoat...I don't understand your reasoning."

"Pish-posh, you know I'm no threat to E'Neskha. That you'd deliver false information simply to place a wedge between us is atrocious. Verifies what I've been telling her all these years, that your advice cannot be trusted." Lucius lounged in a chair beside his sister, his overconfident demeanor nettling Sameya. Judging by the conceit in his eyes, he thought he'd won.

"Do you believe him, E'Neskha?"

"Which part? Your misinformation or his innocence?"

"Either, and both." She watched her, gauging the leader.

E'Neskha was silent a long moment before she responded, and not to her question. "You've got your mates to keep you busy now. You don't need me, and I've been restless this last millennium. Maybe I should've stepped aside sooner." She shrugged. "I hadn't thought about it until all this mess with the rebellion. All things must eventually come to an end."

Sameya stomped to the table and slammed her palms facedown on the tabletop. "Do. You. Believe. Him?"

The Empress wouldn't meet her gaze. "He's my brother, Sameya, we'll leave it at that."

"Have you lost your fucking *mind*?"

"You'll mind your tone," Lucius said condescendingly.

Sameya ignored the arrogant bastard.

"What reason does Lucius have to lie?" E'Neskha shot back, her bottom lip trembling.

No way was the Atlantian leader that gullible. That they shared the same blood softened her. Maybe it *was* time E'Neskha yielded her throne, but there wasn't a chance in hell Sameya would allow Lucius' behavior to go without repercussions.

Utilizing her siren speed, Sameya zipped to Lucius and drenched him in a serenade. He screamed and slapped at his forehead as E'Neskha vaulted to her feet. "Sameya!"

"No closer, E'Neskha, or I'll reap him." The coldness in her voice halted her leader's approach. She plugged the male siren with her special magic, the magnitude of the effects more pronounced on someone as strong as him. But he still held no chance of evading her control.

With his sister staring on in horror, Lucius finally gave up the fight and went limp in his seat, his hands dropping into his lap. He twitched as if suffering the delayed twinges of an electrocution, but with his mental struggle against her song eliminated, he had become her puppet. At her mercy, he'd do her bidding with no hope of E'Neskha superseding Sameya's song.

The other woman's hands shook as she lifted them in prayer-like fashion below her chin. "Please don't harm him, Sameya. He's all the family I have left."

When I'm done with him, you will be all he has left.

"I'm disappointed you'd turn your reign into a mockery like this, E'Neskha." Sameya couldn't understand her leader's tolerance for Lucius' comportment. "Being your brother doesn't grant him indefinite liberties. He is still accountable for his actions, yet you won't hold him to that standard."

E'Neskha notched her chin higher.

But Sameya wasn't finished and continued to talk. "You've given him everything he's ever wanted." She had, too. His parents had died while he was young, just like Sameya's parents had. The Empress had raised him from his early teenage years into adulthood. "Are you going to give him this, also?"

"It's the only thing I have left to give, and if he wants it...." E'Neskha didn't finish the sentence, but her meaning was clear enough.

"Pity." Her mates must've sensed her intention because they moved a little closer as if they expected her former Empress to make a go for her. "I won't allow him the position."

"Sam—"

"*No!*" She notched her thumb into the base of Lucius' neck. "You're commanded to tell your sister everything, Lucius."

Standing at the male siren's back, she couldn't see his face, but his sniffles told her he'd begun to cry. He spilled all...how he coveted E'Neskha's power and the respect her people gave her. How he felt worthless stacked against a sister bearing such high accolades, and a sibling who placed more clout in Sameya's opinions than his. Growing weary of waiting for her to concede her position, he'd incited discord among the Atlantians. The disharmony was easy to come by, telling Sameya the people were ready for a change.

He'd formed a resistance and given instructions to those closest to him to do *anything* to gain his seat as Emperor, even if that meant E'Neskha's death. Knowing if his sister were murdered, Sameya wouldn't accept a fatality without a formal inquiry, he'd concocted her kidnapping and demise, as well, at the hands of a griffin with only one requirement...a power he could dine on for centuries.

Sameya would've killed him for that alone, but the sorrow on the Empress' tear-stained face stayed her ruthless judgment. "My gift to you, E'Neskha, is Lucius' life." She stepped to face the male siren and met his gaze. "I allow you to live only because of your sister. You're prohibited from ever making a bid for the Atlantian royal seat. From today onward you're exiled from Atlantis, forbidden to return, and you're to never raise arms against your sister. You'll be faithful to her, as she deserves, for the years of love and compassion she gave to you. If you *attempt* to break any of my commands, you'll be reaped immediately."

She released him and faced her former leader. "E'Neskha, I'll expect you to depart Atlantis as soon as you formally surrender your position and swear in a temporary ruler." The Empress nodded and Sameya went on. "Where's the witch?"

"The kitchen," the Empress said in a watery voice.

Frustrated by the turn of events, Sameya headed for the kitchen. Falling in beside her, Gabriel easily matched her pace as he clasped her hand in his. She could feel Maximus at her back, but both of her guys were silent.

Kat sat at the kitchen table picking through a bowl of candies. The witch looked up when they entered.

"It's time for you to return home." Sameya opened a portal to the earth realm and indicated it with her hand. "Now."

"Is everything okay?" Kat peeked at the men as she rose from her seat.

"No. But the Atlantian future isn't devoid of hope. We'll see you soon."

"Go, Kat," Maximus said as he placed his palm low on Sameya's back.

No one spoke as the witch went through the green mist. Once she disappeared, Gabriel squeezed Sameya's hand, as if he could sense how numb she felt. "I'll break the serenade as soon as we're on Earth, Gabriel."

"I knew you did it to protect us all."

She peered up at him. Thank goddess, she had these men in her life. They'd make leaving her homeland a little easier. It didn't matter that she'd already been thinking of leaving Atlantis with her guys. What struck her most was the finality of it all.

Her vampyr palmed her shoulder. "Sameya—"

"I'm okay." She was a long way from being okay, but thankfully the only hint she would fall apart any moment was the twitter in her voice.

She hadn't expected things to proceed in this manner. She should've known E'Neskha would go soft when it came to Lucius. He might be her brother, but he was more like her son.

Silence stalked them as they strode to her apartment. The moment the doors closed behind her, Sameya went to her hands and knees and wept. She was losing her past to gain a future. The memories would remain, but she'd never peer at the mystical waters again. Never watch the golden fish catch the sunlight as they jumped across the Great Lake during spawning season. Never again take a hike up Blue Chimney Mountain.

Gabriel scooped her into his arms and sat on the sofa, cradling her. She shifted to straddle his lap and wrap her arms around him, as she buried her face in the curve of his neck. His embrace the solace she needed to calm her mixed-up emotions.

She could live with never seeing her birthplace again. These men were her future. Being with them felt right. And she'd have the comfort of knowing she'd saved Atlantis from a ruler that would've resulted in her homeland's decline. The things she'd seen in Lucius' head that she hadn't forced him to share...he would've debilitated Atlantis and its citizens.

"I'm sorry you're upset, Sameya." Reminiscent of a feline, Gabriel rubbed his cheek against her hair. "Maximus and I will do everything in our power to make you happy."

The sofa shifted, she suspected it was Maximus taking a seat beside them.

Leaning back, she confirmed the vampyr's presence as she met her cat's gaze. "Don't misunderstand my grief, Gabriel. The idea of never seeing Atlantis...." She choked up all over again. He captured her face and kissed her forehead.

"I understand." Maximus shifted onto his knees and massaged the back of her neck. "My family disowned me for mating Gabriel."

How horrible! "I'm sorry, Maximus."

"I'm not. He's worth the sacrifice...when he's not being a pussy." He winked at the shifter.

She smiled as Gabriel growled at Maximus. The guys chuckled. Amazing how quickly these two had burrowed into her heart. "You two are my future." She kissed both of them, astonished how important they'd become to her in such little time. "Take me to your...no. Take me to *my* new home and officially claim me."

She wanted to be theirs more than she'd ever wanted anything in her life.

"'Officially' doesn't matter. You're already ours, *naleah*. We"—Maximus motioned between himself and Gabriel—"never planned to give you up."

Sameya peered between them.

"Nope," Gabriel confirmed. "We were committed to convincing you we're worth keeping around."

"Kidnapping you if necessary," Maximus's deadpan was so convincing she was uncertain of his sincerity.

Gabriel nodded his agreement.

Shaking her head at their alpha-*ness*, she climbed off the tiger's lap. "I need to talk with Dart, see if she'll go with us. And the Zions—I assume Thrax and Nero will join me, but I can't take it for granted."

Wearing a smug expression, her vampyr leaned against the cushions. "I already worked out a deal with Dart. She's agreed to join us."

Impressive. But shocking Dart had shown herself. Even the Empress had never laid eyes on Sameya's brownie. "What'd you agree to pay her?"

"Reese Cups." A lopsided grin exposed a fang. Soon they'd be inside her. At the idea, anticipation shivered through her. "A large bag once a month."

Sameya laughed. "What a hard bargain Dart drives."

"I asked her to pack your things and deliver them to our home."

Arrogant to assume she'd depart with them.

"I spoke with the Zions." Gabriel looped his arm over Maximus's shoulder. "They expected to live with you wherever you reside."

"You two thought of everything." She wasn't sure how to feel about that. "And you were both confident I would depart with you."

Maximus adjusted her position, giving her no time to react to her sudden placement. Sprawled across their legs, with her head in the cat's lap and her butt across the vampyr's thighs, she scrutinized them, surprised with her abrupt relocation.

Her bloodsucker laid his arm across her abdomen. "Gabriel and I want you to be prepared about...his family."

She shot a glance at the tiger, her nerves twittering through her belly.

Gabriel put his fingers through her hair. "We have a marital custom. While they've accepted Maximus as one of their own, we never participated in the custom because we wanted to wait for you."

Refusing to jump to conclusions, she waited for them to explain.

"If you don't want to do it, we won't." From her tiger's probing stare, she gleaned how important this ritual was for him.

"It won't mean we're any less mated or married," Maximus said quickly. "The pride will still recognize our relationship."

Whatever the tradition, it was obviously important to Gabriel. "Go on."

She attempted to sit up, but Maximus applied pressure to her belly. When she met his gaze, he thrust his palm beneath her shirt and cupped her breast, applying slight pinches to her nipple. Biting back her groan, she ignored his smirk. The conceited vampyr knew how his touch affected her.

Gabriel tilted her head back to meet her eyes. He licked his lips, and she noted his nervousness. "We mate with my pride in attendance."

Sameya processed the idea. "You want us to have sex while they watch?"

"It's the custom." He shrugged. "And I like being watched."

She liked observing him. The first time she'd seen them together, they'd been having sex on the balcony, and they'd been pandering to the crowd on Bourbon Street. She was no prude; it was common for soirees in Atlantis to end in explicit displays of carnal pursuit. The *Hall* had seen more action than Sameya cared to recollect. She'd never been watched before.

A tingling at the base of her skull suggested there was more to his request. "If we don't do the custom, how does this affect us?"

Gabriel hesitated. "Any of our children will not be recognized by the pride."

"Or ours," Maximus said. "I've been adopted into the pride."

Unfair to punish children for the actions of their parents, and she couldn't deny any child—especially any of her own—the blessing of family and community. "We should do it."

The gold of her tiger's eyes flashed, proof he liked that she'd agreed. "I don't want you rushing into a decision. Think about it, Sameya."

"I'm not rushing the decision." She pulled Maximus's hand from beneath her shirt and kissed his fingertips. "However, I won't tolerate anyone touching either of you." She would've never guessed she was the jealous type, but let someone touch one of her men…. "I'll serenade them before I permit it."

"Fitting. Only Gabriel and I can touch you." Her vampyr bent over and licked her pussy through her pants. "Want me to tell you what I plan to do to you while they watch?"

"No. Surprise me." She rolled quickly before either of them could halt her departure. "But I plan to give at least one of you a blow job while they watch."

Maximus's eyes glowed green, and his fangs bit into his bottom lip.

Gabriel slashed his fingers through his hair and muttered, "Fuck me."

She grinned and sashayed out of the room as Maximus said, "She'll be the death of us."

"A fine death it'll be." Gabriel's purr carried.

Making her men happy pleased her tremendously.

Chapter Twenty-Six

They'd left Atlantis and Sameya hadn't allowed melancholy at the loss of her homeland to set in. A bright future with mates she adored was her primary focus.

Dart was in heaven in the guys' "estate", as Dart called it, and in the first week, Sameya had stumbled upon the brownie humming as she cleaned. The Zions had found paradise in the thousand acres on which the house sat. She'd never seen them happier.

Before doing the mating custom, Gabriel wanted her to spend some time with his pride. He thought she'd be less self-conscious of getting dirty with them if she knew his family better. Honestly, she was impatient to showoff her mating marks. She'd been with Gabriel's family a week, with the ritual to occur momentarily.

The tiger's sister, Bethany, was a surprise. Eight months pregnant, his sibling was a delight, frank and to the point. Her mate was a quiet man who doted on his wife and adored his woman. She and Sameya got along famously and went off for long walks, discussing the differences in their life. She thought it helped her better understand Gabriel's easy manner, but also his determinedness to protect her like any alpha shifter.

The first day of her arrival, his mother, Gabby, had greeted her with a hug, as if they were long-time friends. She suspected the other woman's open affection made all the difference in her reception among the close-knit group.

It bothered her that she hadn't thought to ask either of her men if they had any siblings. She'd had a heart-to-heart with Maximus that evening and discovered he was a single child like her. He hadn't been close to his family, but he'd had a cousin he'd thought of as a brother. They hadn't spoken since he chose to mate their tiger. The hurt in his eyes as he talked about his clansmen had Sameya itching to pay forward a little pain to them all. How dare they abandon him because nature put him with a different species!

Taboo union? Many thought so. Their children would be powerful, but more importantly they would be loved regardless of their decisions in life.

Sameya touched her belly as she peered at herself in the mirror. A baby. Which of her men would get her pregnant first? It was unlikely they'd know until the infant bared fangs or shifted.

Bethany came up behind her and adjusted a strand of her hair. The other woman had insisted Sameya wear her hair up, so Gabriel and Maximus would have easy access to mark her neck during the ceremony. Sameya knew the hairstyle wouldn't remain so tidy, but she'd humored her soon-to-be sister-in-law.

Bethany ran a finger along the column of Sameya's neck. "Just think, the next time you look in the mirror, you'll bear their marks."

A nervous twitter panged through her stomach.

"Don't be nervous. We all go through the ceremony."

How did Bethany do that? Her uncanny empathy to read people was kind of spooky at times. "I'm not nervous about being with them." And she wasn't. "It's just...." She shrugged. "I don't know. It's hard to explain, but sex with them is personal and special, and I've never had anyone watch before."

The other woman leaned against her back, wrapped her arms around Sameya's belly, and rested her chin on her shoulder. Bethany's hugs were something she was getting used to. The other woman was extremely affectionate.

"Sex in the pride is rarely private. You're the only one letting it get in your head." The baby moved against Sameya's spine, and its momma grinned. "I can count the number of times I've had private sex on one hand." She giggled like a schoolgirl. "Gabriel and Maximus are crazy about you, you know that, right?"

She nodded. They made her feel special, treated her like she was a priceless commodity. "They're pretty amazing, too."

"Of course they are. Gabriel's my brother, and my parents only create amazing offspring." Bethany offered a teasing wink. Sameya chuckled as the other woman went on. "Trust them, they'll take care of you and make you forget all about us."

Appreciative of Bethany's support, Sameya squeezed her hand.

"It's almost time." The tiger stepped back and gave her a once over. "You're going to blow their minds in this outfit."

Sameya surveyed her wedding gown—if it could be called that. She felt sexy for sure wearing it. And Bethany's, "I'd so fuck you right now," had sealed the decision on the purchase while at the same time sending Sameya into a fit of giggles.

Made in two parts, the top was a black, diamond-beaded corset that pushed her breasts upward. The waistline of the black, silk skirt was also dotted with diamonds and hung so low on her hips, a slight tug and the garment would be pooling on the floor. The silk flowed past her ankles, and if not for the slit that ran all the way up her leg to the top of her thigh, she would've tripped over the material. Beneath she wore a red thong, the bold color intended to tantalize her men. According to Bethany, her black four-inch strappy high-heels were "fuck me" shoes.

"Trust me," the female shifter had said at the bridal store, as Sameya modeled the shoes with the dress. "Those won't be coming off." She'd pointed at the heels. "They'll insist you wear them while they fuck you."

Such frankness from Gabriel's sister had had color burning Sameya's cheeks as she'd glanced about to make sure none of the clerks had been near enough to hear the scandalous comment. Bethany had smiled her satisfaction with a flicker of something wicked lighting up her blue eyes.

A knock at the door pulled her attention off her reflection and recent memories.

"It's time."

Her belly dropped.

"Stop that!" Bethany swatted Sameya's arm and hooked their arms elbow-to-elbow. "You don't have to do this, you know?"

Steeling her spine, Sameya squared her shoulders and notched her chin higher. "Yes, I do." She exhaled slowly. "I want to do this for them and for our children."

That reality settled her anxiety.

Arm-in-arm with Bethany, Sameya entered the Ceremonial Chamber. In the center of the room was a king size bed made up with white silk sheets. Members of the pride were seated in chairs situated about the room. The only seat unoccupied was the one beside Bethany's husband. She'd been forewarned that before the ritual was over, there'd be others who'd be partaking in carnal delights. She wasn't sure what she thought about being the cause of an orgy, so she'd decided not to dwell on the possible outcome.

Maximus stood next to the bed wearing a black tux and a top hat. She smiled at him and met his silver-blue eyes. His gaze slid down her body, and his eyes flared into his vampyr, glowing green. Damn, but he looked handsome in his finery. Beside him the alpha leader of the pride, a young, powerful man, paled in comparison to her vampyr.

Gabriel was nowhere in sight.

"Where's Gabriel?" Her stomach plummeted. She knew he hadn't changed his mind, so maybe he was running a bit late.

Bethany patted her hand. "Patience, sweetie."

"Who gives this woman to these men?" The alpha of the pride held her gaze.

What a weird question. No one else had the right to give her to them. "I do."

The leader grinned and Bethany giggled. "My husband and I give her to them." When Sameya frowned at her, Bethany explained, "It's customary for a pride member to grant permission." Sameya opened her mouth to tout the idiocy of that, but the shifter kissed her cheek. "I'm delighted to call you sister." Gabriel's sister squeezed her hand and went to the seat beside her spouse.

"Sameya, do you accept Maximus and Gabriel as your mates?" The leader asked.

"Yes." Her voice rang loud with confidence.

"Gabriel and Maximus, do you accept Sameya as your mate?"

"Yes." Her vampyr's fangs slid out and over his bottom lip.

"Yes," Gabriel said from behind her. Electricity sparked in the air, and she guessed he shifted to his fur.

"Allow the ceremony to commence with the Mother's blessing." The alpha leader squeezed Maximus's shoulder and strode to an empty chair she hadn't noticed located behind the bed.

The purring at her side alerted her to Gabriel's presence. He rubbed his body along her legs, and she ran her fingers across his fur.

"In cat fashion, he's marking you as his," Maximus's husky voice explained.

"I am his." She went to her knees and wrapped her arms around his neck. She buried her face in his fur. "I love you, Gabriel."

His purring became louder.

"Come, Sameya." When she looked up, Maximus had extended his arm toward her.

She licked her lips and rose to her feet. "I'm both of yours, Maximus." Her tiger nudged her toward her vampyr. When she was mere inches from him, she felt the static in the air signifying Gabriel's shift into man. His finger slid along the hemline of her skirt at her lower back. Her skin tingled where he touched.

"This garment makes me want to fuck you senseless." Gabriel's finger dragged up her spine.

"Me too." Her vampyr's eyes hadn't stopped glowing since getting his first gander of her.

Sameya had no idea how to proceed. What came first? Were there any rules? Anything they had to do to make the mating official among the pride?

They must've sensed her uncertainty, because in the next moment, Maximus went into action, his fingers in her hair, dislodging the pins. The hairpins hit the hardwood floor with pings as her hair tumbled around her shoulders. Gabriel nudged her hair aside with his chin and licked her neck. One of his hands landed on her hip and the other palm flattened against her thigh. His touch shifted to the inside as it moved upward. He cupped her pussy, and everything quickened. Her breath came in short pants, her pulse leapt, and her skin prickled with anticipation, while moisture surged from her core.

Her tiger placed nips up her neck before pressing his lips against her ear. "Mmm...wonder what these panties look like."

"We should find out." Maximus tugged her forward and spun her about. As he sat on the edge of the bed, he pulled her back against his chest between his parted legs.

She scrutinized Gabriel. His golden gaze was honed on her, intense and penetrating. And after his shift, he was naked.

One man came to her dressed in finery, the other in his fur.

Maximus shoved a hand into her corset, his thumb swishing back and forth across her nipple as Gabriel knelt. Gripping her skirt her tiger pushed the divisions on either side of her knees. Palms on the top of her thighs, he pushed the silk upward. His scrutiny lowered to her pussy. "Red, Maximus, they're red. And lacy."

The silky material of her skirt was shoved upward quickly to her waist. Afterward Maximus and Gabriel readjusted her position. She found herself sitting on the vampyr's legs, with hers dangling on either side of his, and she was tugged forward so her bottom rested against the edge of his knees.

"Sexy." Maximus pinched her nipple as he fingered the edge of the panties. He lowered his head and captured her lips in a kiss. His tongue pushed between her lips, claiming her like he marauded a village. His typical embrace, he demanded her sole focus.

Until Gabriel hooked his fingers behind one of her knees and pushed her leg toward her body. He kissed up the inside of her other thigh. She moaned into Maximus's mouth when Gabriel tongued her pussy through the lace.

He plied her clit with swirls and sucks through the material, teasing arousal out of her. Whimpering, she dug her fingers into Gabriel's hair. Maximus lifted his head to observe her for a moment, before peering at the tiger between her thighs.

The vampyr's gaze flicked to hers. "Watch Gabriel, *naleah.*"

She did as he requested. Gabriel stared at her as he manipulated her desire. His mouth killing her with unanswered gratification. Maximus freed her breasts, cupping them in his palms. She squirmed, as the foreplay was amped up a notch.

"Your breasts flush so pretty with your arousal." Maximus adjusted her upper-body at an angle, so he could draw her nipple into his mouth.

Closing her eyes, her head drooped over his arm. With one hand, she attempted to guide Gabriel with his oral play. He didn't cooperate. Her other palm knocked Maximus's top hat off his head as she clutched at his hair. Licks, nips, and sucks against both areas of her body had her mouth parting and her groans painting the air.

Maximus blew on her wet flesh. Sameya panted with want, her belly clenching.

"I'm going to move these aside." Maximus circled a fingertip against the top edge of the thong. "Make her come, Gabriel."

The lace was tugged to the side as her vampyr watched her. Cool air hit her hot flesh. Gabriel's tongue dragged slowly over her exposed pussy and she gasped, tightening her grip on both their heads.

"She wants to come, Gabriel."

"Yes." *Gods, yes I do!*

Gabriel pressed two digits into her languidly, until she wanted to scream her frustration. Maximus ripped the panties and used the same fingers that'd been holding the material aside to spread the folds of her pussy, granting Gabriel full access to her sensitive flesh.

Her tiger purred as he lapped around his digits pumping into her. They moved quicker as he tongued her clit. Sameya shuddered and held her breath. The flat of his tongue hauled back and forth against her nub. She climaxed with a strangled half-scream.

She trembled in their embrace, as Gabriel's purr grew noisy and he licked away her release.

"Perfect," Maximus said as applause erupted from the witnesses.

Having forgotten the audience, they startled her with their ovation.

"Ignore them," Gabriel said after he applied a final lick and pulled her down to straddle his thighs. His mouth was on hers and his tongue in her mouth a second later.

Chapter Twenty-Seven

The minute squeak of springs indicated Maximus moved behind her.

"This has got to go," Gabriel said when their kiss ended. He dragged the corset up and over her head. He tossed it over his shoulder and buried his face between her breasts.

Maximus ran his palm over her hair. She peered up at him as Gabriel made use of his mouth on her breasts. His cock scrubbed against her folds. Suddenly, she wanted to suck on Maximus's dick so bad her mouth watered in anticipation.

"Take off your jacket and shirt, Maximus." She went to work releasing his pants. He made quick work removing his other garments. Digging her fingers beneath the waistband of his slacks, she pushed the material down his legs. His erection sprang free, a spot of moisture beading on the head, and his piercings glinted in the light. Palming the base of him below the stainless steel gracing his cock, she licked the crown as she pumped her hand along his length.

A hiss surfaced from between his teeth, his fangs heavy and longer than she'd ever seen them. She pressed her lips against the head, pulled back the foreskin and met his gaze. "I love you, Maximus."

She eased him into her mouth, and he gasped with his fingers digging in her hair, as Gabriel caught a nipple between his teeth. In response, she sucked Maximus to the back of her throat.

"Goddamn," he groaned. Clenching her head in both hands, he held her head motionless as he fucked her mouth in long, slow thrusts, while holding her eyes.

Her tiger lifted his head from her breasts, caught her hips and shifted her at the right angle to impale her on his cock. She gasped around Maximus's length, her channel quivering around Gabriel. Sameya struggled to catch her breath as Maximus bent over to kiss Gabriel. When their embrace ended, Gabriel said, "Ride me," before he joined her in the oral play.

Maximus sucked on the fingers Gabriel offered him. Those same digits found their way to her bottom, sliding into her as Maximus's erection glided down Gabriel's throat. She whimpered at the sensation of the invasion. A tiny smile on her tiger's lips said her response pleased him.

She followed the removal of Gabriel's mouth with her tongue along the underside of Maximus's length. Together they licked the head, taking turns to swirl their tongue around the pierced crown.

"Enough!" Maximus yanked both their heads back by their hair. "We both want to be inside you when we mate you and come. Any objection?"

She shook her head. "No. I'm ready to belong to you both."

Taking her hand Maximus drew her to her feet, as Gabriel hooked his fingers in the skirt and tugged. The silk glided down her legs and pooled at her feet. Both men caressed her with their gazes, and then Maximus was guiding her to the bed with Gabriel following.

"Love the fucking shoes," Gabriel said.

She grinned at the tiger as the vampyr pointed to the bed.

"Sit." Maximus watched her as she sat on the edge of the mattress.

Unsure of what he planned, she peered up at him. "Here?"

He nodded and went to his knees in front of her, palming her knees to part her thighs. "Do you accept me as your mate, Sameya?"

She touched his jaw. "Yes, Maximus, I accept you as my mate. Do you accept me as yours?" The words sounded so formal even though they weren't planned.

"Yes." As she ogled him his fangs elongated and he licked up the inside of her thigh. An inch from her core, he swabbed over the area housing her femoral artery. "My mate, I mark you as mine."

His teeth buried in her skin, and she cried out at the bliss. The rush of heat his claiming triggered, made her go limp, but Gabriel caught her before she collapsed against the mattress.

The tiger stared into her eyes. "His marking you is the most amazing elation. I know. Embrace it."

There was nothing else she could do but embrace the sensation. The bliss rendered her powerless, her mind a haze of ecstasy. Moments later, the climax that washed over her left her warm and calm, rather than frazzled and wiped-out as was typical. And the connection with the man was amazing. She had no words to describe it. Only that she could *feel* him inside her, as if he were a part of her.

Maximus's fangs retracted, his tongue ran along the wounds, and he rose from between her legs. "Officially mine." The satisfaction in his eyes triggered every pheromone in her body. He kissed her hard and fast, and then whispered against her lips. "Mine." He looked at Gabriel. "Your turn."

He left her to lean against the headboard. He crooked his finger at her. "Come to me, *naleah.*"

With pleasure. On her hands and knees, she crawled to him. When she neared, Maximus gripped her hips and guided her to straddle his thighs. Without preamble, she accepted his cock to the hilt, his piercings scrubbing the right spots on the way in.

Sameya dropped her head back and moaned at the joy of his thick length submerged deep inside her. She clenched his length with her feminine muscles on the glide up, but relaxed on the thrust down.

"That feels so good."

"Yes, you do," he agreed, with his hands on her hips.

The bed shifted and Gabriel moved in behind her. His dick bumped against her backside. "You're my mate." Not a question like Maximus's before he mated her, but rather a claim of ownership. She should've known they'd approach the mating differently.

"Yes." She turned her head to peek at the tiger over her shoulder. "And you're mine."

Gabriel kissed her shoulder. "Are you ready to have us both inside you?"

She shivered at the thought and nodded. They'd prepped her for a week with toys and no matter how much she begged they'd refused to take her together. The guys wanted to wait until today, a special moment to introduce her to double penetration. As wound up as they had her libido, she was cager to accept them.

Her tiger placed a hand to her back and pushed her forward against the vampyr's chest.

Her vampyr nuzzled her neck as her tiger lubed her bottom, pressing his fingers into her. He pumped them, going deeper with each plunge and didn't stop until she whimpered in need.

He withdrew his digits and moved closer, his thighs hitting the back of her legs. Gabriel placed the broad head of his erection against her anus.

"Relax." Maximus's fangs grazed her skin, drawing a fine bead of blood that he licked away.

An appetizer for my mate's bloody palate.

Gabriel slid his hand up her back and then down to the curve of bottom. Back and forth his palm soothed as he pressed into her slowly. She moaned, her eyes widening as his head breached the tight ring. The minor sting faded, and he eased the rest of the way in effortlessly.

The fullness was more intense than when she'd had the dildos inside her when they fucked her. And it felt so much better. Together they were claiming her, making her theirs.

Panting, she peered at the pride leader over Maximus's shoulder, his raised dais giving him the best vantage point to watch them on the bed. His wife was giving him head, his hand on the back of her head guiding her. But they meant nothing to her. All that mattered was her vampyr and her tiger were finally mating her.

Her men remained buried deep inside her for a long while, allowing her to adapt to the sensation. Both her guys pulsed and she wanted them to fuck her like they always did, in a frenzied state of desperate need.

Where'd they suddenly come by their control?

Goddess, it was amazing at how full she felt, how complete this moment seemed, and she gloried in the sensations. The mating serenade suddenly burst forth and blanketed the room, surprising her with its strength, but indicating she fully accepted them as hers. The song couldn't have come at a more perfect moment.

"Never stop singing for us, *naleah.*" Maximus ran his fangs over her neck. "As one flesh we become united." His incisors buried into her.

Her tiger adjusted his position slightly, slipping the rest of the way into her until his pelvis pressed against her butt cheeks. She groaned as her ass accepted the widest part of his shaft, embracing the final burn. Leaning over her, he wound her hair in his hand, anchoring her head into a stable position. Maximus's gentle laps and sucks made her pussy throb. She wanted to demand they fuck her now, but somehow managed to execute patience and allowed them to guide the pace, as she always did in the bedroom.

"Your song enthralls me the same way you do, baby." Gabriel's lips moved against her shoulder as he spoke. "As one flesh we become united."

The tiger flexed his hips and his cock left her body. She whimpered wanting him back inside her. No sooner had the thought entered her mind, he thrust back into her ass and with a roar sank his tiger canines into her shoulder.

Sameya gasped at the sudden claiming. Her guys moved in unison, driving into her as one and withdrawing as a unit in perfect synchronicity.

I won't last. The intensity of them inside her was too much to hold off her climax for long.

The sizzle where their teeth penetrated her indicated the permanency of their mating, and her heart soared with the power of their emotions. The serenade song flourished, and she wouldn't be surprised to discover fine cracks in the windows afterward. Because of the song, the moans and sighs from the viewers grew louder and rowdier.

"Love you both," she whimpered over and over again, as a connection between the three of them bonded them permanently. She could feel them. They were part of her and not because they were moving inside her. A piece of them had joined her.

The pride leader pushed his wife to the floor on her hands and knees. His gaze locked on Sameya's, he released his pants. He tossed his wife's skirts to her waist and thrust into her from behind. The woman screamed at his penetration.

Closing her eyes, she focused on the plunges of her men. Throbs of pleasure greeted their thrusts in, their drags out, back in...the repetition of the movements turning her breathing erratic. Focused on the sensation of them inside her, she never wanted the moment to end. But she knew her orgasm built. It would be unstoppable with the way her body quivered in anticipation of the release. Soon, she'd come, and she'd be just as helpless to the bliss as she was to impeding it.

Their drives grew stronger, the wet sticky sounds of Maximus's cock in her wetness evidence of her arousal. Gabriel pounded into her so hard, he knocked her against Maximus and she buried her face against his shoulder. Each of his thrusts was hard enough to elicit a grunt from her.

Her belly burned hot, and her limbs began to tingle. Her breath grew reedy thin as her vision blurred and her song elicited a high-pitched warble. Sameya came, screaming, as if the universe fractured around her. Shaking with her release, she went completely limp against Maximus. Her climax spawned theirs. Maximus was the first to go, groaning loudly against her neck as he spewed deep into her. He sucked hard, imbibing on her blood as he filled her with his semen. Gabriel roared around his teeth in her shoulder, his bite becoming harder as his seed filled her with hot spurts.

Gabriel collapsed, sandwiching her between them, both buried to the hilt inside her. Her song faded with her release, but she had no doubt it'd return often. From all directions soft sighs and moans filtered about the room.

Maximus was the first to retract his teeth, licking the wounds to seal them. Gabriel licked around his teeth, purring as he laved the oozing wounds.

"I love you, *naleah*," Maximus whispered against her ear.

Gabriel's teeth left her shoulder, the hot glide of blood slithered down her collarbone. "I love you, too, baby."

He withdrew from her ass, and she flinched at the tenderness she hadn't felt during the sex. Maximus shifted, licking the blood off her skin and sealing the wounds Gabriel created. Sitting up, he brought her with him, his cock still buried deep inside her. He kissed her before kissing Gabriel over her shoulder. Afterward, she angled her head to accept Gabriel's embrace.

She'd found her future and happiness in taboo kisses. Everyone should be granted the privilege.

"I love you both." She thanked all the gods for gifting her with two strong males.

Sameya shifted a leg, her heel catching on the silk sheet. Amused when she realized she still wore the stilettos, she laughed as she kissed both her mates.

Gracen Miller

OTHER BOOKS BY GRACEN MILLER

The Road to Hell series

Madison's Life Lessons (prequel)
Pandora's Box (book 1)
Hell's Phoenix (book 2)
Genesis Queen (book 3)

Stand Alone Erotica

Fairy Casanova
Elfin Blood
Taboo Kisses

~About the Author~

Gracen is a hopeless daydreamer masquerading as a "normal" person in southern society. When not writing, she's a full-time basketball/football/guitar mom for her two sons and a devoted wife to her real-life hero-husband. She's addicted to writing, paranormal romance novels and movies, Alabama football and coffee...addictions are not necessarily in order of priority. She is convinced coffee is nectar from the gods and blending coffee and writing together generates the perfect creative merger. Many of her creative worlds are spawned from coffee highs.

To learn more about Gracen or to leave her a comment, visit her website at:

www.gracen-miller.com

Made in the USA
Columbia, SC
01 July 2018